## A TURN OF THE CARDS

"It's Bennet," Abby told Elmer. "He's dead."

The man glanced around the booth as if expecting to see a body in the corner. "Bennet? What happened? Heart attack?"

"I think it's murder," Abby replied. "You go for the police and I'll keep an eye on things until they get here."

Elmer nodded, put on his cap, and turned away. "Right. Quick as I can."

The dark cloud was departing as quickly as it had come. Abby took a penlight from her purse and, steeling herself, returned to the tent for another look.

This time it struck her immediately. There was a knife in Bennet's back.

She resolutely ignored the corpse and examined the surroundings. There was a second chair at the table, opposite Bennet, and a coat tree standing in one corner. A long, dark dress and shawl hung from one hook, and a black wig perched on top. A Tarot deck spilled face down on the floor, directly below Bennet's dangling hand, as though he were pointing to it. Two cards, faceup, lay on the table.

Abby moved closer. The top card, lying at right angles to the lower card, showed a tower tilting to one side as though about to fall. Small figures were either jumping or falling from its parapet.

She recognized the lower card as Death.

# MURDER BY TAROT

## —A MAC AND ABBY McKENZIE MYSTERY—

## AL GUTHRIE

## ZEBRA BOOKS
## KENSINGTON PUBLISHING CORP.

ZEBRA BOOKS

are published by

Kensington Publishing Corp.
475 Park Avenue South
New York, NY 10016

First printing: January, 1992

Printed in the United States of America

# Chapter One

Abby MacKenzie looked around the room with a sense of accomplishment. After months of work, conversion of the front of her Queen Anne style home to an arts and crafts store was complete. She was pleased that the charm of the old house had not been lost in the process.

Opening for the Labor Day weekend was definitely possible.

Possible, but not necessarily desirable. She looked out of the bay window, down the length of Twilly Place. What a mess! A building under construction on the east side of the street had kept trucks running in and out, churning up mud that had hardened into ruts, and turning potholes into bottomless pits. Yet today, instead of busy carpenters, the only sign of life on the short cul-de-sac was a young girl.

The child was perhaps eight, no more than nine years old. She wore shorts made from a pair of worn jeans, a sleeveless green blouse, and sandals. Her long auburn hair was tied back with a green ribbon.

Abby was surprised when the girl, instead of using the driveway as a shortcut to the creek as many children did, stepped onto the wide porch that ran along two sides of the house. Abby opened the screen door.

"We're not open for business yet, honey."

"Isn't this Mr. McKenzie's office?"

"Well, yes. Upstairs, but—"

5

The child's solemn face betrayed a momentary uncertainty, then she took a deep breath and said, "I want to hire him."

Abby grinned. "What would *you* need with a private detective?"

The girl scratched her peeling left shoulder. "It's con — it's private."

"Confidential, huh? Well, I'm Mr. McKenzie's associate. You can tell me."

"It's about Fidget. She ran away."

"Fidget?"

"My dog."

Abby suppressed a laugh. "You want to hire a private detective to find your dog? You know the police will be glad to —"

"I can pay. Honest."

"It's not that. What's your name, honey?"

Instead of answering, the girl reached into the pocket of her shorts and drew out a business card. She gave it to Abby and said, "You have to give it back. I only got one."

The edges were bent and there was a stain on the back. It had originally been the card of R. Daugherty, Masonry. The name KIM had been carefully hand-printed in front of the initial R. "So you're Kim Daugherty." Abby pronounced the last name as Daw-er-tee. "What does the —"

"Dock-er-tee. Everybody gets that wrong."

"Sorry. What does the R stand for?"

"My daddy's name is Roy. But my middle name is Royal."

"Really? What a nice name."

"It was my grandma's name." Kim smiled for the first time. "Daddy says it means I'm a royal pain."

Abby laughed. "I'm sure you're not. And your father is a mason?"

"He's a bricklayer. That's what I'm gonna be."

"I see. Now, about your dog, have you asked at the dog pound? Maybe they've already found Fidget."

"Daddy asked. He said they might find Fidget by acci-

6

dent." Kim screwed up her eyes and seemed close to tears. "But they won't—you know—beat the bushes, he said."

Abby's heart went out to the girl, but the idea of Mac hacking his way through the underbrush calling, "Here, Fidget!" was almost too much. She turned away to hide her twitching lips and was surprised to see her husband standing on the stairs.

He grinned at her and came into the room. "So you want a private detective. We're kind of expensive, you know."

Kim blushed. "I've got ten dollars and thirty-two cents at home." She fished in the pocket of her shorts and brought out a wadded dollar bill and a Snickers bar. The dollar had become welded to the candy by heat "I could give you this now and the rest when you find Fidget."

Abby covered her mouth and smothered a laugh as Mac raised his eyebrows. The laugh turned to a gasp of surprise as he held out his hand and took the mess from Kim's hand.

"Throw in the Snickers, and you've got a deal, Miss Daugherty."

Kim's face broke into a smile that threatened to swallow her ears. "I *told* Shirley I could and you would!"

Mac cleared his throat and adopted a professionally serious expression. "Can you describe the subject, Miss Daugherty?"

"Uh huh. She's a miniature poodle. All white. And she can't hold still for two minutes." Kim fished in the same pocket to which she had returned her business card. "I brought this." She handed Mac a yellow Department of Agriculture rabies vaccination certificate.

"That's very helpful. When did you see Fidget last?"

"Yesterday. She didn't hang around the table for Sunday dinner, so we knew she was gone. We looked all over."

"Has she wandered off before?"

"Uh huh. Lots. But she always comes home by supper time."

"Where does she usually go?"

"Different places." Kim's eyes widened. "But—maybe

7

the witches got her this time. Because why didn't she come home?"

Mac smiled. "There aren't any witches around here. I wouldn't worry about that."

"That's what Daddy said, but—well, Mom's not so sure."

"Well," Mac said, "witches or not, I'll get right on it, Miss Daugherty."

As Kim Daugherty skipped up the street, Abby turned to Mac and shook her head. "What brought on that bit of insanity?"

"Call it McKenzie's last case."

"So you're still determined to be a storekeeper?"

She could see he intended to ignore the question. "And what is the great detective's first ingenious move?"

"Adopt a suitable disguise; cocker spaniel I think. Consult my snitch, the doberman. Interview the victim's enemies—"

"Miniature poodles don't have enemies."

"How about the lady with the torn-up petunia bed? The neighborhood cat? The Yorky she threw over for the Chihuahua?"

"Chihuahua?"

"These Latin types always get the ladies."

"True. If I told you what I think of Ricardo Montalban—"

"Please don't. I'm insecure enough as it is." He looked out of the window as Kim turned the corner. "But I'm already sorry I gave in to this whim." Mac sat on the old glass-fronted counter. "It'd be a shame to disappoint her."

Abby nodded. "They've already checked with the dog pound. Do you suppose they've advertised?"

"Sarahville doesn't have a dog pound, just a contract with a local kennel to hold strays for them. And our animal control officer is whatever cop got stuck with the job this month. I'll check with him—but after that—well."

"You'll just have to beat the bushes."

"Care to join me?"

"No thanks. The village inspector is due today."

"Want me here?"

"What for? It's just routine. What could he find?"


Leichtdorf Road shimmered under the August sun. Mac squinted against the glare and left the shelter of his car. Shaking his head at his own folly, he muttered, "McKenzie's last case!" For ten bucks and change. He chuckled. Of course the fee was contingent. That kid drove a hard bargain.

A high berm ran along the east side of Leichtdorf, concealing what Mac knew to be an abandoned gravel pit. Beyond the berm there was a sheer drop of a hundred feet to the rocky shore of a small lake where numerous springs had filled the pit. He had once tried fishing there. No luck.

At first taking Kim as a client had seemed an amusing bit of whimsy, a break from the boredom he sometimes felt dealing with Abby's store. He turned to the west and found the path leading to the bottom of a still older pit.

But then the animal control officer suggested he was probably looking for a traffic victim, one of many to be found along any road.

Negotiating the path required frequent handholds provided by saplings that grew from a steep slope that dropped fifty feet to a marshy bottom. This pit had been worked to the level where flooding began, and then abandoned. So instead of a lake there were shallow ponds. It must be very old, indeed, because it had been invaded by second growth trees and heavy undergrowth.

If the dog *was* dead, how could he escape telling Kim? By reporting to her parents? Let them tell her. Leave a box of Snickers for the girl, coward that he was. Lacking a handhold, Mac descended the last ten feet in a rush and fetched up against a block of sandstone. He examined the abrasions on his palms and cursed most sincerely. This was definitely his last case.

He leaned back against the stone to rest a moment. After

9

he'd nearly gotten Abby killed on a previous case, her objections to giving up his one-man agency had become muted. Well, today's case involved no danger to anyone. He blew on his smarting hand. No serious danger, that is.

He straightened up and looked around. The trees and steep walls effectively blocked the bright sun, leaving the pit bottom ten degrees cooler, damp and gloomy. For some reason Mac felt reluctant to make his presence known by unnecessary noise, a feeling similar to his reaction to cemeteries. He shook off the feeling and shouted, "Here, Fidget."

The only answer was the scream of a jay.

He followed the path around the edge of a pond, at one point startling a community of frogs into mass swan dives and rapid breaststroking. The pond joined a second pond, the water at the juncture narrow enough to be leaped. Someone had preceded him, perhaps by days, leaving a deep water-filled footprint on the other side. Mac made sure his own jump carried him to dry gravel.

Calling from time to time as he followed the path, Mac only succeeded in silencing the birds and interrupting a rabbit's lunch. The path ended at narrow-gauge rails overgrown with weeds. The tracks extended for fifty yards to the west where several rails had been torn up. To the east, they entered a tunnel that passed under Leichtdorf Road.

Mac entered the tunnel and shouted the dog's name. The twelve-foot-high corrugated steel lining of the underpass made his voice sound like it was coming from the bottom of a barrel.

Emerging on the east side of the road, he stepped into blinding sunlight. This pit was larger, with little vegetation bordering the deep lake. Although the berm cast a long shadow in the afternoon sun, the heaps of sand and gravel at the far end of the pit were sunbathed. The only signs of a once-active mining operation were the rusted steel rails running halfway around the lake, and a small shack which had begun to tilt leftward.

Mac considered a complete search of the pit, but decided

the undergrowth and wildlife of the older area would be more attractive to Fidget. He shouted once more, then retraced his steps under the road and followed a barely perceptible path that split off west of where he had first encountered the tracks.

He might have missed his only clue in the Canine Caper entirely, if the onset of boredom hadn't made him susceptible to idle curiosity. He noticed a coil of barbed wire a bit off the path, and wondered why it should be lying in a gravel pit. Then he remembered Farrel, at the local junk and collectible store, saying people paid good money for these rusty barbs. The treasure hunting instinct took over and he pushed his way through the undergrowth for a closer look.

The wire had been in the same place for many years, a fact attested to by a stunted oak that had grown around one strand. And there, entangled, was a dog collar.

Mac took the rabies registration form Kim had given him from his shirt pocket and matched the numbers to the metal tag hanging from the collar.

There was no doubt Fidget had been here.

Without benefit of wire cutters, it took several minutes and a scratch on the back of his right hand before Mac retrieved the collar. That done, he spent a few more minutes bending a rusted section back and forth until metal fatigue gave him a two-inch sample of the barbed wire to carry away.

He saw a convenient log back near the path. It looked like a good place to sit, nurse his wound, and think about the significance of his find.

Not only was it a convenient resting place, it also held another surprise; a small book propped against one end of the log. It had a brown leather cover with gilt lettering worn into illegibility. The title page read, *The Ancient Religion*.

# Chapter Two

The village board had embraced an ambitious plan for creating a historic district in hope of attracting business and improving the local tax base, but Sarahville's long tradition of incompetent management continued unbroken.

A film of yellow dust had settled on Abby's counter, compliments of the grading crew working on the parking lot across the creek that flowed behind the house. By now there should have been a pedestrian bridge, but crossing the creek still depended on stepping stones—provided the water wasn't too high.

Abby smiled at the perspiring inspector. "Well, I hope you didn't find too much wrong. I'd like to open for business soon and take advantage of the Labor Day weekend."

The inspector wiped his brow and hitched his blue work pants over a substantial pot for the third time in five minutes. To no avail; they immediately started a slow slide back to their accustomed place. "Shouldn't be a problem," he said. "Common sense and a little give and take." He placed his clipboard on the kitchen table.

"Would you like something cold to drink?"

"You wouldn't have a beer, would you?"

Abby got a can of Stroh's from the refrigerator and placed it on the table along with a glass. The inspector sat down and popped the top of the can. He ignored the glass, took a healthy swallow, and sighed in satisfaction. "Nothing better on a hot day." He glanced at Abby, then his gaze slid down her body and jumped from her knees to a corner of the ceiling. He tapped his clipboard with his forefinger. "Most of this ain't too bad. Course, once it's taken care of I have'ta come back and look again."

Abby sat down, putting most of herself out of sight under the table. "Of course Mr.—Mr.?"

"Douglas Kazmierski." The inspector nodded absently, as if lost in thought. "What kind of business did you say this was?"

Since the display cases in the front were full of yarn and needles and the dining room filled with the paraphernalia of the amateur artist, the question made her wonder if he had paid any attention at all during his inspection. "Art supplies and craft goods. You know. Knitting, macrame, that sort of thing."

"Sure. My mother used to make doilies. Everything flat in the whole house was covered with 'em." Kazmierski sipped his beer. "Now, when I come back, you understand I may find something I missed the first time."

Abby straightened in her chair and frowned. She was beginning to understand where the conversation was headed. "May I see the report?"

Kazmierski hesitated—then slid the clipboard across the table.

Abby glanced at the first sheet, flipped to the second, and focused on one item in disbelief. "Sprinklers! You can't be serious."

Kazmierski's smile bordered on a smirk. "It's like I told my wife. With nine hundred pages of village ordinances and building codes, it'd be a miracle if I couldn't find something wrong."

Abby's nostrils pinched as if suppressing a blast of fire and smoke. "And no matter how often you come back, you can always find more, is that the idea?"

Kazmierski's smile vanished. "Oh, no. There has to be

13

an end sometime. A lot of it is a judgement call. For instance, the water heater."

"What about it?"

"It looks new, but when I checked the file before coming here, I didn't see a permit."

"Since when do you need a permit to replace a broken water heater?"

"I know just how you feel. Most people don't know about that. But I figure that's in the past, and who needs a fine. Right?" He took another sip and wiped his lips on the back of his hand. "But sometimes the mayor gets on a crusade, like. I heard him say something about cracking down on permits." He pushed the beer can aside. "But why borrow trouble. Right? A bigger problem is, this is my busy season. Once you fix a violation it could take me a while to get back around to you." His smirk had returned. "When did you say you gonna open?"

Abby rose from her chair and leaned across the table. "I have every intention of opening for the Labor Day weekend. And if you think—" The squeak of the screen door interrupted her and she turned to see Mac enter.

"Hi, Hon. I'm back." Mac laid a book and a piece of rusty wire on the kitchen counter and, smiling broadly, advanced on Kazmierski, hand extended. "I'm McKenzie. Everybody calls me Mac." Shaking hands briskly, he drew a chair close to the inspector and pulled the clipboard over. "This our inspection report? Well, doesn't look too bad. Sprinklers, huh? We're not big enough for sprinklers. I checked that out myself."

Looking uneasily at Mac, Kazmierski said, "It's a pretty big house. Course, you can appeal."

"But an appeal takes a long time." Mac handed the clipboard to the inspector. "We have ten days to correct these before we're cited, right?"

"Wait til you hear this next part," Abby said. "Go ahead, Kazmierski. Tell him about your nine-hundred-page book!"

14

"Kazmierski? That's your name?"

"Douglas Kazmierski."

Mac draped his arm around the inspector's shoulders. "I bet they call you Kaz. Right? Inevitable. Just like me and Mac."

Abby was now convinced that her husband had lost his mind. "Mac! You don't seem to understand what's going on here!"

Mac waved Abby's objection aside. "Tell me about this book, Kaz. Is that the ordinances and the building code?"

Kaz tried to move away, but Mac patted his shoulder. "Don't you worry about a thing, Kaz. I have to see Stan today anyway—"

"Stan?"

"Stan Pawlowski. Chief of Detectives. You know him, don't you."

"Yeah. Not really *know* him, you know, but—"

"Stan and I are old buddies. I'm surprised you didn't know that, Kaz."

The inspector's brow, recently cooled by a can of beer, was again becoming moist. "I'm new here. Just started two weeks ago."

"And so busy already," Mac said. "Well, I'll save you a lot of time. See, as soon as I explain the entire situation to Stan"—Mac massaged the inspectors shoulder—"he'll bring *his* nine-hundred-page book. We'll go through it *very* carefully. And I believe we can get an expedited hearing on the sprinklers. Pays to know somebody, right Kaz? Next time you come, everything will be perfect."

Kaz stood up and grinned weakly. "That ain't necessary." Quickly scribbling on the report sheet, he said, "I think you're right about the sprinklers. Just take care of them boxes downstairs and the front door lock. We'll call it square. Okay?" He placed the report on the table and headed for the door, hitching up his pants as he went.

Mac stood at the window until the sweating inspector

had scuttled across the yard and climbed into his blue pickup. Then he turned to Abby, grinning with obvious self-satisfaction. The grin quickly faded. Abby was not amused.

"I admit it was fun to watch him ooze out of here," she said, "but that doesn't solve the problem."

"He won't be back."

"What about all the other people?" She waved a hand in the direction of Twilly Place. "Construction out there is way behind schedule. It wouldn't surprise me if that wasn't Kazmierski's fault. That man should be in jail. Or at least fired."

"Okay. Okay. I'll talk to Stan. See what he knows about him. Maybe there have been complaints." Mac opened the refrigerator. "I just came home for lunch, not an argument." He took out a package of boiled ham and sniffed suspiciously. "How long has this been here?"

"Two days. When will you see Stan?"

"After lunch. Make me a sandwich, will you Hon? I have to wash up."

Abby, still fuming, took a bread knife from the drawer and attacked a loaf of rye. Mac ran water in the sink and started to wash up. By the time she spread hers with mayonnaise and his with mustard, Mac had dried his hands. She pointed the knife at him. "I don't understand how you can just dismiss this instance of petty graft. If everybody—"

"I *said* I'd talk to Stan."

"Just to placate me. You really aren't upset by this, are you?"

"Born and raised in Chicago?" He shrugged. "At least here I can run him off. When I was a kid it wasn't that easy. Guys like him were part of the cost of doing business."

Abby took a vicious bite out of her sandwich.

Mac, laughing, came to her side. "Calm down. You'll open on time, and maybe we can put a spoke in Kaz's

16

wheel." He bent down to kiss her. "Did I tell you I hate mayonnaise? Next time smear your lips with mustard. Put a little spice in your life."

Abby smiled in spite of herself. "Would you like jalapeño lipstick?" She sighed. "Okay. Change of subject. How is the case going, gumshoe?"

"I found Fidget's collar," he said.

"You're sure—?"

"The numbers on the tag check. It was tangled in barbed wire. Somebody rescued the dog and took it away."

"Why leave the collar?"

"Even without a squirming dog attached it was hard to get it loose. Easier to just unbuckle it and take the dog. Probably a kid." He got the book and wire from the counter. "Kid didn't think about the tag. Or maybe didn't want to. That way he can keep her."

"Where did you find it?"

"A gravel pit on Leitchdorf Road. It's so old it isn't posted anymore. It's an attractive nuisance as far as kids are concerned." He laid *The Ancient Religion* on the table. "I figured it might be the same with dogs, so I checked it out."

Abby picked up the book. "What does this have to do with it?"

"Probably nothing. I found it near the collar. Want to know how to cure warts? Or give them to your neighbor?"

Abby opened the book to a woodcut of a gargoyle perched on the edge of a cauldron. "Good heavens!"

"Not good. And not heavenly, for sure. Think it might be worth something?"

Abby examined the title page. "Looks like it was privately printed. I don't suppose they were burning any witches in 1843, but it could still get somebody a ride out of town on a rail."

"I might check with Farrell," Mac said. "About this

too." He tossed the wire on the table. "People collect this stuff."

Abby, engrossed in the book, nodded. "What are you going to tell Kim?"

"I'll think about it on the way out there."


Roy Daugherty's five-acre remnant of a farm contained a square two-story complete with lightning rods, a red barn, and a steel pole building. The house gleamed with fresh white paint, but the barn paint had peeled and faded until weathered gray wood showed through in several spots. A red pickup was parked near the steel building. Fence posts were set in concrete around the front yard, but there was no fencing in sight.

Mac parked on the rutted gravel drive near the back door. The front door was unusable due to a missing porch and stairs. He was about to knock when a man in jeans, tee shirt, and a Cubs cap came out of the barn and approached at a fast walk.

From thirty feet away, the man shouted, "What the hell do you want?"

Not a greeting to make you feel welcome, Mac thought, but he descended the three stairs and started toward the man, hand out for a friendly shake. "I'm—"

"I know who you are." The man now stood a foot from Mac and leaned forward, bringing their noses within six inches of each other. "You're a private dick hangs out with the cops. You tell the goddamn mayor to stay out of my business. The next one he sends I meet with a shotgun!"

Noting that the man was about thirty-five, broad shouldered, and obviously in good shape, Mac put up his hands and backed away. "Whoa. Mr. Daugherty—"

"Get your ass off my property!"

"Okay. Okay." Mac continued backing toward his car. "I just wanted to tell you about your dog."

The screen door swung open and Kim erupted from the house. "Daddy! Wait!" She ran in between Mac and her father. "Mr. McKenzie came to see me!"

The man's eyebrows rose and he turned his deeply tanned face to Kim, then back to Mac. "What business you got with my kid?"

"She asked me to find her dog."

"You found her!" Kim said. "Where is she?"

Mac shook his head. "Sorry, Kim. But I did find this." He took the collar from his pocket. "It was tangled in barbed wire. Somebody must have unbuckled it to get Fidget loose, so we know she's okay. My guess is they took her home and if you put an ad in the paper saying where the collar was found they'll bring her back."

The child danced up and down impatiently. "Daddy, let's go do it now."

Daugherty put his hand on her shoulder and drew her close. "Take it easy, Kim. We'll do it." Turning to Mac, he said, "Come on in and have a beer." Without waiting for Mac to accept, he steered Kim toward the back door.

Mac assumed the offer was an apology. "A beer sounds good. Chasing after strays is hot work."

Daugherty stopped at an old pop machine on the screened porch. It was labeled DR PEPPER, but when he pushed an unmarked selection button, a can of Bud dropped down the chute.

"Can I have one, Daddy?"

Pressing the Dr. Pepper button delivered Dr. Pepper. Daugherty retrieved a second Bud, handed it to Mac and motioned toward two wicker chairs. Kim sat on the floor with her back to the wall.

"So tell me about the dog," Daugherty said.

Mac described his search of the gravel pit. "It looks like somebody found Fidget tangled in the wire. Since they didn't bother to get the collar loose after the dog was out, I'd guess it was a kid."

Daugherty nodded. "Kids like that pit. I won't let Kim

19

go down there." He pointed south, toward the rear of his property. "There's a strip of farmland the owner leases out for corn, then the edge of the pit. So it's close by, but too steep at this end to get down." He sipped at his beer. "I checked it out when the dog went missing, but didn't find anything."

"When was that?"

"Fidget took off between nine and noon on Sunday. We started looking about two. I guess I hit the pit around three-thirty or four, maybe."

"Somebody must have found her before then or you'd have heard her bark."

Kim, finished with her drink, frowned fiercely. "You have to find her, Mr. McKenzie. I can owe you some more money."

Mac chuckled. "The dollar you gave me is enough, Kim. Anyway, I don't think Fidget was kidnapped. More like rescued."

"Then why didn't they bring her back?"

"They forgot the collar and don't know who she belongs to."

Kim got up and came to perch on her father's knee. "They could find out, if they wanted."

Daugherty patted his daughter's shoulder. "A dollar? You private dicks come high, don't you?"

Mac laughed. "That was a retainer. Ten more if I brought the dog home. Actually, I'm out of the business. My wife is opening a store—"

"I heard."

Mac addressed Kim. "It was probably some boy that found Fidget. Maybe he took her home and tried to get his parents to let him keep her. But they'll be watching the lost and found ads, so chances are you'll have your dog in no time."

"I'll call an ad in today," Daugherty said.

"What was all that commotion when I first got here?" Mac asked.

Daugherty looked like he was about to spit. "The mayor and his building inspector got a little graft going."

"Kazmierski?"

"You know him, huh? The little—" He glanced at Kim. "You saw my fence posts?"

Mac nodded.

"I got a permit for a fence. Kazmierski comes around after the posts are in and tells me I was supposed to wait until he measured the holes, to make sure they're deep enough. I can pay up or he'll make me dig 'em up and start over. I run his ass off the place."

"But you haven't finished the fence."

"Next a cop shows up with a citation. Dig 'em up or get fined. Next day Kazmierski is back, only this time he stays in his car. Says I'm running a business here and never been inspected. Maybe he'll find a reason to close me down."

"Can he?"

"Nah. I was grandfathered when the village passed the ordinances he's talking about. But if he gets a complaint about a health hazard, that's a different story. When I saw you, I figured you were sent to snoop around and find an excuse for him to come back."

"But you mentioned the mayor."

"Well, figure it out. Could he get away with this crap if the mayor wasn't getting a split? I went down and raised hell about it. The mayor turns around and says, 'You must've misunderstood. Kazmierski's just doing his job.' So I turns around and says, 'Job, hell. You send your stooge back, he'll get a twelve-gauge up his ass.' "

"Not too smart, Daugherty."

"Yeah? Next day the citation was dropped. You gotta know how to talk to politicians."

In 1926 a semi-retired banker of boundless optimism built a three-story building of dull brown brick; Sarahville had its first bank and high-rise. The bank went under in

21

1932. The Police Department, finally full-time and salaried, took over the building in 1947. By 1950 rapid growth demanded new facilities, including room to house a circuit court and a salaried police force. Debate over the bond issue was lengthy and spirited, and the new building was too small by the time it was finished.

So the old bank building still housed, among others, Capt. Stanley Pawlowski.

Stan put two cups of murky coffee, brewed eight hours earlier, on his linoleum-topped desk. "So the great McKenzie is down to working lost and found." He combed his fingers through dark hair graying at the temples. "It's a good thing your wife's a business woman. At least you won't starve."

Mac looked at the window propped open with a two-by-four and the finger-marked wall. "From the looks of this place maybe you should talk Julie into getting a job."

Stan's broad face wrinkled in disgust. "We can't even get the streets fixed around here, so I guess I can't complain."

Mac took a sip of coffee, shook his head in disbelief and put the cup down. "I've tasted better kerosene. Tell me—you had any reports on our new building inspector?"

"Kazmierski? No. He hasn't been here very long. What's the problem?"

"Shakedown. He tried it on Abby. I ran him off."

"No kidding? He must think he's still in Chicago."

"What are you going to do?"

"How'd he do it? Overt demand for money?"

Mac sighed and slumped back in his chair. "No. Just a lot of hints. He makes things tough, then waits for an offer."

"Not much I *can* do. You can file a complaint, but it doesn't sound like we can make a case. If you hadn't run him off we could try putting a wire on you. But if he don't make a demand, and you made an offer, that's entrapment."

22

"What if you just take it to the mayor? To Bennet?"

"Kazmierski is Bennet's nephew. And that Bennet ain't no prize either. Well, I think we'll be rid of him at the next election. He's been around long enough for his high-handed ways to make him a lot of enemies."

"But in the meantime, Kazmierski's home free."

Stan shrugged. "The best way to handle it is for everybody to refuse to pay. Then when he starts dragging his feet or coming up with petty crap to stall people, they march on the village board. If there's enough of you they have to take notice. Either Kazmierski straightens up, or they can him."

"Think it'll work?"

Stan shrugged again. "Trouble is, a lot of business people think a payoff here and there is part of the cost of doing business. Also, if they already paid him, they ain't about to talk." Stan drummed his fingers on the desk. "Why don't you take on the case for somebody that hasn't paid up? You might get something on him. I can't run anything undercover around here. Everybody knows my guys."

Mac shook his head. "I'm out of the business."

"Except for lost dogs."

"Which reminds me. Anything funny going on in the gravel pit on Leichtdorf?"

"All the time. Guys use it for a target range, thinking they're out in the country. But it's inside Sarahville, which makes discharging a firearm a misdemeanor. Once a year at least we get a report of a fire at night. Usually older kids with a six-pack. Two years ago, a drowning. Twelve-year-old went swimming."

"About what you'd expect for a spot like that. Anything else?"

Stan laughed. "Yeah. Witches! Satanic cults. Bogeymen."

"You're putting me on."

"About a year ago a guy went down to fish the other

23

pit. You know, through the tunnel. On the way, he found this dead cow. Swore it had been mutilated."

"Was it?"

"We had a vet check it out. The carcass was badly decomposed. Scavengers been at it. Use your imagination and you could believe what you want. But this guy talked it up and the rumors started."

"Just the one instance though?"

"Well, for a while we got phone calls. Strange lights at night. Missing pets. Somebody found a black candle, or so he said. It's kind of died down now."

"Did you ever find anything? Any evidence?"

"Did you expect me to?"

Mac leaned back, grinning. "How about a book of witches' spells?"

"Come again?"

"*The Ancient Religion,* it's called. 1843. A collection of recipes for the practice of witchcraft."

Stan chuckled. "Where'd you run across that?"

"Where the dog got hung up. How do you suppose it got there?"

"I think a village flake was attracted to the spot by the rumors. Wanted to try out the one that makes your mother-in-law disappear in a puff of smoke."

"Why leave it?"

"Maybe it didn't work. Or maybe the bogeyman came out and ate him."

Mac laughed. "Is that what you call deducing from the evidence, Sherlock? And why 'him'? Aren't witches always 'hers'?"

"Women steer clear of the place. Too isolated. Too gloomy. Too many bugs. Men go there to fish, shoot holes in beer cans, pretend they're Daniel Boone without getting too far away from the nearest tavern. So—what do *you* think?"

"I can think of some I'd nominate for village witch— but they don't use magic. And when it comes to flakes,

24

the list is over-populated." Then, sobering, he said, "I just hope we don't have a flake that needs a dog for ceremonial purposes."

It hadn't taken long to sort out cooking responsibilities in the McKenzie's two-business household. One meal of Mac's infamous chili had settled the issue. Abby cooked on four days, Mac prepared spaghetti or barbecued in season on one day, and they ate out twice each week. Chili was limited to twice a year, preferably when Abby was away for the day.

Mac arrived in time for Abby's meat loaf. "This whole kitchen is hot enough to boil potatoes," he said.

"I knew lighting the oven was a mistake as soon as I did it," Abby admitted, "but you've been agitating for meat loaf, so—instead of complaining, go set the table on the porch."

Mac gathered plates and cutlery. "Daugherty is going to run an ad for the dog."

"Then I suppose Kim will soon have Fidget." She took the bacon-topped meat loaf from the oven. "Now how about *my* dog—Kazmierski? Did you see Stan?"

He carried out the vegetables. "Not much help there."

"I don't believe it! I can't believe Stan isn't even interested."

"He's interested." Mac cut the meat loaf, placed a slice on each plate, and speared a potato for himself. "It's just that not much can be done without a complaint." He raised his hand, forestalling Abby. "And you don't have a basis—not without a demand for money."

"Maybe I could call Kazmierski back and pretend I've thought it over, you know, all worried about opening on time. Ask him if there isn't some way—"

"You forget." Mac added creamed corn to his plate and began scattering pepper over everything. "He's signed off on the inspection."

25

"I hate it when you're right."

"Your meat loaf's getting cold."

"How can anything get cold in this weather?" Abby stirred her corn with a fork and stabbed the meat. "I'm not going to give up on this, Mac. Maybe I'll talk to some of the other people."

"No harm in that, I guess. But anyone that knows anything has already paid up and won't talk. Giving a bribe is a crime too, you know."

Abby sighed. "Okay. Maybe I'm wasting my time. What are you doing tommorrow? You haven't forgotten about my booth for the Founder's Day Arts and Crafts Fair, have you?"

"I better get busy on the few legitimate violations Kazmierski found. He scratched them, but they need to be fixed. The booth is almost ready."

"Good. This is too good a chance to miss. Great advertising for the shop."

"That's the part I'm not clear on. How will an exhibit of your own paintings—"

"It'll draw in the local amateurs and they'll be exposed to the proprietor of the shop where they can get all their supplies as well as someone to talk to about technique and the lonely life of the artist."

"Are you lonely, Artist?"

Abby smiled. "What are you going to do about it, Sailor?"

"Ask me again in the cool of the evening."

"I don't think this evening will have a cool." Abby looked out over the backyard that sloped to Running Fox Creek. "My flowers are starting to droop again. I better get out the hose."

"And I'll put in a little time on the booth."

"Is there anything more you can do about Kim's dog?"

"No. Chances are Daugherty's ad'll get the job done. If not—"

"If not?"

Mac got up to pour coffee. "Then I'm afraid Fidget has a new master." He hesitated. "At least I hope so."

"What else could have happened?"

"Suppose someone freed the dog from the barbed wire, and then she ran off. And got hit by a car. Or into a fight with a raccoon."

"Don't be such a pessimist."

"And then there's that book."

Abby's eyes widened. "Oh, Mac! Surely you don't think—"

"No. Of course not. The idea's ridiculous."

# Chapter Three

Abby spent the next morning, Tuesday, proving that Mac was right about the business community. She limited herself to merchants of the Olde Sarahville district. She knew all of them, and having interests in common made it easier to broach the subject.

The old, established businesses, with one exception, had not been favored with Kazmierski's attention. The exception was the Running Fox Tavern where an outdoor beer garden was under construction. Proprietor Rudy Wilking admitted Kazmierski had raised some unreasonable objections, even though the plans had been approved by the village. Rather than offer a bribe, Rudy referred the matter to his attorney and heard no more about it.

The new merchants, those trying to open for the fall season, had seen the inspector. A remarkable acheivement, since Kazmierski had been on the job only two weeks. All but one claimed to have passed inspection with flying colors. Abby felt sure they lied, and the one exception confirmed that belief. Max Hyland of the Hyland Music Company, recently moved from Chicago's northwest side, smiled when she asked if Kazmierski had given him any trouble.

"Trouble? Why should there be trouble? You have to go along with the boys, Abby. It's cheaper in the long run." When asked point-blank if he had paid Kazmierski, Max Hyland tried to sell her a rebuilt player piano.

With each interview her frustration grew until she decided it was time to let it spill over on the mayor. Or to give him his correct title, President of the Board of Trustees, Lawrence Bennet.

The Bennet Insurance Agency in the Hill Grove Shopping Center occupied a small storefront wedged between a dress shop and a bakery. The window displayed several dusty sun-faded brochures and a potted rubber plant with brown-tipped leaves. As Abby opened the door an attractive, dark-haired woman in a light sundress came out. She ignored Abby, who was still holding the door. Squinting against the glare, the woman put on her sunglasses before moving from the shelter of the doorway.

Abby, already in a bad mood, muttered "You're welcome," and watched as the woman walked away, hoping her three-inch heels would sink into the sun-softened parking lot asphalt. When nothing so interesting happened, Abby entered the relative gloom of Bennet's office.

She waited a moment for her eyes to adjust. The outer office was empty. A single desk held a telephone, blotter, and calendar stand. Hearing the sound of throat clearing, she moved toward the inner office. Passing the desk she noticed the calendar was open to May eighteenth. Did that mean there had been no activity for nearly three months?

"Anybody home?" she called.

Lawrence Benett emerged, straightening his tie and rolling down his sleeves. "Yes. Can I help you?" He was a tall man, mid-fifties, and just begining to thicken around the middle. Broad cheekbones and a completely bald scalp made his head seem disproportionately large. His smile revealed perfect teeth. "I'm sorry. I know we've met, but—"

"I don't believe we have. I'm Abigail McKenzie. Perhaps you saw me at a village board meeting. I've attended several."

His smile broadened. "McKenzie. Of course. I saw your

29

picture in the paper after that unfortunate business last spring. Your husband is a detective."

"Yes. McKenzie Associates. And I'm opening a store in the Olde Sarahville district. Abby's Arts and Crafts. That's why I'm here."

Still smiling, he nodded. "I know. A type of business that should do well in that sort of environment, once the full potential of our plan is realized." His gaze swept over Abby. He looked into her eyes. "But I'm sure you'd do well in any—"

"Yes—well, I'm beginning to wonder if this great plan will be realized in my lifetime."

"Please come in. I'm sure I can handle all your insurance needs." He gestured toward the inner office. "There's a special program designed specifically for the small merchant—including an annuity with tax advantages. Never too soon to plan for retirement, you know." Bennet took her arm and Abby allowed him to guide her to a seat. His hand felt uncomfortably warm.

"Insurance isn't what I had in mind," she said. "Actually it's about the village inspector."

"Doug Kazmierski?" The mayor seemed suddenly wary. "What about him?"

"Surely you must have had complaints."

Bennet retreated behind his desk. She noticed his calendar was turned to the correct date, August third. Bennet picked up a leather trucker's wallet, the sort with a chain that could be fastened to a belt, and put it in a drawer. His high forehead wrinkled in thought. "Complaints? No. Can't say that I have."

"He scares you into thinking you'll never open for business. But he leaves the clear implication that for a few dollars all problems will disappear."

Bennet's tone sharpened. "A bribe? He asked you for money?"

"It was obvious that an offer by me would be accepted."

30

"But he didn't ask for money." Bennet frowned. "I'd hate to think Doug—I know he talks a lot. Likes to impress people with how difficult his job is. Perhaps you misunderstood."

Abby shook her head. "Not likely."

"Now, Mrs. McKenzie. You couldn't swear he solicited a bribe, could you?"

Abby's lips tightened. A flush of anger and frustration rose. "Perhaps I should explain more fully. Kazmierski is too smart to solicit a bribe. But he makes his power to harrass very clear. Then he smiles that oily smile and says, 'Of course, a lot of this is up to the judgement of the inspector.' At which point you're supposed to say let's make a deal. Otherwise, he'll keep you shut down indefinitely."

"I don't see how that's possible."

"He cited me for lack of a sprinkler system. Do you know what a sprinkler system costs? In a house like mine? Ruining the restoration, undoing everything we've done?"

Bennet came around and sat on the desk. He leaned forward, placing a hand on her shoulder. "Believe me, Mrs. McKenzie—may I call you Abigail?—I appreciate the problem. But we can't ignore something as important as fire safety."

"A sprinkler system is not required in a business place of less than five thousand square feet. We don't have anything like that amount of space."

"Well, then." Bennet smiled. "If Doug has made a mistake—"

"Oh, it's no mistake. I'd have to appeal. I'd win of course, but it could take weeks. And then he gets to reinspect, and find another violation, real or imagined."

"Well, when you explain it like that—" Bennet folded his arms and leaned back. "Still—I mean, you didn't actually *offer* a deal. You can't be sure how he'd react. Isn't that true?"

Abby stood up. "When my husband made it clear we intended to fight, he signed off and scuttled out of there like someone had set fire to his tail."

The air-conditioning was not working as efficiently as it might, but Abby didn't think that accounted for the sheen of sweat that had appeared on the mayor's forehead. "I will certainly check into it, Mrs. McKenzie. If any of the other merchants—"

"You don't expect them to admit they've paid off, do you?"

Bennet stood up. "That's a very serious accusation. I'd advise you not to repeat it in front of witnesses."

"Why not? Are you going to sue me?"

"Not I," Bennet said hastily. "But your fellow merchants—Look. I promise, if I find any proof, I'll take immediate action."

Abby moved to the door. "And I promise *you*, McKenzie Associates will also be looking into it."

"That's really not—"

Abby didn't wait for Bennet to finish. She walked briskly through the outer office and into the sunshine. Only the pneumatic closer prevented her from slamming the door on her way out.

Reckless in anger, Abby turned abruptly to the right and ran headlong into a passing pedestrian.

"Whoa there, Abigail," he said. "Who you about to kill?"

Startled and embarrased, Abby looked up into the face of Elmer Johnson. His characteristically raised left eyebrow and half-smile gave him the look of someone constantly amused by the world's foolishness.

"Sorry, Elmer. What was that?"

"You looked like you were ready to murder somebody."

"Guess I better calm down before I get in the car."

"Good idea. You came out of there with a face that'd scare a man to death."

"I suppose so. Unfortunately it didn't work on our wor-

32

thy mayor." Abby laughed. "I did make him a little nervous though."

"Let's get out of this hot sun while you tell me about it." Elmer took her arm and pointed toward Swanson's. "Milk shakes on me."

"Milk shake? Good heavens, I won't be able to eat lunch the rest of the week." Nevertheless she fell in with him as he started toward the ice cream shop. Elmer was building the line of combination shops and apartments on Twilly. Abby hoped he was willing and able to join her complaint about Kazmierski.

As they turned into Swanson's, Abby noticed the woman from Bennet's office. She was sitting in a red mustang applying a fresh coat of lipstick. Abby wondered why anyone would choose to sit there this long. The car must have been turned into an oven by the sun. Unless she was waiting for someone. Bennet perhaps?

Settling into a booth with a sigh of relief, Elmer said, "This summer's sure been a hot one. Won't mind a mite when fall comes."

Abby nodded. "I hope to have the store open by then. That is, if I don't have any more trouble with the inspector."

"Kazmierski givin' you trouble, little lady?"

"You know him? Has he hit you too?"

"Not me." Elmer unwrapped a straw and sipped at his milk shake. "I suspect he's hit on the contractor buildin' my stuff, but the contractor's been around. Probably had the bribe figured into his bid when he took the job."

"Do you know that for sure?"

"Nope. Stands to reason, though. Kazmierski will hit on my tenants as they get ready to open shop. Is this what you were jawin' at Bennet about?"

Abby dipped a spoon into the thick shake. "He's in on it, I'm sure. But I think he'll tell his nephew to lay low now."

"I expect you're right. But I'd sure like to put this thing

33

on Bennet's doorstep. See, I'm planning to run for village board president—"

"You? In politics?"

"I got an investment to protect. Them sleeping beauties on the board ain't done anything right since rocks were new." Elmer spooned up a lump of ice cream from the bottom of his malt glass. "Gonna get these signs painted: TIME FOR A CHANGE. VOTE FOR JOHNSON. Change from what? Incompetence and graft. But I need facts, before I get sued for slander."

"How long has Bennet been getting away with this?"

"Ever since he first got on the board, before he ran for President. Not this building inspector stuff. That's just since his nephew got the job when old Kenny retired. Kenny was slow as molasses and a stickler for goin' by the book. But honest."

"So what did he do before Kazmierski?"

"There was some talk Bennet was the guy to see if you had a zoning problem, or your liquor license was in trouble. That kind of thing." Elmer slurped the dregs of his glass. "As a Trustee he got on the right committees. When he made President, he got his friends on the right committees."

"In a small place like this, didn't people catch on?"

"People don't pay attention unless it's their own corns get stepped on. But things mount up. I'd say the mayor's coming to the end of his string. The next election will be a tough one for him, if a halfway decent candidate runs against him."

"Well, I've done my bit," Abby said. "Even threatened a full investigation by McKenzie Associates."

"Mac still set on gettin' out of the detecting business?"

"Definitely."

"Never understood why. None of my business, of course."

Abby was hesitant about discussing the problem with anyone. Elmer was a friend of Mac's, but not as close as

34

Stan. After all, Mac and Stan had grown up together on the streets of Chicago. And Elmer, country boy manner or not, always had an angle. She shrugged.

"Let me guess," Elmer said. "He spent most of his life galavantin' around in the Air Force, leaving his first wife to fend for herself. Then he retires, moves back here to give her a solid home life, and takes up detectin' for these big aerospace companies all over the world, leaving her to fend again. And then, while he's out of town, she gets killed by a burglar. The boy's got a guilty conscience and he's gonna stick to you like glue."

Surprised, Abby said, "That's about it, Elmer."

"And I suppose gettin' the two of you damn near buried didn't do much to change his mind."

"He won't even talk about it any more."

"But he ain't turned in his license?"

"No, he's just letting it run out at the end of the year."

"And you're the associate in McKenzie etcetera."

"In a way, I guess. What are you getting at, Elmer?"

"So how about if I'm your client? You're after Bennet anyway. This way you get paid for your time, and I get the full report." He wadded up his napkin and shoved it into his empty glass. "Of course, since this is what you might call a public service, I expect we can negotiate your rates down."

"Why don't we call this *your* public service, and leave the rates alone?"

Elmer grinned at her implicit acceptance. "Now don't get me wrong, little lady. I surely do respect what a woman can do when she sets her mind to it. But experience tells. You suppose Mac would—"

"Not a chance, Elmer. I'm your man."

Grinning, Elmer patted her hand and said, "Good girl." He paid the check, obviously pleased with himself.

They stopped on the sidewalk for a moment and Abby looked around the nearly empty lot. The heat was taking its toll of daytime business, most people saving their

35

shopping for the evening hours. The woman from Bennet's office was still sitting in her Mustang. She was staring at Abby.

"Elmer, do you know the woman in that car over there?"

Elmer glanced over his shoulder. "Magdelena Kazmierski? The inspector's wife."

Startled, Abby turned and looked directly at the woman. The Mustang's engine started and the car roared out onto Harper Road.

"Why do you suppose she was watching us?"

"I have that effect on all the ladies," Elmer said, and walked off chuckling.

Abby grinned briefly, then looked after the disappearing Mustang. The woman had sat in her car, in the heat, the whole time Abby and Elmer were enjoying their malts. Why? If it hadn't been obvious that Abby had spotted her, would the woman have followed her? Or Elmer?

Well, to hell with that. She had a more serious problem. Elmer assumed she would soon be in over her head and Mac would have to bail her out. Mac, who would swallow his anger, who would be insufferably patient and understanding when she told him what she had done.

Any chance of trapping Kaz into soliciting a bribe was gone. What other avenue was open? None of the other merchants would talk. Not only had she taken a case Mac wouldn't touch, it was a case with nowhere to go.

She walked slowly toward her car. But that was no longer true, was it? After all, Kaz wasn't the real problem, was he? Now the focus was on His Honor. She picked up the pace, walking briskly in the heat. How much investigation could Mr. Lawrence Bennet stand?

Maybe she wouldn't tell Mac about their new client. Not right away.

# Chapter Four

Fire regulations require three feet between the top of stacked material and the ceiling. Inspector Kaz, before he decided on a whitewash in lieu of a citation, noted that cartons in the McKenzie basement violated that rule by six inches. The basement, though gloomy, would be pleasantly cool compared to the ninety degree, high humidity day above it. Mac decided to restack the cartons. The job took about three-quarters of an hour.

Then he sat on the stairs to consider his next move.

Maybe he'd take care of the front door lock. Born to a family where do-it-yourself was an economic way of life, he was a fair hand at most of the trades and particularly fond of carpentry. On the other hand, he knew little about running a retail business. Knew little and, he had to admit, cared little. Maybe he should hire out to Abby as janitor and maintenance man.

Staying with his own business was out of the question. It had been easier than expected to translate his experience into a post-retirement career. His clients were aerospace firms. No need to advertise. They knew him by reputation. Some had been at the wrong end of his investigations for the Air Force Inspector General. It was nice, clean work: check security systems, occasionally a case of industrial espionage. But it meant long periods away from home. Not until his wife died did he realize how much she had sacrificed for his job.

After a period of depression, Abby had drawn him out of his shell—dragging him into investigating the murder of her sister. That ended in near disaster for them both, as had the next case she pushed him into.

Maybe he could specialize in lost dogs.

His thoughts were interrupted by the doorbell. He found Kim Daugherty standing on the porch peeling a patch of sunburned skin from her shoulder.

"Good morning, Miss Daugherty. Any news?" He opened the screen door and motioned for her to come in.

Kim shook her head. "Mom said it's too soon. Maybe tomorrow somebody might call."

"So what brings you all this way?"

"Do you have a—uh—a card, like for being a detective?"

"Business card? Sure."

"And could I have one?"

"Since you're my client, I don't see why not." He reached under the counter where Abby had placed a supply of his cards. "Take two. They're small." He'd have to remind Abby to get rid of them.

"Thank you." Kim's grin was infectious.

Mac laughed. "You're welcome. Is that all you wanted?"

"Uh huh."

"It's a pretty long walk from your house to here, Kim. Don't your folks mind?"

Kim stuffed the cards into her pocket and looked around the room, pretending a great interest in the woodwork.

"They don't know you're here, do they?"

"It's okay. Honest."

"Tell you what, Miss Daugherty. I'll give you a lift home, and on the way we'll get an ice cream cone. Okay?"

Kim's answer was a broad grin and a quick nod.

Mac decided to drop in on Farrell afterward, so he took

38

*The Ancient Religion* with him, placing it on the dashboard.

"Are you going to the library, Mr. McKenzie?"

"Why—oh, I see. You mean the book. I found it in the gravel pit."

"Can I see?"

Mindful that some of the woodcuts would raise more questions than he cared to deal with, Mac said, "It's very old. I'm afraid some of the pages might crumble."

"My mom had a book like that once. She said I couldn't look at it and couldn't wait to get it out of the house."

"Really?"

"Must have been like that magazine Daddy gets. I'm not suppose to look at that either."

Mac grinned. "Well, this book isn't anything like that. Just real old stuff. Not very interesting."

As Mac pulled into the rutted driveway of the Daugherty home a thin woman in a cotton housedress appeared at the door. Seeing Kim get out of the car, she stepped outside, shoved a strand of hair behind her ear and said, "Just where have you been, young lady?"

Kim licked at a trickle of melted ice cream that was running down her arm. "Mr. McKenzie bought me a cone."

"That's very nice, but where were you?"

Mac got out of the car, leaving the door open to catch the slight breeze that stirred dust in the yard. "She stopped in to see me, Mrs. Daugherty. It seemed too hot for such a long walk, so I brought her home."

"Kim, how many times do I have to tell you about wandering off like that? Now get inside. I'll deal with you later."

Those words must not have posed much of a threat because Kim bit the bottom out of her cone and skipped off to the house while draining the rapidly melting ice cream into her mouth.

Mrs. Daugherty, frowning, shook her head. "I don't know what to do with that girl. One of these days her wandering'll get her in trouble." She smiled and the worry lines cleared from the corners of her eyes. She suddenly seemed very young. "I want to thank you for taking so much trouble with Kimberley. Over her dog and all."

"I'm just sorry I couldn't find Fidget. But your ad should get some result."

"I hope so. That girl's driving me to distraction. Between her and—well anyway, thanks."

"This coming on top of your problems with the village you mean? I know Mr. Daugherty seemed pretty upset."

Her face tightened momentarily, then she smiled. "Can I offer you something, Mr. McKenzie? Wouldn't take but a minute to make coffee."

"No thanks." He reached into the car and retrieved the book. "Ever see anything like this?"

Her eyes widened. "My, that seems very old." She took a step backward.

He pushed the book toward her and she accepted it reluctantly, flipped a few pages, turned pale, and quickly handed it back to him. "Witch's curses!" She backed up farther. "Why'd you bring it here?"

Surprised at her strong reaction, he tossed the book onto the car seat. "It's just a book I found in the old gravel pit. I was going to ask a friend if it was worth anything as an antique. You don't believe in that sort of thing, do you?"

"Of course not!" She combed her fingers through blonde-streaked brown hair and laughed. "Not really." She motioned toward the tree line that marked the pit's edge. "You found it in there?"

He nodded.

"You know, they found animals in that pit all cut—" She gasped and covered her mouth. "You don't suppose

40

Fidget was taken by one of them devil worshippers?"

"No, I don't. Really. In the first place, there haven't been a lot of animals. Just one cow, and no matter what you heard, it died of natural causes. And if there was some kind of crazy cult around here the police would have heard of it."

"I'm not so sure. They don't take it serious. I called because there was a car parked on Leitchdorf and you could hear somebody chanting—like in church? Only you couldn't hear the words exactly. The police came and—"

"You heard chanting? From the bottom of the pit?"

Her expression was intense as if she willed him to believe. "It must have been loud."

Mac looked across the cornfield to the line of scrub trees that marked the edge of the pit. "That's a long way." And the pit itself would tend to contain the sound. "Have you ever heard shots coming from there?"

"Shots? Guns? No. Never. Why would I? I mean who would be shooting?"

"Some people use it for target practice, that's all." Never heard gunshots, but could hear chanting. Rampant imagination. "And you saw a car from here?"

"No." She looked into the distance as if visualizing the scene. "You can't see it from here. I saw it on the way home from the Jewel. I put the groceries away, then Fidget went running off into the corn." She pointed in the direction of the pit. "I went and called her out of there when I heard it. Fidget must of heard it too, the way she came tearing out to me."

"Fidget generally come when she's called?"

"Unless she's after a rabbit."

"Have you ever been down in the pit?"

"Once. Roy took me fishing. The place gives me the willies."

"Kim ever been there?"

"She better not! I catch her she won't be able to sit for a week!"

41

Mac hoped she was right about Kim not going to the pit. At Kim's age the pit would have been the first place he'd go.

Growing up took a lot of the fun out of life.

But if she were down there when some mighty hunter was bagging his limit of beer cans — well, accidents happen.

As Mac got into his car Mrs. Daugherty said, "If you want to know about stuff — in the book — see Madame Gladys."

She entered the house before he could ask who in the hell Madame Gladys was.


Mac, lost in thought, didn't remember his intention to check with James Farrel until he parked outside his own garage. Rather than drive the short distance, he walked down Twilly Place to where it met Main and stepped onto Farrel's porch, grateful for the shade. The sign painted on the fascia read TWILLY FEED AND FARM IMPLEMENTS.

Hiram Twilly, one of the early English settlers in northern Illinois, established his business in 1850. In the midst of German immigrants, he managed to hang on and prosper. The store was a large two-story building. The broad porch with the wide plank floor was a place where items could be displayed and farmers linger out of sun or rain to discuss the state of the weather and the price of corn in the Chicago market.

The rear of the second floor had a loft door where feed and seed corn could be lifted in by rope and tackle, and stored. The front half housed the Twilly family. The prolific Twillys, with six children (eventually adding six more) soon found the upper level too confining. They built a house some distance behind the store. Much later the gravel drive to the house became Twilly Place, and the Twilly house became home to the McKenzies.

Mac entered, immediately aware of the mixed odor of

furniture polish, dust, and mildew. He paused to let his eyes adjust to the dimness and glanced around at a shop crowded with a jumble of collectable junk and aisles that resembled a maze. Most of Farrell's business consisted of items from the turn of the century through the thirties. Only a few pieces were true antiques, and Jim would probably wind up selling those to other dealers.

Mac spotted Farrell's unkempt red hair rising from behind a wardrobe that stood in the middle of the room. Walking farther into the shop, he saw the proprietor's short, wiry figure standing on a step stool. He was rubbing a spot on the oak back with a rag.

Farrell stepped down. "Hi, Mac. What's new in the keyhole-peeping trade?"

"Not much, Jim. How's the junk business?"

Farrell gestured toward the oak wardrobe. "I just got this piece in. Think Abby'd be interested?"

"What were you up to? Adding a few years to its age?"

"There's a manufacturer's label burned into the back and covered with crud." He gestured with the rag. "Just trying to clean it up with mineral spirits."

Glancing around, Mac said, "Speaking of cleaning, will you ever straighten up this mess?"

"Certainly not." Farrell grinned. "My customers are rummagers. They want to find a treasure I'm too stupid to recognize. If the place was neat, they'd think I knew my business and stop trying to take advantage of me."

Mac held out the book of spells. "Without taking advantage of *me,* what do you think of this."

Indicating his soiled hands, Farrell disappeared into a back room. Mac heard running water, then Farrell came back wiping his hands on a paper towel. He inspected the book's cover, then laying it on the counter, opened it to the title page. His eyebrows rose as he continued to page through it, finally inspecting the marbled end papers.

"Not my line, Mac. If I had it in the store, I'd get an opinion from somebody in the book trade. If it was worth more than a nominal amount I'd have him sell it on consignment. In my shop, it'd just be a curiosity. Maybe fifteen—twenty bucks tops. I can let you have a couple of names of people who'd know."

"Thanks, I'll take them. Anyone local that might be into this kind of stuff? A collector?" He chuckled. "Or a witch, maybe?"

"Yeah, as a matter of fact." Raising his voice he called, "Mr. Ingram? Someone here I'd like you to meet."

Unaware that there had been anyone else in the store, Mac turned to see a tall, very erect, white-haired man approach. He had bushy eyebrows and wore a dark suit and tie in spite of the temperature. He came forward with measured tread, as if walking in a procession.

Farrell said, "Charles Ingram, meet Mac McKenzie."

Charles Ingram extended his hand and clasped Mac's firmly. His eyes flicked to the book on the counter. He said nothing.

"I see my book interests you," Mac said.

"Old books are always interesting. May I?" He picked up the book and examined it.

Charles Ingram's deep voice reminded Mac of a radio announcer he had listened to as a child, but he couldn't remember the name. "What do you think?" he asked.

Ingram replaced the book on the counter. "May I ask where you got it?"

"Found it. You know anyone around here that might be interested? Or might have lost it?"

The man shook his head.

Mac waited, but Ingram kept silent. "Well, I suppose I could advertise."

"That might not be advisable," Ingram said.

"Why not?"

"You can't tell what might respond." With that Ingram turned and left, the screen door banging shut behind him.

"Did he say *what* might respond?"

Farrell laughed. "Ingram is a little—unusual."

44

"Just a little. Voice reminds me of — who? Franklyn MacCormack? Pierre André?"

"Before my time. Charles is one of my regular browsers. About a year ago he bought an old wrought iron candlestick and six months ago a plexiglass pyramid. Said it was a gift for his landlady."

"Pyramid?"

"You never heard of pyramid power?" Farrell leaned on the counter, bringing his face closer to Mac. In a stage whisper he said, "Keep your razor blade under it and it never gets dull. Preserves food." Straightening with a grin, he said, "Sleep under it and it does something. I forget what."

Mac laughed. "What does he do besides haunt you?"

Farrell shrugged. "Don't really know. Based on his age and the fact that I've seen him around at all hours, I'd guess he's retired." He punched Mac's arm. "Course, I could say the same about you."

"Lives here in Sarahville, I suppose?"

"Yeah. Out near Liechtdorf. I think."

"That's interesting." A coincidence? "I found the book near there."

Farrrel nodded. "Looked to me like he recognized it. Didn't you think so?"

"Why not claim it, then?"

"If you were a collector of strange stuff, I suppose you would. But if you were really into this — well, would you say, 'Hi, I'm your neighborhood warlock and that's my operating manual?' "

Mac laughed. "Guess not. Well, if he doesn't want to claim it, I guess it's mine."

"Until the next full moon, when you turn into a frog."

# Chapter Five

Except for exchanging tales of the day's activities (Abby's edited to avoid her commitment to Elmer) the McKenzies enjoyed a quiet Tuesday evening. Abby, preoccupied with planning an attack on Bennet, failed to notice Mac was also lost in thought.

By Wednesday morning Abby had a plan of action. Step one: consult back issues of the newspaper at the library for background on Bennet's political activities. Step two: question people touched by that activity.

She could ask, but would they answer? It seemed easy on TV. The private eye barges in on the widow demanding to know where she was when the cyanide was dropped in her husband's drink. She, clad in a black negligee as a sign of mourning, swears she was in bed with the victim's partner at that exact moment, and her recent purchase of rat poison was pure coincidence.

In real life people weren't that forthcoming. Mac once told her people spoke out of self-interest. The detective's job was to figure out their angle, and interpret their words accordingly. She could do that.

Couldn't she?

Wednesday and Thursday she split her time between dealing with suppliers, finding lost invoices, planning a grand opening sale, and researching the Lawrence Bennet story. By Friday she was ready to visit a couple of the losers in past elections. She learned they had undertaken a run for the office after much arm-twisting. Defeat had been a relief. Their subsequent interest in Bennet's career was less than obsessive.

Saturday she visited local businesses and discovered a reservoir of ill will where Bennet was concerned, but no specific misdeeds that anyone could, or would, document. It appeared His Honor was near the end of his political string; any opposition candidate, not named Adolf, would probably win.

By Sunday the pressures of business and frustration with her investigation had turned Abby into an unreasonable grouch. Mac tended to what he called his janitorial duties and tried to stay out of the way.

But Abby would have none of that.

Sunday evening she arranged an impromptu training session for Mac. "If you're going to switch from private investigator to shop clerk, there's a lot more to it than minor repairs and opening boxes." She installed him behind the counter and cast herself in the role of customer.

"I want to knit this sweater, and I should get ten stitches to the inch. But I can't get the gauge right. It always comes out with too many stitches. What should I do?"

"Try Elsie's Resale Shop. They have some nice used sweaters."

"Mac, be serious."

"Okay. I give up. What's the answer?"

"You tell me to use the next larger needle size. Got it?"

"Got it."

"And if the guage is off the other way?"

Mac hesitated. "The next smaller size?"

"Good. Now—"

"What's the prize?"

Abby's lips tightened in disapproval. "A repeat cus-

47

tomer." She leaned on the counter. "I don't think you're taking this seriously, Mac. We're due to open in less than three weeks, you talked me out of hiring anybody, and as far as I can see the only thing you can do is sweep up."

Mac's eyebrows rose. "Talked you out—Wait. You were crying about needing to keep costs down until the business showed a profit." He spread his arms as though appealing for justice. "I *volunteered* to help out. And I think I've done a *little* more than sweep—"

"Do you want to argue, or do you want to learn?"

Mac waited a beat while his face shifted to neutral. "Shoot, teach."

"Now, I have this pattern and it calls for twelve skeins of eighty-five grams each." Abby scanned his face to be sure he was paying attention. "But the yarn I want to use comes in three-and-a-half-ounce skeins. How many skeins do I need?"

"Gotcha. Now you're on my turf. Technical. Scientific. Be right back." With that Mac went up the stairs two at a time.

Abby impatiently tapped her foot until he returned carrying a pocket calculator and a copy of *CRC Standard Mathematical Tables*.

"This will only take a minute." He turned to the metric conversion factors. "Ounces, right? Let's see. Apothecary, fluid—ah, avoirdupois. That's 28.3499527 grams. Now what was the problem again?"

"Forget it, Einstein. The customer decided to take up basket weaving."

"I suppose you can do that problem in your head and make change at the same time?"

"At least I can make change without counting on my fingers." Sighing the sigh of martyrs she said, "All right, we'll just have to work on that. Let's try you on art supplies."

48

"I may not know much about art, but I know what I like."

"Mac!" Abby shook her head. "Now I'm a customer that has taken up watercolors. Try not to say anything stupid." She forced a rather grim smile. "Excuse me. I've been painting bowls of wax fruit for six months and I'd like to try something more challenging. What do you suggest?"

Mac folded his arms and stared at Abby for a moment. Then he suggested just what she could paint and stalked out of the room.

Startled, she said, "Now what's gotten into you?"

She was only trying to help him, wasn't she? If he *insisted* on muscling into her business, he'd—Okay. Wrong term, muscling. After all, he wouldn't say that about *her,* if he found out she was playing shamus.

Would he?

Was there any doubt he had a lot to learn? Okay, so maybe she had been just a little rough on him, but if he insisted on turning himself into a ribbon clerk—

No, what he wanted to be was her partner. She turned to the stairs where he had disappeared. But damn it, Mac, you know you aren't cut out for the retail business. Go back to doing what you do best.

Then maybe he could take over Elmer's case.

And rescue her from a commitment she should never have made? Was that what she was after? Was she *really* becoming that manipulative?

If she was, it was Mac's fault.

Bill Norris, her first husband, often disappeared in times of crisis, usually to work some con game, or to keep a step ahead of the law if the scam went sour.

Mac, on the other hand, was always there. Almost to the point of being underfoot. No, that wasn't fair; he'd been a great help in getting the store ready. And he was always understanding. Well, *usually* understanding. He *wanted* her to lean on him.

But that was no excuse for her behavior. She'd gotten herself into this mess. She'd see it through alone.

Meantime, there were amends to make.


By Monday morning the McKenzie household was back to what passed for normal and Mac bid Abby a lingering farewell before leaving in the station wagon for a tour of the area hardware stores and lumber yards.

She opened the front door, to take advantage of any breeze that offered itself, and found a slim, well-dressed woman standing on the porch.

"Oh. I wasn't sure you would be open."

"I'm sorry. We won't open until Labor Day weekend." Abby appraised the woman's dress, fawn-colored in a silky material, her string of pearls and high heels. All that on a summer day that promised to set a new record high before it was over. Not exactly the type to crochet afghans. Maybe she painted plaster figurines. Abby had considered adding a line of green ware, but she really didn't have the space.

On second thought, she couldn't see the woman in paint-stained jeans, either. "What sort of craft are you interested in?"

"Craft?" The woman nervously fingered her pearls. "No. I'm looking for the Detective Agency. Aren't you Mrs. McKenzie?"

"Yes, I am, but—"

"My name is Esther Bennet. Madame Gladys referred me to you."

Thoroughly confused, Abby said, "Madame who?"

"Gladys. You know her, don't you?"

"No, I don't think so. Bennet? Are you—"

"The mayor's wife. Yes."

"Well!" Sensing a break in the case, Abby said, "Come in. Would you like coffee? The pot's on."

"No, thank you. I don't have much time. And my problem is rather urgent."

"Mr. McKenzie isn't here right now. But I'll be glad to pass on—"

"No, no. Madame Gladys specifically said I was to see you."

"Me? There must be—well, never mind. Come on into the kitchen. There really isn't anywhere to sit out here. As you can see, the store is nearly ready, but there are still a few things to be done. Well, I suppose I'll still be saying that on opening day."

Abby seated Mrs. Bennet at the table, offered coffee again, and was refused again.

"What exactly did you want my husband to do, Mrs. Bennet?"

"As I said, it's you I want." She touched her blond hair as though reassuring herself that nothing was out of place. "You see, I'm planning to divorce my husband."

This statement, catching Abby by surprise, also presented a dilemma. If Mac were here, he'd promptly tell the woman he did not handle divorce work. On the other hand, the statements of a disgruntled wife might provide valuable insight to Bennet's dealings. Then again, was it ethical to obtain the information under the pretense of considering her as a client?

"Before you begin, Mrs. Bennet, you should know that Mac has never handled a divorce case."

"This isn't about the divorce exactly. I have plenty of grounds for that. I want you to find out where he hides his assets."

"His assets? Well. I see." She didn't. "Tell me more."

Mrs. Bennet looked around the room, as though uncertain how to begin. "The checking account has barely

51

enough to run the household, and our savings account has been closed."

Closely watching the woman's face, Abby judged her to be within a year or two of her own age, although she had at first appeared younger. The fine lines at the eyes and the crease at the corner of the mouth had been minimized by expert makeup, and she obviously took care not to expose herself to the sun. Her skin was smooth and pale, with just a hint of color applied to the high cheek bones.

Considering the woman's clothes, pearls, and a large diamond ring, Abby felt sure a reduced checking account must be a new experience for her. "How long ago did this happen?"

"About six months ago. The business account is down to a hundred dollars. Aside from the furnishings and car, and a heavily mortgaged house, that's all I know about. Yet he's always done reasonably well in the insurance business."

"Does he gamble? Drink?"

Mrs. Bennet's voice lost its uncertain tone and her eyes narrowed. "His only vice, pursued with great enthusiasm, is women. I'm sure he's concealing income so he can lead the life of the great lover." She snorted. "That must be another hidden asset. *I've* never seen any evidence of his skill."

"Then perhaps there *is* no money. He could easily spend it all on his—hobby?"

"But he's been acting—strangely. He spends less time in the office and he's developed a sudden interest in fishing, of all things. He's nervous, as if under some pressure I don't understand. And with all that, he's written a lot of insurance in the last three months. Much more than usual."

"How do you know that, Mrs. Bennet? From what you've been telling me, I wouldn't have thought he'd talk much about his business. Not if he's deliberately concealing his income."

"He has one of those trucker's wallets he uses for trips to the bank. The last time I peeked it contained over thirty thousand in checks." Mrs. Bennet had become brisk and businesslike. "That money never appeared on any bank statement. He must have an account somewhere. If I don't find it before I file for divorce, it will disappear forever. I'll be left to pick over the crumbs."

"And you've no idea where he might have this account? Has he been going into Chicago, perhaps?"

Mrs. Bennet shook her head. "You may not believe this, but I've come down to checking the odometer on his car. And examining the oil company credit card bill. If anything, in the last six months he's put on less than normal mileage. The money must be nearby. There are plenty of banks in the surrounding villages."

"Maybe he's using someone else's car. A lady friend perhaps?"

Mrs. Bennet's eyes widened. "I never thought of that!" She began to rummage in her purse. "Madame Gladys was right as usual. I see I can leave this in your capable hands."

"No. Really. I can't. Mac *definitely* would not approve. And the truth is, there might be a conflict of interest. I'm investigating your husband—"

"Whatever for?"

"It's confidential. But it has to do with the way he's handled some of the village business."

"I don't see any conflict." Mrs. Bennet pulled a checkbook from her purse. "You're out to nail the bastard, and so am I!" She started writing a check. "Take my case and I'll tell you everything I know about Lawrence. In addition to your fee, of course."

"That's a very tempting offer, Mrs. Bennet, and be-

53

lieve me I'd love to accept. But you see, if I'm right about your husband, then part of the money you're looking for may be the result of criminal activity. It could be seized by the police. And there's always the IRS. They'll want to know if he declared it."

Mrs. Bennet looked dismayed. "You mean, I might not get anything?"

"I really don't know. But if you've been signing a joint return, you better check with a lawyer."

There was a sudden rush of color to Mrs. Bennet's cheeks and she threw her pen on the table. "That bastard! He not only screws me out of my share, but I could go to jail!"

The woman was so obviously upset that Abby almost reached out and patted her hand. She restrained herself. What was Mrs. Bennet's first name? Esther, that was it. "I don't think you have to worry about jail, Esther. Not unless there's evidence you knew what was going on."

Grim-faced, Mrs. Bennet shoved the check across the table. "Take this, Mrs. McKenzie."

She should have known Mrs. B was not the informal type. "As long as you understand the situation, Mrs. Bennet." Abby picked up the check and tapped it on the table. "I'll see what I can find out."

"If you find the money, just tell me. I'll take my chances on getting my share. If not, I'll still have the pleasure of seeing him rot in jail." She grew thoughtful. "Could help me with the IRS too, couldn't it? Isn't there a reward? Ten percent I believe."

"You said your husband had done pretty well in the insurance business. Frankly, I wouldn't have guessed from seeing his outer office. It's dusty, the plants are dying, and there is a general sense that little business gets transacted there."

"Oh, that's Mrs. Tarbell. She always made sure those

54

things were taken care of when she was his secretary. But since she's retired—"

Remembering the calendar in Bennet's outer office, Abby hazarded a guess. "On May eighteenth?"

"How did you—of course—*that's* why Madame Gladys sent me to you. You have the gift!"

"Gift?"

Mrs. Bennet leaned back, smiling. "You're psychic!"

"Really, Mrs. Bennet. There's nothing psychic about—" Madame Gladys. Where had she—had Mac mentioned her? "Who is Madame Gladys?"

Leaning forward, still smiling, she said, "You really *must* meet her. She's a neighbor of yours, you know. Moved in over Kurtz's bakery about a month ago. I first met her at a psychic fair in Rosemont and convinced her that Olde Sarahville would be a much more suitable location than Lincoln Avenue in Chicago."

"Psychic fair?"

"She's really marvelous. The things she can tell you. She occasionally does tea leaves, but her real gift is with the Tarot."

"And you believe all that?"

"She sent me here, didn't she? Now I must be going. I'll be late as it is." Mrs. Bennet stood and started to leave.

"But you were going to tell me all about your husband!"

Over her shoulder, Mrs. B said, "Of course! We must get together soon."

Disappointment at Mrs. B's abrupt departure was quickly overcome by elation. I'm on his trail now, Abby thought. Hidden assets. A spy in the enemy camp. This private eye business is a snap.

Now, if I can just find where he hides his money. The checks. Start there. Were they made out to the insurance company or—no they must be made to Bennet. Otherwise Mrs. B wouldn't—but she might because she could easily estimate his commission. Or did independent agents deduct their commission before sending the money on? She'd have to find out.

In any case, the money hadn't flowed through his business or personal accounts. So there must be an account Mrs. B didn't know about. Without an account cashing the checks would be a problem and he'd need to write checks to the insurance company. How do you go about finding an account? Couldn't just call banks at random and ask.

Follow Bennet until he visited his money? No telling how long that would take, and she still had to get ready for Founder's Day.

Abby sighed and poured a cup of the coffee Mrs. B had refused. Maybe the private eye business wasn't such a snap after all.

Her train of thought, which had just entered a dark tunnel, was derailed by a loud knocking at the back porch screen door. She hurried out to admit two women.

The one that had done the knocking was tall, thin, and dressed for a safari. Khaki pants with numerous large pockets, a matching jacket or shirt (Abby was never quite sure which these things were meant to be) with many additional pockets, and horn-rimmed sunglasses. She was in her late fifties with short dark hair graying at the sides.

"Understood the shop wasn't open for business, so we took the liberty of coming around back. I'm Irene Quill." A brief chuckle and she continued, "Friends call me Goose. Can't think why."

Abby extended her hand and it was firmly grasped. "Glad to know you—Goose. "I'm Abby—"

"Yes, we know. This is my chum, here, Estelle

56

Prestwick. Nobody would dream of calling her anything but Estelle."

The other half of the duo, a bit younger and much shorter, had been standing quietly by, smiling gently. Her violet eyes widened as she said, "Pleased to meet you, Mrs. McKenzie." She wore a floral print dress and medium heels. If there was any gray in her brown hair it had been artfully concealed.

"Just Abby will do. Won't you ladies come in? As you said, I'm not open for business yet, but the coffeepot is on."

"Thank you," Goose said. "Skip the coffee if you don't mind. Lots to do this morning. We were referred by Madame Gladys."

Abby sighed. "Of course. Isn't everyone."

"Don't want you to get the wrong idea. Don't hold with a lot of superstitious nonsense. Spirits, seances, things that go bump in the night. Scientific turn of mind myself."

"Absolutely," Estelle said. "Of course there *is* evidence for ESP and precognition. Perhaps you are familiar with Professor Rhine?"

"Of course, Estelle. Everybody's heard of him. Mustn't insult Abby's intelligence."

"As a matter of fact," Abby said, "I'm a little hazy—"

"And the ancient astronauts," Estelle continued. "Not to mention UFO's and the work of Hynek."

Goose nodded. "Ancient astronauts. Just climb in the Andes, as I have. The evidence is plain to see."

Impressed, Abby said, "You mountain climb?"

"Used to. Don't mind admitting I'm getting a bit on for the sport. Touch of arthritis. Came on about the time I retired."

"Well, if you'd take your marigold tea, dear—"

"I'm sure Abby's not interested in all that."

Looking for some clue as to why Madame Gladys,

57

whoever she might be, had sent these two, Abby asked, "Retired, you say?"

"Civil servant. Military before that. Graves registration."

"Goose insists on telling the most awful stories. I simply refuse to listen."

"Someone has to do it."

"Just why *did* the Madame send you?" Abby asked.

"Need some detecting, of course."

"At least Madame Gladys *says* we do."

Goose frowned at her chum. "Hasn't steered us wrong yet, has she?"

"No. But he's such a pleasant gentleman."

"Is he? Abby, here, will soon find out."

Abby took a sip from her cup to give her time to sort out what she had heard. The coffee was cold, and she realized that, up to this point, there was nothing to sort. But at least she could straighten out an obvious misconception. "You must understand that it's my husband who's the detective."

"But you're his associate," Estelle said.

"In a way, yes, but—"

"And you're the one investigating Lawrence Bennet." It was clear Goose was not asking a question.

"Bennet? How did you know about that?"

Estelle smiled gently.

Goose laughed. "Madame Gladys. Sees all, knows all. Not literally. Too many unknown factors. Psychic phenom's not a hundred percent reliable."

"But I must admit," Estelle said, "she is more reliable than most."

"I see Abby is champing at the bit and we're holding her up. Let's get to it. Several months ago Lawrence Bennet sold us annuities. Estelle, Charles, and me as well."

"Charles?"

58

"Yes, he rents the apartment over the garage. Nice fellow, though a bit peculiar in some ways."

Not willing to get sidetracked again, Abby asked, "The annuities. What about them?"

"All seemed aboveboard to me. Estelle and I in similar circumstance. Pension, a bit in small investments. Fairly comfortable. In any case, this Bennet convinced us there were tax advantages to putting what we had into this annuity thing."

"And now you think it was a bad investment?"

"Can't say that, exactly."

"We really can't say that."

"But there it was," Goose said. "She laid out the cards and pointed it out. If we didn't do something, we'd lose it all."

Estelle's lip trembled. "A disaster."

"Putting it mildly. We're not rich, you know."

"How much did you put into this, exactly?"

"Ten thousand. Each."

"I see. But my husband—"

"Madame Gladys was most particular about that. It was *you* we were to see."

"Said you'd soon sort it out. Just let us know the rate. We're not rich, as I said. But we can't afford to lose it all, so I suppose we must bear the cost."

Abby gave in to fate's maneuvering. Or the Madame's. "We'll work out something on the bill. You're not the only client after the same thing, so I suppose it's not fair to charge you each full price for the same hour. Did you bring the insurance papers?"

"Of course. Estelle?"

Estelle Prestwick took a thick envelope from her purse and gave it to Abby.

"And what's his name—Charles. Are his papers here also?"

"Oh no," Estelle said. "Charles is very independent.

59

He said he'd take care of Mr. Bennet himself!"

"All talk. Well, no doubt you'll have further questions for us, once you've examined all that." Irene Quill, a.k.a. Goose, dipped into one of her many pockets and handed Abby a calling card. "Give us a jingle. Perhaps you'd like to come around. Estelle does a fine lunch."

Abby saw them to the door and watched them drive away, her mind in a whirl. Yesterday she had been frustrated by the lack of concrete leads to Bennet's shenanigans. Today she was up to her eyeballs in leads. And clients.

Clients! Oh, God, what would Mac say? How had she let herself in for this? Had she broken any laws by taking four clients for the same case? Had she broken her marriage vows? Or was it a commandment? Thou shalt not meddle.

She tossed her cold coffee in the sink. Especially after the bitchy way she'd behaved yesterday. And he had dismissed the entire incident at the first hint of apology, which almost made her mad all over again.

But all had ended well. She poured a fresh cup, and carried it to the front sales room. Looking at the clutter of catalogs spread over the counter, she felt a decided lack of enthusiasm. She carried the cup out onto the porch.

The street scene was a bit more encouraging than it had been last week. A crew was cleaning up construction debris from Elmer's building, and the exterior looked finished. She had to admit he'd done a good job. It was a single structure divided into six shops, each with an apartment on the second floor. The units had been given separate fronts so they appeared to be separate buildings. The entire project had a turn-of-the-century appearance.

A lone female figure walked in the middle of the street, kicking up dust, and heading toward Abby. I really must put up a sign telling people we won't open till September, she thought. Although, she had to admit, none of those coming to the door so far would have cared whether the store was open or shut. She hoped that wasn't a sign of things to come.

This one didn't look like a typical customer either. She wore the prescribed adolescent uniform: tight jeans, tee shirt, white sneakers, no socks. Her long blonde hair was pulled back in a pony tail. The figure arrived at the McKenzie front walk and Abby revised her age upward by a decade. Definitely not a teenager. As the woman mounted to the porch Abby pushed her estimate of age up another notch. Over thirty. But she had a sunny smile, a full set of freckles, and a slim body barely topping five feet in height.

Abby smiled a welcome and wondered if she too had been sent by Madame Gladys. "Good morning. I'm Abby McKenzie, proprietor of this yet-to-be store."

The woman held out her hand. "Hi. I'm Gladys."

# Chapter Six

In addition to a number of necessary lumber and hardware items, a demonstrator at one store beguiled Mac into buying a tool that could slice bricks. He decided it might be best to smuggle the gadget into the basement rather than explain why he might need a sliced brick.

Station wagon loaded at last, he headed for home. Reaching Leichtdorf Road, thinking of Kim and her dog, he turned south and headed for the Daugherty place.

Roy Daugherty called through the screen door, inviting him to have a beer. Wiping his brow, Mac accepted with thanks, and joined Daugherty on the porch. He had just taken the cold can when Mrs. Daugherty came out.

She wore a skirt and blouse and her hair fell to her shoulders in soft waves. Much less the harried housewife than Mac's first impression of her. "I'm glad you came, Mr. McKenzie," she said. "Could you talk to Kim?"

"Come on, Fran," Daugherty said. "Mac's got better things to do than worry about our kid. Besides, they all do this kind of thing. What's the big deal?"

"*You* don't have to take the phone calls." She turned to Mac. "If she hadn't blacked out the number, *you'd* be getting the calls."

"At least *he* wouldn't get bent out of shape about it. Hell, kids are kids."

Mac's head swiveled back and forth between the combatants. "What does my number have to do with this?"

"You remember giving Kim your card?" she asked.

Mac nodded.

"Well, she put her name on. K. R. Daugherty, Secret Agent. And changed the phone number. But it still says McKenzie Associates."

Smiling, Mac said, "That seems harmless enough."

"Sure," Daugherty said. "Kids play those kind of games."

"Oh? Well I got a call from Wanda Grossman this morning. Wants to know what my kid's doing peeking in her window. When she hollered at her, Kim shoved your card in front of her, said 'official business,' and ran like hell."

"So what's old round bottom all excited about," Daugherty asked.

"Grossman's out of town and she's *probably* entertaining. Lord only knows what Kim saw. When I asked Kim she just stared off in the distance and said 'not much.' "

Laughing, Daugherty said, "Okay. I'll talk to her. You want to join in, Mac? Maybe you can scare her into behaving."

Mac felt a bit uncomfortable with the idea of scaring small children, but agreed to explain that his card was for official use only. "But what I really stopped in for was to see whether the dog showed up."

Mrs. Daugherty shook her head. "I think maybe that's behind her private eye fantasy. She wants to find Fidget."

"I'm sorry about that, Mrs. —"

"Just Fran, please. When you call me Mrs., I feel

63

like Roy's mother." She glared at her husband. "Not that he doesn't need somebody to grab him by the ear sometimes."

"Guess I better get back to earning my fee." Mac drank the last of his beer. "I really thought the ad would turn something up."

"If you could—"

"Can't ask the man to drop his business to hunt for a dog, Fran."

"No, it's okay. Losing a dog is serious business to a kid. And I *did* promise her. Is she around?"

Grinning, Daugherty said, "She's in her office." He pointed to the barn. "Go right on in."

The inside of the barn, dimly lit by sunlight filtering through gaps in the siding, contained the tools and materials of the mason's trade. A horse stall, the only remaining sign of the building's farming origins, occupied the far corner. Kim was not in sight. Faint sounds came from the stall. Mac approached quietly.

The stall, or office, was furnished with a three-legged stool and a refrigerator carton that served as a desk. The great detective herself lay on the floor, one leg raised, balancing a bucket on her foot.

"How's the case going, Secret Agent Dougherty?"

The bucket crashed to the floor and Kim scrambled to her feet.

"Sorry," Mac said. "Did I scare you?"

Kim stared at the floor. "Mom told me I wasn't supposed to show anybody your card. Are you mad?"

"No, I'm not mad. But you really shouldn't peek in people's windows. How would you like it if somebody peeked in yours?"

"Isn't that what you do, Mr. McKenzie?"

Mac laughed. "Not usually. What private detectives do mostly is ask people questions and then think about the answers."

"What if nobody wants to talk to you?"

"Yes. Well. That can be a problem. Maybe it's because you're asking questions that aren't any of your business. What do you ask?"

Kim sat on the carton/desk and kicked her heels against its side. "Mostly I asked if they had my dog."

"That's okay to ask. Wouldn't people answer that?"

"Some did," she admitted. "But some didn't."

"Did they say why they wouldn't answer?"

She shook her head. "Mrs. Grossman didn't come to the door. I could tell she was home 'cause her car was there. When I looked in the window she got awful mad." Kim blushed. "She was kissing with somebody."

Mac forced a serious expression on his face. "You know, Kim, a private detective's work is always confidential. You have to promise not to tell what you see or hear."

Kim stared at her knees and kicked the carton rapidly.

"Promise?"

She nodded and her expression brightened as they left the subject of Mrs. Grossman behind. "That spooky man in the garage wouldn't come to the door either. And when I tried to peek in he pulled down the shade."

"What spooky man?"

"I don't know his name."

"He was in his garage?"

"He lives upstairs. Nobody was home in the house."

Mac didn't find this entirely clear, but let it pass. "Why do you say the man is spooky?"

Her face lit with pleasure. "He looks like the man

65

who plays Dracula. Only different. And he stared right at me through the window and his eyes got really big and he raised up his hand and made a sign in the air."

"Then what happened?"

"He pulled down the shade."

Mac leaned against the wall of the stall and thought about this for a while. Then he asked, "How did he look different than Dracula?"

"He was real old. Even older than you."

"That *is* old. But Dracula is old too."

"His hair was all white, and some was growing out of his ears."

Mac grinned. *"Really* old! Can you tell me where he lives?"

"Uh huh." Her voice dropped to a whisper. "Past the pit of hell."

Startled, Mac said, "The pit—where did you get that name?"

"That's what Mom calls it. She says it's evil and I should stay away."

"Do you? Stay away?"

Kim jumped off the carton. "Are you going to arrest him?"

"Dracula? No. But I'll go talk to him. And don't go near the pit again. It's not evil, but it can be dangerous."

Mac stopped at the intersection of Leichtdorf and Stuart Roads. Kim said the house was past the pit, but did that mean on Leichtdorf which ran along the east side, or on Stuart, a curving gravel road that ran approximately parallel to the southern edge?

He chose Stuart. There were several houses on half-acre lots, each lot including a heavily wooded strip bordering the pit's edge. If this was where the mysterious Dracula lived he might have to try each house.

His search was brief. The second house had a three car garage behind it with an apartment above. This made immediate sense of Kim's description; the man in the garage who lived upstairs. And the people in the house still weren't home as he discovered by ringing the bell.

The house was at least fifty years old and in need of a new roof. Greater care had been given to the front yard. The lawn was recently cut and, unlike the dormant grass baking in most yards this dry August, was green from frequent watering. A bed of gladioli ringed with petunias added color.

The backyard was shaded by several trees and the grass grew with less authority. But here too foliage plants ringed each tree and bordered the gravel drive. Mac climbed the outside stairs that led to a small porch above the garage.

He rang the bell. There was no answer. A shade was drawn over the window in the door and the window on the right. He pressed his ear to the glass, but heard nothing.

Descending, he walked behind the garage. A narrow strip of weed-infested grass separated garage from woods. The entrance to a path was guarded by flanking tree stumps. The rear wall of the garage was pierced by two windows. Mac rubbed away some of the grime coating the glass, but saw nothing of interest; a lawn mower, a snow blower, several bags that might have contained fertilizer, and assorted gardening tools.

Mac passed between the stump sentinels and followed the woodland path. It was free of vegetation or dried leaves and from time to time he noted a footprint in the dust-dry dirt.

A hundred yards into the woods he nearly stepped off the edge of the pit. He leaned forward carefully and looked down.

To his surprise he saw a wooden ladder. Obviously homemade, about fifty feet long, it ended where the slope became less precipitous. A path with several switchbacks continued on to the bottom. Dracula, it seemed, had a private entrance to the Pit of Hell.

Farrell said Ingram lived near Leichtdorf. Kim's description of the man over the garage, allowing for a strong measure of imagination, fit Ingram. So assume it *is* Charles Ingram.

Mac was about to turn away when he saw someone moving in the pit. It was only a brief glimpse before the figure disappeared in the trees, but he was fairly certain he had seen a mane of white hair.

The book was found near the dog's collar. Ingram recognized the book, but denied it. Ingram spent so much time in the pit he had made his own entrance.

Mac grasped the top of the ladder and gave it an exploratory shake. It appeared to be firmly anchored. Most of the area consisted of sand and gravel deposited by the last glacier, but this edge of the pit was an outcropping of solid rock.

So Charles Ingram, seated on a log to practice incantations, heard Fidget yelping. He freed the dog and carried it up the ladder, leaving the book behind. But where was Fidget? Not in the garage. Probably not in the apartment or the house; ringing the doorbell would have been answered by yelping and barking.

Mac descended rapidly, noting the ladder was pinned in place by steel stakes. He could think of several reasons for Ingram to take the dog, ranging from the macabre to a love of animals. But why leave *The Ancient Religion* behind? Had he been startled or disturbed?

68

By what? Mac thought of nothing plausible.

Except—what might disturb Charles Ingram wouldn't necessarily be apparent to anyone else.

The trail from ladder's end to pit bottom was not too steep and he was soon moving along the only path leading away into the undergrowth. After a few yards it turned west, paralleling the pit edge. Another hundred yards and he came to a path that branched north. But Charles Ingram, if it was Ingram, had been heading west.

He could see the west wall of the pit looming just ahead when he came upon a clearing with a large boulder in its center. The top of the boulder was fairly flat, forming a natural table. A wrought iron candlestick stood on the table—or altar?

A smaller boulder just to the right of the trail suggested a stool and Mac sat down to think things over. He hadn't begun to think before he caught a flash of white out of the corner of his eye. As he turned his head a ball of fur struck him in the chest and toppled him backward.

He looked up into a hairy face and a pink tongue that was trying to wash his nose. He reached up and scratched the dog's ear. "Well, hello, Fidget. Where the hell have you been?"

# Chapter Seven

Abby sat across the kitchen table from Madame Gladys. "You are certainly not what I expected."

Gladys grinned and slipped into Gabor Hungarian. "You expected maybe Maria Ouspenskaya and a were-wolf?"

"Something like that," Abby laughed.

"You should see me in my professional rig. Golden earrings, makeup, purple dress, and babushka. As a matter of fact, you'll see me at the Founder's Day Arts and Crafts fair. I'm not sure if I'm listed under art, or craft."

"Some of each, I expect. As a matter of fact, I'll have a booth there."

"I know. Right across from mine."

"Was that a psychic flash?"

Gladys shook her head. "I don't leave stuff like that to chance. First time I signed up for one of these things I found myself between a guy frying bratwurst and a woman who made dolls out of toilet paper rolls. The worst part of it was, it was a mile away from the beer tent."

"I thought booth assignments were first come, first served."

"The village clerk hands out assignments. She's a client. Ever been to a fortune-teller? Excuse me—we like to refer to ourselves as psychics these days."

"Never. You don't seem to take it too seriously your-self."

Gladys leaned folded arms on the table. "Depends. A lot is show biz. But not all."

"So sometimes you have a—what do you call it? A vision?"

"No, dollink. It is what the cards reveal." She drew a deck from her purse and fanned out the colorful medieval drawings of the Tarot on the table. "Care for a demonstration?"

Fascinated by the strange cards, Abby asked, "Does each one have a specific meaning?"

"A range of meanings, the interpretation shaded by the cards that surround it. And the meaning is changed when the card falls upside down. Leaves scope for the reader's psychic ability." She gathered up the cards and handed them to Abby. "Shuffle."

Feeling a bit foolish, Abby complied. "Do you always use the cards? No tea leaves? Crystal ball?"

"I can do either, but there's not much challenge. Any fool can look into a crystal ball and claim they see visions. The cards keep you honest, because the client can see exactly what the reader sees. I keep a crystal sitting around for atmosphere, but I haven't used it since my carnival days."

When the deck was thoroughly mixed Gladys sipped her coffee and wrinkled her nose. "I'm afraid I've let this get cold. Would you mind?"

Abby dumped the cold coffee in the sink and poured fresh for both of them.

Gladys drank deeply and said, "Thanks. I needed that." She set her cup aside and laid the top six cards from the shuffled deck faceup in a patterned sequence. "The card in the center is the questioner's present circumstance."

71

"Questioner? I get to ask questions?"

"This is a general reading. We can do another later, if you want. As you see, the card is The Magician. You are a creative, self-reliant person. You are capable of guile, and in your present circumstance may resort to trickery and deception."

"Makes me sound like a swindler."

"I said in present circumstances. You are also strong-willed."

The next card lay on top of The Magician and at right angles to it. It was a picture of a smiling man dangling from a gibbet by his left foot. "The Hanged Man. He crosses you. You are in a time of transition, not sure which course you will follow."

Abby nodded in agreement and Gladys tapped the card above The Magician. "Your destiny, if current trends continue. The Empress. You will become a successful businesswoman and a motivator of your husband."

"This tells you about Mac too?"

Gladys shook her head. "No. It tells me how *you* feel about him. He's too easygoing, unless his interest is engaged. Then he's stubborn."

"That's Mac all right."

"This card to the right, The Chariot, is the past. It seems you have escaped from much turmoil and adversity. You agree?"

Abby's smile was a bit lopsided. "You could say that."

"The card at the bottom is the recent past. It's called, The Lovers"

"Looks sexy," Abby said.

"Again, it shows trials overcome, leading to romance and love. You are a lucky woman."

Abby's smile widened. "*I* think so."

Gladys became Madame Gladys as her expression darkened. "Here to the left we have the future." She tapped the horned figure, The Devil. "This represents evil, or black magic. I can not be more specific. Take warning."

Abby shook off a momentary foreboding and laughed. "Look both ways before crossing? Or am I about to be hexed?"

Gladys smiled and shrugged. "Let's see what the rest of the cards say." She laid four more cards on the table. The first was the Wheel of Fortune. "It seems you are approaching the end of a problem. Whether the result will be good or bad depends on other factors. Such as," she tapped the next card, "The Emperor. A male authority figure, no doubt your husband, a man of war-making tendencies."

"Mac?"

"You don't agree?"

"Well—yes, I suppose I do."

"And this card, Strength, indicates a strong desire to challenge the hidden forces at work." Gladys looked up, meeting Abby's gaze. "That may require guile."

Abby, sure now that this entire reading was being staged to manipulate her, said nothing.

Madame Gladys disappeared and Gladys returned, grinning. "And this last card, The Sun, means success, and perhaps a new friendship."

Abby leaned back in her chair, arms folded. She studied the card layout, memorizing the cards and their position. "If I were to get a book—there *are* books?"

"Lots. I sell a few. Some at the library too."

"So if I looked up the meanings, they would agree with what you just told me?"

"You could get alternative readings. But if any of

these cards were different, my reading would not be possible."

"So your reading is a combination of the luck of the draw and psychic intuition. Right?"

Gladys laughed. *"This* reading is just fitting the cards to my research. A little time with the newspaper files and talking to some locals filled me in on your past. Observation tells me a lot about your present. And like all good fortune-tellers, I'm pretty good at reading character."

"No psychic input here at all?"

"Not a bit."

Abby relaxed. "Are you this frank with all your clients?"

"Hell no. Most of them wouldn't want to know. And I *do* have my psychic moments."

"But what if the cards had fallen differently?"

Gladys reached into her purse and took out another deck of cards. "This is the deck you shuffled. When I asked for fresh coffee I rang in a cold deck. The whole thing was a setup."

"Giving away the secret? Isn't that against union rules?"

"You'll never be a steady customer anyway. Too set on controlling your own destiny. What you just saw was what I do to hook a mark. Once they're in, no more cold decks."

"No dealing seconds? No marked cards?"

"Strictly legit. Sort of. The general reading is like your loss leader, you know? Drags 'em in so you can push stuff with a decent markup."

Abby glanced at the clock. "How about lunch? Just sandwiches."

"I'll settle for a piece of fruit, if you have it."

"Bananas, canteloupe, and plums."

74

"Plums? Love 'em. Expect your husband soon?"

"Hard to say." Abby placed a bowl of fruit on the table and selected a banana. "Now explain why you've been shilling for his business. Not that we don't appreciate the thought."

"A fortune-teller spends more time listening than talking. You'd be amazed at the things people tell me. And then *they're* amazed when I read the same thing back to them from the cards."

Abby nodded. "But how did you know I was checking on Bennet? I'm sure my client doesn't consult cards, tea leaves, or the stars."

"His wife, Esther, consults all three. She was the first one to call after I hung out my shingle."

"So when Mrs. Bennet mentioned her problem you figured I was already working on His Honor and might as well add her. More coffee?"

"No thanks. Maybe a banana."

"But what made you think Estelle and Goose had a problem?"

"*They* thought they had a problem. Bennet's been stalling them about statements, not answering phone calls. They're afraid to face their own suspicions. And Mrs. Bennet more or less confirmed it by telling me how he's been acting, and how the assets have evaporated."

"Why not tell them to call the insurance company? That's cheaper than a private investigation."

"Okay. Suppose they did. And suppose the deal *is* phony. Then what? Go to the cops?"

"Why not?"

"They arrest Bennet, he claims he spent the money, cops a plea, does maybe a year, digs up the cash, and takes off. Who needs that kind of justice? Money's better."

"I see your point, but if he has it in a bank some- where, I don't see how anybody can get their hands on it. Except the police, of course."

"Forget about banks. He knows his scam can come apart any minute and the first thing that'll happen is a search for accounts that can be frozen." Gladys opened her purse. "Mind if I smoke? Lousy habit, but I can't kick it."

Abby brought out the ashtray she kept under the sink and put it on the table. "You mean he'd keep all that money buried in the petunia bed? Even so, there's no guarantee they'd get theirs back. They'd have to stand in line with anybody else he's cheated."

Gladys raised an eyebrow and blew smoke at the ceiling. "First find the money. *Then* we'll see." She grinned. "No use worrying about the future till it gets here."

"Strange talk for a fortune-teller." Abby picked up The Hanged Man. "Time of transition, huh? Which card says a Gypsy is stage-managing the change?"

"My child, you are a skeptic."

"I can swallow a coincidence as well as the next one, but today is a bit much. First Mrs. B. Then the strange ladies. Then you. All between breakfast and lunch."

"It does seem fate is riding you pretty hard. But it's really simple. I heard from Mrs. B two months ago and then got an update last week. Goose and company were in to see me two weeks ago. I didn't tumble to their problem right away. Just felt uneasy about it."

"And what did you tell them all?"

"The usual smoke. The trends aren't established yet. Future's cloudy. Keep in touch for late bulletins. Then Mabel came to see me yesterday, and the whole thing

76

fell into place. Called them this morning and told them to see you. Then decided to stop in myself before you came looking for me with a butterfly net."

Abby thought this over and decided it was all just barely possible. "Okay. For now." She grinned. "Why not give me a reading? I'll ask the cards where the money's gone."

"Ask me something else. I've already struck out on that one." She stubbed out her cigarette and produced a deck from her purse. "This is the one you shuffled. What will it be?"

Abby thought a moment. "The only other problem—tell me how to find Fidget."

Gladys started laying out the cards. "This is The Pope and he's upside down. Impotence. Probably means you can't do anything about the dog because it's your husband that's looking."

"How did you know?"

"Fran Daugherty."

"Is every woman in town your client? And how come no men?"

"It is not macho, dollink. They come, but if I tell who they are, they crap."

Abby laughed and nodded. "If Mac ever went to a psychic—not that he would—he'd die before he'd tell anyone."

"Maybe we can change his mind. Whoops! The Pope is crossed by The Fool. Inverted." She laid down a card showing a man carrying a hobo's bindle. He seemed unconcerned about the dog trying to tear out the seat of his pants. "I'd say someone made, or is about to make, a bad decision. Well, let's look at Destiny."

She turned the next card and started to place it on the table. The blood drained from her face. Hand

77

trembling, she placed the card back on the deck. "These cards must have gotten mixed up in my purse. We'll have to skip the reading."

Abby flipped the card faceup and stared at Death.

# Chapter Eight

Mac struggled to his feet, keeping a firm grip on the undersized poodle. She lived up to her name, wagging her tail enthusiastically, her whole body moving in counterpoint.

Anxious to get the dog home, he rapidly retraced his steps to the ladder. Ascending proved difficult with Fidget under his left arm. He wondered how Charles Ingram had managed. He set the dog on the ground at the top of the ladder, taking a chance on her scurrying off. Instead, Fidget fidgeted impatiently in front of his face while he crawled off, apparently preferring human company to lonely wandering.

When she jumped into the station wagon he examined her carefully. Her coat was clean and free of burrs.

Before the wagon rolled to a stop in the Daugherty's drive Kim was running to meet them while Fidget tried to scratch a hole through the window. The excited squeals and frantic barking brought Fran Daugherty out, and Mac turned to her with a broad and foolish grin.

"I assume you know this dog?"

"Where on earth did you find her?"

"In the pit." He watched Kim and Fidget racing

79

around the yard until Kim fell exhausted and the dog stood on her chest, tongue dripping. "She seems to be in good health."

"Somebody must have had her then," Fran said. "She couldn't have been down there all this time."

Mac saw no reason to stir up trouble by mentioning Charles Ingram. "I guess you're glad to get her back," he said, beginning to wonder if that was true. Fran was not smiling as expected.

"At least that's one good thing today. It'll take her mind off her father."

"Trouble?"

She sighed. "His damn temper. The police arrested him a little while ago. Now I have to find a lawyer. Do you know any, Mac?"

"Sure. Why was he arrested?"

"Bennet and that Kazmierski drove up. Soon as he saw them he grabbed his shotgun and ran outside. The mayor no sooner opened his mouth and said something about business when Ray fired a shot in the air and ordered 'em off the property."

"And?"

"A police car was passing. He stopped and ran up with his gun out hollering for Ray to drop it. Then he pushed him up against the wall, handcuffed him, and took him away."

Amazed at Daugherty's stupidity, Mac said, "Did he have to start a shooting war? Couldn't he just order them off?"

"Sometimes he don't think. Specially where the mayor's concerned." She blushed. "I'll never forget the time he shoved the mayor's face in a punch bowl!"

Mac sighed. "Okay. Let me make a call. If my lawyer's available, we'll take Kim and Fidget over to my place and I'll take you to his office."

* * *

Abby sat behind the cash register in her store and stared moodily at the schoolhouse clock on the wall. When Mac got home, she would be asked how her day had gone. How could she tell him that? How could she describe Mrs. Bennet, Goose, Estelle, and Gladys without telling him he had three new, and unwanted, clients? Four, counting Elmer.

If she kept silent, tried to carry out the commitments she had made on her own, their relationship would deteriorate into a string of lies.

But if she told him, how would he react? Would he sigh and say, "That's all right, dear. You meant well."

She could stand *anything* but that. Better all-out war. She sighed deeply and walked out to the porch. There really was no option, she'd have to tell him. And no time like the present. Mac's station wagon had just turned into Twilly Place.

He stopped in front instead of driving around back, the car door opened and Kim jumped out followed by Fidget. Kim ran up the walk grinning broadly and gained the porch ahead of the dog who had stopped to sniff the scent of those that had gone before.

"Fidget's back! Mr. McKenzie found her. Ain't that great!?"

"That's wonderful, honey." Turning to Mac who had come up the walk a distant third to Kim and her dog, she asked, "How did you manage this on a shopping trip, Oh Great Detective?"

"Kim can tell you about it. Right now I have to take Fran Daugherty to see Metlaff and you've volunteered to babysit. Mind?"

Abby glanced at the station wagon and noticed for

81

the first time the woman sitting in the passenger seat. "Metlaff? Why?"

"My Daddy's in jail, but Mr. McKenzie is gonna get him out and put the mayor in jail."

"Well — at least we'll get your Daddy out."

Mac left immediately and Abby ushered her two charges into the kitchen. In the case of Fidget, that involved stopping at every doorway to call the dog back from excited exploration. She supplied Kim with a glass of milk and a banana, Fidget with a bowl of water and slice of salami. Fidget gulped the meat, ignored the water, and leaped into Abby's lap. After several frantic attempts to climb Abby's chest to lick her face the dog jumped down, curled up at Kim's feet, and fell asleep.

"I can see why you call her Fidget. So tell me. Where has she been?"

"Somebody must have had her, I don't know who. And then she ran away and fell in the Pit of Hell and Mr. McKenzie rescued her."

"That certainly sounds exciting. Did Mr. McKenzie tell you that?"

Kim nodded vigorously. She stuffed the last of the banana in her mouth and chewed slowly while propping her chin on her hand. "Will Mr. McKenzie bring my Daddy home?"

"I'm sure he will, Kim. Do you know why he was arrested?"

"He tried to shoot that fat man that made him dig up the fence. But a policeman made him miss."

"But why does he want to shoot anybody?"

"Because they're politicians, Daddy says. Politicians are always bad guys."

About to launch into a civics lesson, Abby thought better of it and pressed for more information instead.

82

"He must have had a special reason, Kim. Besides the fence. Do you know what it is?"

Kim shook her head. "But he really is a bad guy. I heard—oops!"

"You heard what?"

"Mr. McKenzie said detectives can't tell stuff like that."

"What detective is that, Kim?"

"Me. I found out all kinds of stuff until Mom made me quit."

Abby laughed. "I bet you did. But I'm Mr. McKenzie's partner. You can tell me. What did you hear about Kazmierski? That's the man that made you take down the fence."

"I know. Daddy said his name and a lot of other stuff I ain't allowed to say. See, I was down in the—" Kim blushed and looked out the window.

"Were you down in that gravel pit, Kim?"

"You won't tell?"

"Promise you won't go down there again?"

Kim nodded.

"Okay. What did you hear?"

"The other man Daddy shot at—"

"What other man?"

"Mom says he's the mayor. He was with Mr. Kazmierski today. But one day he was down in there with his fishing stuff—"

"Mr. Kazmierski?"

Kim shook her head. "The mayor. And he went through the tunnel. *Then* Mr. Kazmierski came down and went through the tunnel too. So I tailed him. That's when you follow somebody and they don't know it."

"I bet you're good at that."

Kim grinned. "They didn't hear me or anything. They

were talking real mad. Mr. Kazmierski said something about nickels and dimes. What does that mean?"

"I don't know. What else did he say?"

"He said he wanted his share. So the mayor goes, 'oh yeah?' And Mr. Kazmierski goes, 'Yeah. Or you'll wish,' and starts to walk away. What do you think?"

"It sounds like Mr. Kazmierski thought he wasn't getting his share of some money. And if Mr. Bennet didn't change that, he'd do something to make him wish he had. Did he say what he would do, exactly?"

"Uh huh. He said he'd kill him."

Startled, Abby said, "Oh, I don't think he really meant that."

"He did so. He goes, 'And stay away from my wife or I'll kill you.' Honest."


Mac looked at the peeling green paint on the wall of the interrogation room and wondered what he was doing here. When Fran Daugherty had asked him to go with Metlaff he had refused. Only Roy Daugherty's lawyer would be allowed in, and anyway, he had to finish Abby's booth for the Founder's Day fair. But Fran insisted that Roy respected Mac and hated lawyers. Things would go better if Mac were there.

At that point Metlaff had put his cigar stub in the ashtray, rubbed a hand across his freckled bald head, and sighed in resignation. He agreed to tell the police that Mac was working on the case. Mac surrendered.

Roy Daugherty was brought in looking subdued and a bit nervous. "Guess I really screwed up this time. But how did I know a cop would come by right then? Sometimes I don't see one by my place for a month. And then that horse's ass says I tried to kill him."

Metlaff eyed Daugherty with a grim expression. Mac

realized the expression meant little, merely reflecting the lawyer's view of life and humanity in general. Nothing personal.

"I would advise you to curb your temper in the future," Metlaff said. "Not that I don't appreciate the business people like you bring me. Now let's stop wasting the time you are paying for. What happened. Precisely."

Daugherty told them, the story differing only in minor details from the one they had already heard from Fran.

"The animosity you bear toward Bennet and Kazmierski. What is its origin? Surely not the fence incident alone?"

Shaking his head, Daugherty said, "Goes back a long way. I knew Bennet when his name was Benkovski, back in the old neighborhood."

"Old neighborhood?"

"In Chicago. We lived around North Avenue and Western when I was a kid. The old man did car repairs in our garage. Liked to be his own boss. Said he had enough of taking orders during the war. Not much money in it—"

"I assume Bennet enters this tale at some point?"

"Bennet hung around the ward office a lot. I was pretty young then, so some of this I heard from my old man later. Anyway, Bennet comes around and tells us running a business in the garage is illegal and there's all kinds of permits and inspections and it's a residential area. But for a few bucks he can fix it with the ward committeeman."

"And like any good Chicagoan, he paid."

"Sure. Figured that's just the way things were. But Bennet kept coming back for more until the old man got sick of it and threw him out. Next thing, an inspector shows up. But we're ready. The old man had gotten to be buddies with the precinct captain, a few more bucks changed hands, only this time with somebody that'd stay bought, and everything was okay."

"And this childhood incident, which you probably didn't understand at the time—"

"Where'd *you* grow up? Sure I understood."

Mac, having grown up not far from the scene of this story, grinned in appreciation. Metlaff was not amused. But then, Metlaff never was.

"Nevertheless, this can hardly be the sole cause of your extreme dislike. Anything else?"

"Yeah. I was about fourteen when he started up with Mary, my sister. She was about seventeen then, but not too bright where guys were concerned, you know what I mean? And he was a lot older. Bein' a kid myself, he was an old man to me. She kept it a secret 'cause the old man would have a fit if he knew."

"He treated her badly?"

"I was coming home from the movies. The Tiffin, you know where it was?"

Metlaff waved off the question impatiently. Mac nodded.

"I saw him with Mary. He had a hold of her arm and kind of pulled her into a gangway." Daugherty's jaw tightened and his fist clenched. "When I got there he had her pushed up against the side of the building and she seemed to be trying to get away so I hollered something. I don't remember what. Mary broke away and ran out past me. Bennet grabbed me by the shirt, rammed me up against the wall."

Daugherty pressed his hands against the table, fingers spread; he looked at the backs, turned them over, inspected the palms. Then he sat back in the armless chair, almost relaxed. "The bastard slapped my face."

86

Mac thought about the effect of this incident on a fourteen-year-old boy. The memory of young Daugherty's humiliation seemed still to strongly affect Daugherty the man. Enough to motivate an attempt on Bennet's life?

Not according to Fran's account. But she *was* his wife.

"Were there any further incidents?" Metlaff asked.

"I heard he got a job up in Lake County somewhere. Anyway, he moved out of the neighborhood."

Metlaff's habitual scowl had deepened. "Your wife told us of more recent events. The incident of the punch bowl. Shouting threats in the village hall. Have you anything to add?"

Daugherty shook his head.

"So the position is this. There is a history of animosity going back many years. There are recent incidents to prove the intensity of feeling has not diminished. The alleged victims claim you shot at them. The police officer cannot confirm or deny your statement that you fired into the air. But on the whole he will tend to corroborate Bennet's claim."

Daugherty's shoulders drooped. "So what can we do?"

"I'm afraid you are in for a night in jail, but there should be no trouble in gaining your release on bail in the morning. Meantime we will take certain steps."

Mac spoke for the first time. "How far from them were you when you fired?"

"Less than ten yards."

"You couldn't miss at that range with a scattergun. Where were they at the time?"

"Kazmierski was on the passenger side. He had the door open and was getting out. Bennet was already out."

87

"Had he moved away from the car?"

"No. He had the door open and was standing behind it."

"What did they do?"

"When I lit the shell? Kazmierski froze." Daugherty's grin reminded Mac of a wolf's snarl. "Bennet ducked. Probably had to change his pants when he got home."

Mac looked at Metlaff and smiled. "Bennet will claim he ducked *before* the shot, which is why he wasn't hit at such short range. But that means the car would have been peppered with buckshot."

Metlaff nodded. "Certainly a point to be argued to a jury. But—there was no proper investigation. The arresting officer's—strike that. John Almeir's report makes no mention of the crime scene. Apparently he decided the word of two public officials and his own eye witness account was all that was needed."

"Almeir? He's the guy that just happened to be passing? Now that is a coincidence."

"Yes. Isn't it," Metlaff agreed.

Daugherty, obviously puzzled, said, "What difference who came by? Who's Almeir?"

"Captain of the village bluesuits," Mac said. "Bennet is his buddy and the main reason Almeir made his rank."

"You mean this was a setup?"

Metlaff sighed in exasperation. "How could they predict your precise reaction? More likely Bennet asked Almeir to be present just in case you behaved as foolishly as you are prone to do. However, one thing is clear."

"What's that?" Mac asked.

"You must make sure Bennet doesn't take the car off somewhere and cook the evidence."

"Me?" Mac was not as surprised as he appeared. Knowing Metlaff, and given the circumstances, he would have been surprised *not* to be asked to investigate. He might have refused, but he *had* promised Kim to get her Daddy out of jail. "Okay." He hated to admit it to himself, but this was a lot more interesting than converting grams of yarn. "Then the sooner the better."

"And I'm sure it has occurred to you," Metlaff said, "that, should you actually observe Mr. Bennet falsifying evidence, the situation would change dramatically."

Mac grinned. "It crossed my mind."

# Chapter Nine

On leaving the interrogation room Mac and Metlaff agreed that speed was essential. Sooner or later it would occur to Bennet that his undamaged car did not support his claim of attempted murder. Mac must be on his tail before that happened.

"You take the Daugherty women home, and I'll get onto Bennet."

"Women? Mrs. Daugherty and who else?"

"Abby's babysitting with Kim and Fidget. While you're there you can explain to Abby that I'll be late. No point in her waiting up."

"Fidget? Strange name for a child."

"You'll like her."

Mac bent a few speed laws getting to Bennet's split-level brick on the north edge of Sarahville. He was relieved to find Bennet's undamaged Cadillac in the drive. Faced with a possible all night vigil, and having eaten nothing since breakfast, he took a chance on driving to a nearby Burger King.

By 7 P.M. he had settled in a half block from Bennet's home with two cheeseburgers and a large coffee. Before he could take the first bite Bennet trotted out of the house, got in his car, and took off heading west. Mac cursed, slipped the lid back on the coffee container, and set off after him.

Tailing the Cadillac presented no problem. Traffic was

heavy enough so that Mac could keep at least two cars between him and his quarry, and light enough that there was little chance of losing him.

At seven-thirty Bennet stopped at the Fox Valley National Bank in Elgin. It was open until eight on Friday night to accommodate weekly paychecks and weekend shopping. Mac got two bites out of a cold cheeseburger before Bennet reappeared and they were off and running again.

This time they travelled north on Route 31, then turned left to the Kane County Savings and Loan in West Dundee. Here Bennet beat the 8 P.M. closing by five minutes, and then moved on to the nearby Sleepy Hollow Motel. He parked at the far end of the rear lot and waited several minutes, apparently looking things over, before he got out and walked rapidly toward the motel. He failed to notice Mac, who had pulled in between two vans.

The motel was a one-story structure consisting of twenty units and a small office. The office opened to the street side, the rooms faced the rear where picture windows overlooked the rolling hills of the Fox River valley. As Bennet approached a room midway in the building, the door opened. Whoever was inside remained out of sight as Bennet entered.

Mac waited until he was sure no one was watching, then walked over and paused outside the room. He hadn't expected anything else, but was still a bit disappointed at the silence and the fully closed blinds. There was a red Mustang parked directly in front of the door. Mac noted the license number on the assumption it belonged to the room's occupant. Then he returned to his cold coffee, cheeseburger, and some guilt.

If Bennet was seeing a woman, this could be a long vigil. Founder's Day was tomorrow. He should be helping

Abby with last minute chores. And she expected him to set up the booth early in the morning. Well, a night without sleep and a little exercise at dawn wouldn't kill him.

He looked at the second cold cheeseburger with distaste and decided there were worse things than starvation.

He would have to explain to Abby why he had changed his mind about the detective business. He was having a little trouble explaining it to himself. He wasn't even sure when he had made that decision. Maybe the turning point had been Abby's little seminar in the art of retail salesmanship. Maybe it was the growing feeling that Abby wasn't really keen on having him underfoot in her store.

Or maybe he just liked sticking his nose into other people's business. McKenzie the neighborhood snoop. For instance, why had Bennet raced around the countryside to make two banks before closing? Neither one was in or near Sarahville. And what was he really doing at Daugherty's place today? Surely not about the fence. Did he really hope to provoke a confrontation that would allow Almeir to make an arrest? If so, why?

And who was in the motel with Bennet?

Mac dozed intermittently from eleven on, finally getting out of his car at two in the morning to avoid a sound sleep. He took the coffee container and uneaten cheeseburger to a nearby trash can and walked around to the front of the motel. The vacancy sign was lit and the night clerk was not in sight. He looked up at the sky and saw that the stars were also out of sight. After four weeks of no rain it looked like the weather was about to dump on Sarahville's Founder's Day.

He strolled back, turning the corner of the building just as Bennet's Cadillac disappeared around the opposite corner. Cursing, Mac broke into a run, jumped into his car, and reached for the ignition. At that moment the door of the motel room opened and a woman came out moving quickly. Mac ducked out of sight, but he needn't have bothered. The woman got into the red Mustang without looking around and left rubber in the parking lot as she roared onto the street.

Resigned to having lost Bennet, and for lack of a better plan, Mac decided to follow the woman.

That turned out to be a lucky choice. Within a mile it became apparent that the Mustang was following the Cadillac and the entire three-car caravan was headed back to Sarahville. The woman in the Mustang kept well back and, when possible, stayed behind another car in the sparse traffic.

Bennet turned onto Leichtdorf Road. That presented a problem, even for an experienced shadow. At this hour there was no traffic and following Bennet around the corner, particularly in a car he would recognize, was bound to give the game away. But the driver of the Mustang was equal to the challenge. She turned off her lights and stopped at the corner where she could see down Leichtdorf.

Mac passed her and continued through the intersection, turning into the driveway of the first house. He turned out his lights and opened his door so that the interior light went on, then closed it again. It was too dark for her to see whether he had gone into the house, but the brief flash of light should convince her that he had.

He waited but an instant before her lights came back on and she turned onto Leichtdorf. He followed and was surprised to find the Cadillac parked about where the steep path led down into the old gravel pit. The Mustang stopped, forcing him to pass. He turned on the street where he had found Charles Ingram's ladder, parked, and trotted back to the corner.

At first he saw nothing in the darkness. Then he gradually became aware of a dark shape at the side of the road and guessed it was the woman, probably looking over the edge of the pit. His guess was confirmed when she suddenly began running along the road in his direction. She paused several times, apparently trying to see into the pit, but Mac knew from experience that, even in daylight, she would see little but dense undergrowth.

It occurred to him that she was trying to track Bennet's flashlight. The beam might be visible intermittently.

She had now reached the southern edge of the pit, and stood directly above the tunnel that ran under the road, and no more than twenty feet from where Mac hid behind a tree. He could now see she was wearing high heels and a knee-length skirt. The darkness washed all colors to varying shades of gray and black.

She glanced around, then back into the pit. Suddenly she ran across the road and climbed the high berm that shielded the second pit. She slipped several times but paid no attention to the damage done to her clothes. In fact, on reaching the top she lay full length on the ground peering over the edge.

The scene held for perhaps five minutes, then she rose and walked back to her car. In a moment she was gone.

Mac retreated to his own car for a flashlight and then ran to Charles Ingram's ladder. Reaching the bottom he followed the narrow gauge tracks to the tunnel. He was about to enter when a movement at the far end caught his eye. Although the night was dark, the tunnel was darker and he could see an indistinct figure silhouetted against the far opening. Bennet? No. Someone else was watching.

Mac approached the tunnel cautiously and strained to

see. After a while his eyes began to water and he had to blink frequently.

The figure moved back toward him, and Mac concealed himself behind a clump of sumac. As the mysterious watcher emerged from the tunnel close to Mac's hiding place he recognized Charles Ingram. Ingram chose concealment on the opposite side of the tunnel opening.

Someone came through the tunnel behind a bobbing flashlight, making no attempt at concealment. This could only be Bennet. He emerged from the tunnel moving rapidly and took the path leading back to the Leichtdorf Road entrance to the pit. As he passed, Ingram rose and followed.

Mac was about to fall in and follow along when the stillness of the night was shattered by the unmistakable sound of a shotgun blast. Mac ran for Ingram's ladder.

It was impossible within the confines of the pit to tell where the shot had come from. But Mac was sure the Cadillac was being decorated. Bennet couldn't have negotiated the winding path, the pools of water, the steeply sloping path, in so short a time. Who had fired the shot?

Reaching the top of the ladder he ran full speed toward where he had parked his car. He reached for the door and suddenly found himself bathed in light. He turned, shielding his eyes against the glare of a flashlight.

"Well. Mr. McKenzie." The voice held a hint of amusement. "What a surprise."

"Who the hell are you?"

"Captain Almeir, Mr. McKenzie." Almeir chuckled. "And you are under arrest on suspicion of burglary."

# Chapter Ten

Mac stood in front of Almeir's desk impassively examining the man's florid face and the strands of black hair carefully combed across a bald dome. Almeir had been reading a report for the past ten minutes while pointedly ignoring Mac.

Finally he looked up, his blue eyes expressionless. "You're in real trouble this time, McKenzie."

Mac, tired of Almeir's game and suffering from hunger and heartburn, fetched a chair from against the wall. He placed it next to Almeir's desk and sat down.

Almeir flushed. "Nobody invited you to sit."

"If I'm not welcome, just say so. I'll leave."

"Leave? No. I've got a long list of questions. And then there's a room reserved just for you."

"First, I get to make a phone call. Then you charge me with something."

"You've got that backward. You don't get a phone call until *after* I charge you. And first—we talk."

Whatever the legal niceties of the subject, Mac felt sure insisting on a lawyer would get him nowhere and merely delay matters. There was no chance the charade would result in a formal charge. This was a matter of personal animosity and would have to play itself out.

And Almeir wanted to know what he was doing at the pit. "I'll make a deal. Let me call my wife. She worries. Otherwise—no talk."

Almeir pushed the phone toward him. "One word about lawyers and you get booked."

The phone was answered on the first ring. Apparently Abby hadn't taken his advice not to wait up. "You should get some sleep, honey. Especially with the booth to get ready."

"What's going on, Mac?"

"I'm helping the police with their inquiries. Has a nice ring to it, doesn't it?"

"You've been arrested? Why? Never mind. I'll get Metlaff down there right away."

"No need. Really. I'll be through here soon. But I'm not going to be much help with Founder's Day. A couple hours sleep and then I have to track down some witnesses."

"Witnesses to what?"

Mac grinned at Almeir. "The more people I can find who saw Bennet's car before somebody mistook it for a moose last night, the better." Mac was pleased to see Almeir's jaw clench.

"Metlaff told me about that," Abby said. "So Bennet *did* falsify the evidence."

"Not Bennet. He was otherwise engaged." Mac smiled at Almeir. "Maybe some other public official."

Almeir placed a finger over the phone hook. "Sign off."

"Got to run, Abby. Duty calls." Mac handed the phone back.

Almeir stood up, his beefy frame topping six feet three inches. "Now we talk."

"Right. Let's start with why you were hanging around the pit at two in the morning, Almeir."

"I'll ask the questions." Almeir leaned forward, his face grim and menacing "But since you ask—we've had residential burglaries along Stuart Road, so I staked it

97

out myself. And guess what I found, Mr. Peeper? I found you lurking in the bushes. Which place were you casing?"

Mac stood up and leaned toward Almeir, forcing him to straighten up. "That story won't fly, Almeir. Burglary investigation is Stan Pawlowski's job. Yours is chasing speeders."

"Don't tell *me* my job. What were you doing there?"

"What do you know about the shot that was fired? Don't tell me you didn't hear it. I bet your ears are still ringing."

Almeir grabbed Mac's shirt. "You want to do this the hard way, gumshoe? We can go downstairs!" He glanced over Mac's shoulder and released the shirt.

Mac turned and saw a uniformed officer, an astonished look on his face, gazing through the glass panel in the door. Mac smiled and raised a hand in greeting.

"Sit down, McKenzie. You're making a spectacle of yourself." Suiting his own action to his words, Almeir returned to his seat. "Now what's this crap about a shot?"

"Sounded like a twelve-gauge. And when I get a look at Bennet's Cadillac I'm going to find buckshot dings on the drivers door and the front end. Probably a shattered headlight. Maybe windshield damage too."

"Daugherty took a shot at Bennet. You know that."

"I can swear Bennet's car was undamaged after that alleged incident. So somebody cooked the evidence." Mac grinned. "I think he's going to drop the charges, don't you? And you won't press it—will you?"

"I'll tell you what I'm going to press, McKenzie. You were found loitering in a suspicious manner in an area that's been hit with a string of burglaries." Almeir leaned back, smiling. "And suppose I go out right now

98

and start tearing your car apart? No telling what I'd find."

Thinking of the set of lock picks in his glove compartment, Mac nevertheless managed to laugh. "I suppose you'd find anything you want to find. But planting evidence does no good without a search warrant."

"I can get a warrant. No problem."

"Now we get to the part where I insist on a lawyer. He'll demand probable cause."

"Suspicion of burglary."

"Okay. I'll explain to the judge what brought me to the scene, and there goes probable cause."

"You were alone. Whatever you say is unsubstantiated."

"I'll admit to tailing Bennet. And back it up by showing I know every move he made, including his stay at the Sleepy Hollow Motel. And if the judge don't buy it, I'll have to defend myself with a press conference. Think Bennet will like that?"

"Why were you following a public official?"

The way Almeir's fist clenched and the vein at his temple stood out gave Mac the uneasy feeling he was pushing his luck. "To keep His Honor from obstructing justice. That should get the press's attention. What do think?"

Mac smiled to show a confidence he didn't feel. "Even if the judge gives you a warrant, my lawyer will insist on having a witness present when you open the trunk. You still get zilch."

Almeir stood up. "You're a wiseass, McKenzie." He walked around behind Mac. "Look over your shoulder now and then. You never know when you might see me." He opened the door. "Now get out."

Mac lost no time in following Almeir's order. He was

tired, hungry, and beginning to get a headache to go with his heartburn. Despite that, it would be a while longer before he could rest.

Mac's phone call had left Abby with the uneasy feeling that she should do something. He didn't need a lawyer. So he said. What about Stan Pawlowski? After all, if you can't take advantage of your friends, who *can* you take advantage of? She glanced at her watch and imagined Julie Pawlowski's reaction to a call at this hour. Better leave that till the sun came up.

She listened to the old building settle for the night.

Mac found Fidget, got involved in Daugherty's arrest, staked out Lawrence Bennet, wound up in police hands. All in the eighteen hours since he left the house this morning.

Why was he so deeply involved after insisting he was through with private investigation? Reluctantly dragged in by concern for Kim Daugherty? Or maybe not so reluctantly.

What did it all mean? Like sitting behind a post at a play, she was missing key parts of the action.

And so was Mac. He had no idea what she knew about Bennet, what she guessed. Even worse, no idea of who his other clients were.

A distant rumble of thunder brought her to the window. It looked like Founder's Day might founder. And not only from the weather. Mac would need sleep. She couldn't expect him to help set up her booth at the craft fair.

She returned to the lounge chair, unwilling to go to bed until Mac got home. She tilted the chair back and stared at the ceiling. There was one thing she could do to help. Mac said he needed a witness to the condition of Bennet's car. Who better than Mrs. B?

A half hour before sunrise the sky began to lighten despite the heavy overcast. Mac stood to one side of the tunnel for ten minutes, listening for any sound that might mean he had been followed. Except for a cricket chorus, there was nothing.

Was he wasting his time coming here? If there was any clue to the Mayor's nighttime visit, he'd have to be lucky to stumble over it. The woman in the Mustang had watched Bennet's flashlight to see where he had gone, what he had done. It was a long shot, but he felt certain the mysterious lady would be back, probably very early. Why not use her as a guide?

Some animal, nocturnal or an early riser, made a faint scrabbling noise to his left. As Mac moved away from the tunnel toward the lake, a startled frog splashed into the water. The larger features of the pit were visible in the morning twilight, including the old shack that Mac intended to use for cover.

The shack was approximately halfway between the lake and the northern wall of the pit. By the time he reached it the dull gleam of a sun obscured by clouds had appeared above the eastern lip of the pit.

The door of the shack stood open and Mac used his flashlight before entering. The floor seemed sound enough, except for a missing board. He stepped in and began his vigil.

By six o'clock his headache had worsened, his hunger pangs had become severe, and every muscle in his body advised him to find a soft place to lie down. His shoulders drooped and he began mentally preparing himself for the climb up Ingram's ladder.

He forgot his fatigue. A woman came out of the tunnel moving rapidly in his direction. She was slim, about five-foot-six and dark-haired. Mac had only seen the woman of the motel in poor-to-no light and couldn't swear this was the same person, but to have another woman show up here at this hour was highly unlikely. She had changed her dress for jeans and a sweatshirt, and her hair was tied back with a ribbon. She carried a canvas tote bag.

As she stepped through the door of the shack Mac smiled and said, "Good morning."

The woman gasped, and turned to run.

"Don't be alarmed. My name's McKenzie. I'll stay here, you stay there, and we'll talk."

She stopped, reached into the bag, and whirled around with a small pistol in her hand. "Don't come any closer! What do you want?"

Mac spread his hands, palms out. "Take it easy. We don't want any accidents with that thing."

She appeared to have recovered from her initial fright now that she was in control of the situation. Her eyes narrowed. "McKenzie." She nodded. "I might have known you were mixed up in this somewhere. Who are you working for?"

"Roy Daugherty."

"Daugherty? Who is Daugherty?"

"Bennet didn't tell you about him? That's hard to believe. What *did* you talk about until two in the morning? Or was the mayor in too much of a rush for conversation?"

Her eyes widened in surprise, but she recovered quickly. "What makes you think I've talked to Bennet?"

"I followed him to the Sleepy Hollow Motel last night. I hung around until he left with you in hot pursuit. And I was right behind you when you got to the pit."

Mac noted the woman would make an excellent poker

102

player. Her face gave nothing away. "By the way, who are you?" he asked. "No use keeping it a secret. I'll know soon anyway."

She laughed. "I thought your wife would have told you. The name is Kazmierski."

Surprised, Mac asked the obvious. "Douglas Kazmierski's—"

"Wife. Right. And if you're thinking of blackmail, forget it. Larry's marriage is shot, and mine's not worth keeping." She gestured with the gun. "Step away from that door."

As Mac complied, she moved up and looked inside. "Don't move. I'll be watching you."

She backed through the door and out of Mac's line of sight. If he couldn't see her, she couldn't see him. Did she expect him to just hang around? He sighed and put his hands in his pockets. Why not? When she came out he'd know what she had come to find.

He regretted that decision almost immediately. She burst out of the shack, gun pointed at his head, hand shaking. "Where is it? What have you done with it?"

Startled, Mac said, "With what? What's missing?"

She stared at him for a moment, then apparently decided his ignorance was genuine. "I'm leaving now. You stay here until I'm gone. If you follow me I'll shoot and claim you dragged me down here." She backed to a safe distance, then turned and walked rapidly away.

Mac, glad to be free of the threat of her gun, made no attempt to interfere. Cursing himself for not having examined the inside of the shack when he first arrived, he stepped inside and looked around.

A board lay near the back wall. His flashlight showed an empty hole where the board had been. Then he saw an open tackle box in the corner of the shack.

It was empty too.

103

# Chapter Eleven

Abby woke feeling stiff and groggy, covered by an afghan she couldn't remember putting on. She found a note from Mac propped against the phone; he would meet her at the fair when she felt up to it. The events of the previous day rushed back, bringing her fully alert.

She hurried through the morning routine, anxious to hear what had happened while she slept. The art and craft exhibition area was deep in the Civic Center park, beyond the parking lot and the carnival midway. Numbered plots had been marked out along a paved walk. Abby's assigned place was at the point where the path curved close to the dense shrubbery that marked the park boundary.

She found her booth all set up, canvas top deployed against sun or rain, paintings hanging on the pegboard back and sides. Two canvas chairs and a folding table were arranged so that customers could circulate through the booth to admire her work. As demanded by optimism, a cash box lay on the table. But no sign of Mac. She opened the cash box and found another note, this one saying Mac had gone to get some much needed rest.

Behind the booth, thirty yards distant, were two large tents; one for bingo later in the day, the other containing long tables and benches. The latter tent was lined on both sides by food vendors. To her right a woman prepared to sell jewelry of her own design, to her left a man displayed rare butterflies encased in plastic.

The space opposite, backing on the shrubbery, contained a small, striped tent and Abby remembered Gladys saying they would be neighbors. That was confirmed almost immediately. Gladys, wearing shorts and sandals, came out and set up a sign that said, MADAME GLADYS, THE FUTURE REVEALED. A second, smaller sign, hanging from a hook on the larger one, said, MADAME IS OUT.

Abby waved, and called, "Gladys! Come have a seat."

Gladys grinned. "Howdy, neighbor." She accepted the offered chair with a sigh. "Putting up that tent by myself is a bitch."

"Isn't it awfully hot in there?"

"It would be, if the heat wave hadn't broken. I don't know whether to be glad it's cooled off or worried about rain. I keep hearing rumbles from the sky."

"The storm seems to be passing north of us. We may be lucky."

Gladys got up and started touring the booth. "You painted all of these?"

"It may not be great art, but it keeps me out of mischief. Of course I haven't had much time for it lately."

"I like your style. Beats the monkey doodle they hang in galleries nowadays." She spent some time examining a painting centered on the back wall. It showed a sunlit graveyard with a broken tombstone surrounded by wildflowers. "I like this one. The Schneider graveyard?"

"You're well-informed for a newcomer."

"Can't live here for long without hearing *that* story. Is it all true?"

"That would depend on what you've heard. But right now I'm interested in *your* story."

Gladys sat down. "What can I tell you? I make a few bucks telling fortunes and try to stay out of trouble. That's about it."

"Maybe I need a reading. What are you charging?"

"One buck."

"That's certainly cheap enough."

"A dollar brings people in just for laughs. But a few will be hooked and come to my place for the full treatment. Ten bucks for the Major Arcana, twenty-five for the full deck, and if I do my job right, repeat business."

Abby had no idea what the Major Arcana was, and decided not to ask. "Maybe you should be out by the midway."

"Everybody'd think I was a carny. Which I was at one time. Back here I'm in the company of respectable business people. Whole different attitude."

"How did you wind up in Sarahville? Wouldn't you do better in Chicago?"

Rising, Gladys said, "I'll tell you later. Right now I'm going for coffee before the crowd starts. Want some?"

Abby, sure Gladys had no intention of answering the question later, watched her slip between the booths and head for the food tent.

A few people had been drifting through the area, although the fair didn't officially open until ten. Now the traffic was increasing and several people had stopped to see her paintings and stare at her price tags.

"Seventy-five? Can you believe it, Evelyn? That frame isn't worth more than forty-five."

"And those colors wouldn't go with your new carpeting, Judith. You need a nice clear red. For accent. You know?"

Abby pretended not to hear and moved out front to look at the threatening weather. Gazing at the sky she almost bumped into a passerby.

"Mrs. Bennet!" Dressed in yellow and white striped culottes and a sleeveless flowered blouse, she had shed the look of tension and worry along with her high heels and

106

pearls. A floppy white hat shielded her from non-existent sunshine. "You're looking very summery today. Now if the weather will only cooperate."

"Scattered thunderstorms, the radio said. We may not get any rain at all. How is your investigation progressing?"

"As a matter of fact, I need your help. You know about the incident yesterday?"

"The shooting?" Mrs. B looked around to be sure no one could hear. "I do hope they aren't too hard on the young man. No doubt Larry deserved it."

"Did you get a look at your husband's car last night? After the shooting?"

"The Cadillac? Let me see—yes. I did see it. He parked in the drive when he came home, so I knew he'd be going out again. Otherwise he would have put it in the garage."

"Did you notice anything different about it? Was there any damage?"

"None that I noticed."

Abby smiled. Just what Mac needed. "Did you see it this morning?"

"No." Lines of tension had returned to Mrs. B's face. "Larry left before I did."

"What did he say about Daugherty?"

"We generally have very little to say to each other. However, he seemed so agitated last night I asked him what was wrong. He said that idiot Daugherty tried to kill him. Frankly, knowing Larry, I considered that an exaggeration." Her smile was grim. "I suppose I said so, and we had one of our usual shouting matches. Then he left. He returned in the small hours."

"I see. And yet you say he left early this morning. But I suppose as mayor he'll have some ceremonial duties today."

"The man usually thrives on public appearances. But

the way he's behaved these last few months—I'm not sure."

"In what way has his behavior changed, exactly?"

"Insurance companies he represents have been calling him at home complaining that his office doesn't answer. When he can't avoid the call he blames the problem, whatever it is, on his secretary. Says she quit without notice and left the paperwork in a mess. Truth is, she gave two months notice. She was very conscientious."

"Two months? He's certainly had time to replace her."

"The man's made absolutely no effort. None at all."

Abby took Mrs. B's arm and steered her across the way, stopping near the fortune-teller's tent. "We don't want to be overheard," she said. "Do you have access to his office? Maybe his files—"

"I've been over every inch of that office," Mrs. B interrupted. She shook her head impatiently. "Judging by his files, you'd think he went out of business six months ago."

"Surely there are things he can't ignore. Insurance claims, bills. What about those?"

"He does the absolute minimum he can get away with. And for the past two months I've found overdue bills in the wastebasket."

"Sounds like someone on the brink of bankruptcy."

Her voice rose in anger. "Then what about the checks I've seen in that trucker's wallet?" She looked at the passersby and dropped her voice. "Two new ones. Just yesterday. Five thousand each."

"And you still have no clue as to where the money is going?" Abby asked.

"None." Mrs. B paused, took a deep breath, and smoothed the lines of anger from her face. She smiled and patted Abby's shoulder. "But I have complete confidence in you. Madame Gladys says your efforts will be crowned with success in the near future." Turning to look at the tent, she asked, "Where *is* she, by the way?"

"Just stepped out. Are you having a reading today?"

"No, no. I understand there are one or two antique dealers here that have depression glass for sale. I have a *passion* for depression glass." She looked around at the nearby booths and showed signs of leaving. "You wouldn't happen to know where—"

"Here's Gladys now," Abby said.

Gladys, bearing two styrofoam cups, smiled. "Mrs. Bennet. How nice."

"Oh. Madame Gladys. I hardly recognize you in casual dress."

"I might say the same for you." Gladys handed Abby a cup. "That color is very good on you."

Mrs. Bennet was looking around again and didn't seem to hear the compliment.

Reasoning that Mrs. B seemed to have few secrets from Gladys, and unwilling to let the opportunity go by, Abby pressed on with her questions. "Have there been any other changes in your husband's behavior? You understand I'm looking for departures from the norm. Even if it seems insignificant."

Mrs. B's expression was vague, as though the collector's lust was upon her. "Changes?"

"How about fishing," Gladys said. "You told me he's turned into a fisherman."

"Well, yes." She tucked a stray lock under her hat. "It's the oddest thing. He comes home in the middle of the day, changes to old clothes, and goes off with a pole and tackle box."

"Sounds like he's lost interest in business."

"But he's never fished. Not before."

"Could it be to cover the time he's spending with a woman?" Abby asked.

"He's never bothered." She tapped her lips with a forefinger. "But you know, he's been very discreet lately. Now

109

*there's* a departure from the norm. For a while I thought it might be Maggy, but she hardly speaks civilly to him."

"Maggy?"

"The weasel's wife. Magdalene Kazmierski."

"Why did you think she was the one?"

"Larry had no use for Douglas. Then suddenly he went to a lot of trouble to get him a job with the village. I thought it was to bring Maggy within striking distance. She's certainly attractive enough—but hard as nails."

"How did she wind up with someone like Kazmierski?"

Mrs. B laughed. "As unlikely a pair as you can imagine." A couple had stopped to read the sign on the tent. She sobered and waited for them to move on. "The story *I* hear is, Maggy's first husband died and left her a lot of debts. Well, Douglas inherited a little money from his father. I suppose that looked pretty good to Maggy at the time. But she long since ran through the inheritance. Now she prods Douglas to do better. Waste of time."

"Remember your last reading?" Gladys asked. "The High Priestess was reversed. That could be Magdalene Kazmierski. Watch out for her."

"Well, I suppose it could all be playacting." Mrs. B nodded. "And the fishing—but that's ridiculous. Surely he could have used some other—I mean a simple business call would do. Why something as bizarre as fishing?"

Abby felt a sudden rush of elation. "That must be it! It's a disguise so he won't look out of place when he hides the money!" She grinned with satisfaction. "Now all I have to do is find out *where* he does this phony fishing."

"Oh, dear. Here comes Larry, looking like a thundercloud. If he sees me we'll probably get into another fight." Mrs. B patted Abby's arm. "I'll talk to you later." In an instant she had disappeared between the booths.

"She doesn't seem to think much of your idea." Gladys

110

glanced at her wristwatch. "Time for me to get ready." She turned abruptly and entered the tent.

Finding herself suddenly alone, Abby muttered, "People come and go so quickly here, said Dorothy." She returned to her booth and searched the path now crowded with optimists ignoring the weather. Bennet was nearly upon her before she separated him from the others.

Mrs. B was right about his mood. His face was grim and he strode along bent forward as if making his way against a stiff wind. Abby was about to try catching his attention when she saw another familiar face in the crowd. Kazmierski's wife, Magdalene—Maggy—a few yards behind Bennet and matching his pace.

Paying no attention to the sign that said Madame was out, Bennet barged in. Maggy pulled up at a booth where hand-tooled leather goods were on display. She appeared to examine a purse, but kept her eyes on the tent. Abby almost laughed aloud as she saw Douglas Kazmierski a few yards behind Maggy. He ducked into a potter's stall, then peered cautiously around a large urn.

Abby could hear Bennet's angry voice, and occasionally the higher pitch of Gladys, but the words were indistinct. She was about to move forward for some shameless eavesdropping when someone tapped her shoulder.

Startled, she turned to find Goose grinning at her.

"Gave you a start, did I?" She stood feet apart, hands in pockets, wearing her safari suit and bush hat. "Sorry about that. Came to see your works of art. Be glad if you could let me know how the detecting goes, as well. Not that I want to press you. Know these things take time."

Abby's annoyance at the interruption was tempered by guilt. She should have called the insurance company about Goose and Estelle's annuities. She smiled weakly.

111

"Things are a bit confusing right now. And with the fair—Where's Estelle?"

"Engaged by fancy paperweights. Collects them, you know." Goose nodded in the direction of the tent. "That where Madame Gladys sets up her crystal ball? Thought I'd pop in and say hello."

"Yes. But she's engaged." Abby glanced toward the tent. "Oh. The sign's fallen over."

"It *has* gotten a bit breezy." Goose held out her hand, palm up. "And I do believe I felt a drop."

"Come into my booth," Abby said. "Fortunately Mac built it with a canvas top."

The few early drops became a light drizzle as they moved into the shelter. Goose examined the way the back and sides were hinged. "Afraid this won't do if the wind kicks up. Nothing to anchor you to the ground. Be a shame to get these paintings wet."

"Maybe I should pack up." Abby looked up and down the nearly deserted path. "Everybody has run for cover." She noticed that Maggy was gone and there was no sign of Kaz.

Goose turned her back on the path and looked at Abby's paintings. "Quite good," she said. She moved deeper into the booth and stopped in front of a portrait of an old woman. "Yes. Quite good."

"That's my grandmother. They're all for sale, except that one."

"An idea just struck me." Goose sat in one of the canvas chairs. "Could I persuade you to do Estelle? I'd pay, of course."

"Estelle? Well, really, I don't do portraits. Hardly ever. As you can see all the others are landscapes."

"You should take it up. The grandmother painting shows that."

"The nice thing about landscapes is, they don't wiggle while you're drawing them."

112

Goose chuckled. "See what you mean. Nevertheless, I *would* like to persuade you."

"But it would be a long time before I could get at it. You understand how it is starting a new business." Abby took the other chair. "I plan on opening for the Labor Day weekend. Then there is the grand opening sale to consider." She cast about for further excuses. "And October is a busy month as people get back to pursuing their indoor hobbies. November is even busier, at least I hope it will be. The Christmas season is so very important."

"No hurry. It will take a bit of doing to get Estelle to sit. She's camera shy and I suppose that will extend to portrait paintings as well. A shame, really. She has such marvelous color."

They sat silently for a while, then Goose craned her neck to peer around Abby. "Why, that's Charles."

Abby noticed a tall, white-haired man striding in their direction. "The Charles you mentioned? The other annuity?"

"Yes. Can't think when the man sleeps."

The man's distinctive appearance made the connection for Abby. This had to be the Charles Ingram that Mac had described. "Why don't you introduce me? I'd like to ask him about Bennet."

Goose shook her head. "Glad to introduce you, but it's no good talking to him. Good tenant and all that, but a bit peculiar. He's fixed on dealing with the mayor in his own way."

"He may get the chance," Abby said as Charles Ingram pulled aside the entrance flap of Gladys's tent. He ducked his head and stepped in.

"Get his chance? What do you mean?"

"Bennet's in there with Madame."

"Really? Bit out of character I should have thought. The mayor is not the type to take stock of the paranormal."

113

Ingram stepped out and continued up the path at his usual pace, ignoring the rain.

"Well, in any case Charles hasn't lingered to make a scene. Couldn't have been in there more than two minutes."

"Just what is Charles's 'own way'?" Abby asked.

Goose looked uncomfortable. "As I said, a good tenant and all that. But much too interested in that witchcraft gibberish. Mind you, there are some unexplained phenomena — Haiti and so on — but that's a different thing altogether." She shook her head. "Black cats. Eye of newt. Lot of nonsense."

Abby laughed. "He's going to cast a spell on the mayor?"

Goose chuckled. "Shouldn't be surprised."

Abby indicated Gladys's sign where it lay soaking in the rain. "Do you suppose I should put it up for her? It says 'Madame is out.' Might save her another interruption."

"No point. Everyone's scampered from the rain. Either gone to the food tent or headed for home. Suppose I should do the same."

"You'll get soaked. Why not wait until it lets up? Or are you concerned about Estelle?"

"She had the good sense to bring an umbrella." Goose nodded in the direction of the path. "Not quite everyone has left. Here comes someone at a run."

Abby watched a man in dungarees, tee shirt, and baseball cap, and wondered where he was going. That unspoken question was soon answered. He swerved left and plunged into the fortune-teller's shelter. But only for a moment. He came out of the tent, glanced toward Abby and Goose, and ran in the direction of the food tent.

"Very odd," Goose said.

"Very. What next, do you suppose?"

"More rain, from the look of it. Founder's Day is a washout, wouldn't you say?"

Abby nodded. "The only reason I haven't packed up is, Mac has the station wagon and I can't get this stuff in the car. I'm sure he's getting some well-deserved sleep, so I don't know how long I'll be stuck here."

"Late night with the boys?"

"Late night following Bennet."

"Aha! Then the case is going forward. What has he found?"

"I don't know," Abby admitted. "We haven't had a chance to talk."

"Fascinating business, detection. Often thought I might have talents in that direction." She frowned at the rain-slicked path. "There's a thought. Do you suppose— No, I suppose not."

Abby shivered. "After all the heat, this change in the weather feels too cool for comfort. Wish I'd brought a sweater."

"I don't suppose McKenzie Associates could use another operative?"

A picture of Irene "Goose" Quill in a trench coat and fedora flashed into Abby's mind and she almost laughed. "I really don't think so. Mac has always been a one-man shop. Sorry."

"Just a thought, as I said. Perhaps—future expansion?"

"I'll certainly keep you in mind."

A woman's voice said, "Mind if I come in out of the rain?"

Abby's "Please do," was automatic as she turned to greet the newcomer. "Why Mrs. Kazmierski, you're soaked."

The woman's hair hung limply to her shoulders and her thin blouse was soaked through and had become transparent. Her canvas shoes and the cuffs of her slacks were muddy. "Afraid the rain caught me at the far end of the park and I made the mistake of trying to make it to my car. I should have waited for it to let up."

Abby glanced over at the leather goods booth where she had last seen Maggy. The exhibitor had wisely packed his stock in cartons and was now loading them into a van. "I noticed you admiring the purses across the way. The rain must have started right about the time you left there."

"Yes. Just a light drizzle. I thought it would stop."

"We've never been introduced," Abby said. "I'm—"

"Abby McKenzie. Yes, I know. My husband told me about you."

"Is that why you were watching me at Swanson's?"

Maggy's smile seemed less than sincere. "I *was* curious. I wondered if you had been complaining to the mayor about Douglas." She looked around. "Has he been here today?"

Not wanting to answer, Abby asked, "Have you met Miss Quill?"

Goose thrust out her hand. "How do you do. Trust you won't catch cold. A bit cool to be standing around in wet clothes."

Maggy ignored Goose's hand. "You're quite right. Since I'm wet already I should have just kept on to the parking lot."

"That occurred to me," Abby said.

"The sooner I get into dry clothes the better," Maggie said. "Thanks for the shelter."

Abby and Goose watched her trot up the path toward the parking lot.

"Wonder how she managed to get so muddy," Goose said. "All trimmed grass, and it hasn't been raining that long."

"From the look of her she must have been out in the rain from the moment it started until now. And Bennet

116

still hasn't come out of the tent."

"Thought you said Madame was in consultation with Bennet?"

"She is." Abby turned in time to see a figure in gypsy costume bend over to pick up the fallen sign. "I could have sworn she hadn't come out of the tent."

"There's a back entrance, you know."

"No I didn't. Why two entrances?"

"She once told me she doesn't like to be seen wandering about at fairs munching a hotdog. So she doffs her costume and slips in and out the back."

"Apparently this time she didn't bother to change."

Goose chuckled. "The Madame was out and the sign, or lack of sign, indicated the Madame was in. Now the Madame is in, and the sign says Madame is out.

"And where's Bennet?"

"Waiting for the rain to stop, I expect."

"Maybe he left the back way with Gladys, though I can't imagine why he wouldn't use a perfectly good path instead of going through the bushes." Abby, growing restless, moved to the front of the booth. "Does Gladys know him? Personally, I mean."

"Shouldn't think so. Well, it doesn't look as though the rain will end any time soon. I must try to locate Estelle." Goose settled her hat firmly on her head, waved to Abby, and started for the food tent at a brisk trot.

Alone, Abby settled in a canvas chair and wondered whether Mac would be coming for her anytime soon. Sitting outdoors with a chill rain falling was not the very best way to spend a day. And they had a lot to talk about.

She looked across at the tent. You'd think Bennet would at least poke his head out to check on the weather. Unless—no. Gladys was too shrewd to fall for the mayor's dubious charms.

Having resigned herself to a lonely vigil, Abby was

117

surprised to see two more damp joggers on the path. One was instantly recognizable as Kim Daugherty. She had only seen Fran Daugherty once, briefly, but she assumed the woman holding an umbrella was Kim's mother. As they entered Abby's booth Fran Daugherty closed the umbrella and shook water from it.

"Hi, Mrs. McKenzie. Have you seen my Daddy?"

"I don't know, honey. I've never met your Daddy. Isn't he still in jail?"

Fran held out her hand. "I'm Fran. Kim's mother. I want to thank you for looking after Kim yesterday. That lawyer was in a hurry and wouldn't let me come in last night." Her smile was brief, but sincere. "You should have seen him when he came out carrying Fidget. That little monster got hold of his cigar. I thought he'd explode."

Abby laughed. "I'd have paid money to see that."

"I guess he's a good lawyer though. I went by the jail this morning and they told me Roy was out and the charges were dropped."

"I suspect that was Mac's doing," Abby said. "He was on Bennet's trail last night. And when he called me, he was with the police. From what he said, I think he caught Bennet falsifying the evidence."

"See," Kim said. "I told you Mr. McKenzie would fix the mayor. He's a great detective."

"I guess he is," Fran said. "Now all we have to do is find your Daddy before he gets in more trouble."

"You don't know where he is?"

Fran shook her head. "He don't have the truck, so he couldn't go too far. I was afraid he might be after Larry—Bennet, I mean. And this bein' opening day here, he'd figure this was a good place to look for him."

"What does Mr. Daugherty look like?"

"Five-eleven. Real well-built. Wearing a Cubs hat and a tee shirt."

"Then that must have been him I saw. Not too long ago either."

"My Daddy's here? Where did he go?"

"Oh, dear," Fran said. "Why didn't he call me? I'd have come for him. And he should know better, anyway. Larry Bennet isn't going to be out here in a pouring rain."

Now that Abby knew the man she had seen was Daugherty, his actions were decidedly peculiar. If he were looking for Bennet, why did he spend so little time in the tent once he had found him? Bennet must have slipped out the back. Yes, that must be it.

"So, what did he do?" Fran asked. "Keep going down this path?"

"He went into Madame Gladys's." Abby nodded toward the tent. "Over there. Then—"

Kim pulled her hand from her mother and shouted, "Daddy!" She ran across the path.

"Kim!" Abby called. "Wait!"

It was too late. Kim had already reached the tent and pulled the flap aside.

"I was going to say he only stayed a minute," Abby explained. "Then he ran off again. Does he know Gladys?"

Fran, watching the tent, nodded. "Sure. She's from the old neighborhood."

Kim, wide-eyed, walked slowly back, unmindful of the rain. Trembling, she put her arms around her mother.

"What's wrong, child?"

Kim turned her wet face up to her mother's. "He killed him. Daddy killed him."

# Chapter Twelve

The gusty wind died and a cloud of ink-like blackness appeared in the southwest. Fran Daugherty clutched Kim tightly. "Calm down, honey. Tell me what happened."

Trembling, Kim raised her head. "It's that Mayor Bennet." She started to cry. "They'll arrest Daddy again!"

Abby touched Kim's shoulder. "Kim. You ran away before I could tell you. Your father was only in the tent for a minute and then he left. I'm sure you don't have to worry."

Fran stared wide-eyed at Abby. She didn't have to say the obvious; a minute was long enough for a disastrous burst of temper.

Abby glanced at the sky. The black cloud moved rapidly, turning day into night. "I guess someone better go and see." Wind sprang to life, whipping the tent flap aside as though inviting her in.

Heart pounding, she stepped into darkness. At first she saw only a vague shape, like a crouching animal. Then, as her eyes adapted, the shape resolved into a man sitting in a chair, his head resting on a card table. His right arm was extended across the table, wrist limp, hand dangling over the far edge. His left arm hung down from the shoulder, nearly touching the ground.

The sound of rain falling on canvas had been faint,

but now a loud drumming filled the tent, announcing a change in the storm's intensity. The tent flap flew open and a flash of lightning illuminated the scene.

She saw his eyes. Open and staring, they seemed to look through her to something not visible to the living.

She backed up, feeling behind her for the exit.

By the time she regained the shelter of her booth she was soaked through. A rivulet of water ran down the path carrying cigarette butts and a gum wrapper. "Fran — take Kim home. Never mind the rain. If the police want to talk to her later — Kim is too upset. They'll have to wait. Okay?"

"Yes, but what about — you know. Him."

"I'll take care of it. Just get her out of here."

Fran took the child's hand, nodded to Abby, and said, "Let's go, Kim. Daddy's probably waiting for us at home."

Abby watched them run, heads down, until they were out of sight. Now she was completely alone. The other crafts people had covered their stock at the first hint of rain, and when it became clear that the weather might turn violent had packed in panic.

She wished she could take the time to do something about her paintings, but the first priority was to notify the police. There had been several patrolling the grounds earlier, but they seemed to have disappeared along with the exhibitors.

She turned at the sound of heavy footsteps on the path and saw Elmer Johnson approaching. He had his head down, arms and legs pumping in runner's style, but not making much more headway than a fast walk. He raised his head as she called his name and veered left into the shelter of her booth.

He took off his golf cap and shook water from it. "How do you like Foundering Day so far, Abby?"

"Am I glad to see you, Elmer. I —"

121

"Like a cow peein' on a flat rock. The weather report says tomorrow will be pretty good, but folks walkin' around are goin' to stir up plenty of mud."

"Never mind that, Elmer. I need you to go for the police."

His eyes widened. "Oh? Somebody rip off your cash box?"

"It's Bennet. He's dead."

Elmer glanced around the booth as if expecting to see a body in the corner. "Bennet? What happened? Heart attack? Where is he?"

"I think it's murder. You go for the police and I'll keep an eye on things until they get here."

"Murder? Bennet?" Elmer shook his head. "He's dead?"

"Yes, Elmer, for God's sake! Murder means dead. Now go. Please!"

Elmer nodded, put on his cap, and turned away. "Right. Quick as I can." He set off, all form and no flash.

The dark cloud was departing as quickly as it had come. The rain decreased in intensity and the sky lightened. She had said "murder," but why? Couldn't it be a heart attack? Had she been influenced by Kim's presumption that her father had killed Bennet? It had been lighter when Kim entered the tent. Perhaps she had seen more clearly. Abby took a penlight from her purse and, steeling herself, returned for another look.

This time it struck her immediately. There was a knife in Bennet's back.

She resolutely ignored the corpse and examined the surroundings. There was a second chair at the table, opposite Bennet, and a coat tree standing in one corner. A long, dark dress and shawl hung from one hook, and a black wig perched on top. A Tarot deck spilled face down on the floor, directly below Bennet's dangling hand, as though he were pointing to it. Two cards, faceup, lay on the table.

Abby moved closer. The top card, lying at right angles to the lower card, showed a tower tilting to one side as though about to fall. Small figures were either jumping or falling from its parapet. She recognized the lower card as The Fool.

Returning to her booth, Abby again felt her isolation. It seemed as though she were the only one left in the entire park. The muscles in her back tensed and she whirled around, trying to see in all directions at once. Foolishness! She wrapped her arms around herself and shivered. She was in no danger. And the police would be here any minute.

Best to keep busy. She took down a landscape from her California days and laid it on the table. Where was her husband? Was he going to leave her here to drown? She lifted the portrait of her grandmother from its hook and was turning away when she caught a flash of yellow through the pegboard holes. Whatever it was, it moved quickly. She froze.

The movement turned the corner and continued along the north wall. She spun toward the entrance holding the portrait before her like a shield. Then the yellow resolved into a slicker-clad figure and she began to breathe again. Police!

"What are you doing here, Mrs. McKenzie? I thought everybody left by now."

"Captain Almeir! Am I glad to see you! He's over there. In the tent."

"He? Who's he?

"Bennet. Didn't—I guess not. Bennet's dead. Murdered."

Almeir turned quickly and started toward the murder scene. Then he turned back. "Just what in the hell did

123

you figure on doing? Wait for the rain to quit and then send us a letter?"

"No! I sent—"

"You stay put." Almeir strode across the path and entered the tent.

Abby glared after him. Overbearing ass! She returned to stacking pictures on the table, setting them down with unnecessary force. "He'll probably muck up the evidence before Stan gets here," she muttered. And where the hell was Mac?

Mac turned into the village hall driveway, wipers operating at full speed. Abby was probably soaked and angry enough to turn the water to steam by now. Well, it had been a rough thirty hours and a man had to sleep sometime. He entered the nearly empty parking lot. How was he supposed to know it would rain? The morning forecast said possible showers, not a rerun of Noah's flood.

He passed one of the few remaining cars and noted two women getting in. They were both dripping wet, especially the one that looked like she was out to bag an elephant.

As he slowed to follow the part-mud, part-gravel path that skirted the carnival midway he saw Elmer Johnson break from behind the merry-go-round. He considered offering him a lift to his car and thought better of it. Elmer was already wet, and Abby was waiting.

He stopped with the wagon's tailgate in front of Abby's booth. Expecting, at the least, a cutting remark about his tardy rescue, he was surprised when she ran out of the shelter and into his arms.

"Mac! I'm so glad you're here!"

He hustled her in out of the rain and, grasping her shoulders, looked into her tense face. "What's wrong, Abby?"

"Someone's killed Bennet." She waved toward the tent. "Over there."

Startled, Mac glanced over his shoulder as Almeir came out of the tent.

"What the hell do you think you're doing, McKenzie? Get that wagon out of here. This is a crime scene."

Mac pushed Abby behind him. "I guess you forgot to put up a barrier, Almeir. And why are you prowling around in there before the evidence tech has been over it? Ever read the police manual?"

Almeir stopped six inches from Mac and poked him in the chest. "I know my business. Now let's talk about yours. You were tailing Bennet last night. Maybe you tailed him this morning too. Maybe I should take you in for questioning."

Mac caught the flash of red and blue lights from the corner of his eye. "Stuff it, Almeir. The real cops just arrived."

The police cruiser followed by Stan Pawlowski's unmarked car stopped well away from the scene. Stan and Bob Henderson got out. Stan beckoned to the man in the cruiser. "I want tape around the area. Include the booths on both sides and the three across the path. And behind those bushes, at least twenty feet." He started toward Abby's booth. "Almeir! Don't stand around with your finger up your nose! Get somebody here and secure the area."

"I don't take orders from you, Pawlowski." Nevertheless, he pulled a radio from under his slicker and walked off muttering into it.

Ignoring Mac and Abby, Stan went to the tent and pushed the flap aside. He flicked on a flashlight and examined the interior without entering. "Get your pictures, Bob. Let me know when it's okay to go in."

Abby grabbed Mac's arm. "We have to talk."

125

Stan stepped toward Abby's booth. "You feeling okay, Abby?"

"A little shaky. I'm all right, Stan."

Stan nodded. "I won't keep you long. Just a couple of questions now and you can come in to make a statement tomorrow." Turning to Mac he asked, "Were you here when she found him?"

Mac shook his head. "I just got here."

"Then your wagon wasn't here when it happened. Go ahead and load the pictures but leave the booth. How did you come to find him, Abby?"

"Me? I didn't —" She hesitated. "I mean, I saw Bennet go into the tent quite a while ago. When everybody else had left because of the rain and he still hadn't come out, I got curious."

"So you looked in and there he was. Nobody else around?"

"By then everybody had gone. I was just about to go for the police, when Elmer showed up and I sent him. I stayed to make sure nobody else went in."

Stan nodded. "Good girl. The rest can wait until we're through here. Go on home."

"Mind if I stay?" Mac asked. "I'll get Abby loaded and she can take the wagon."

"How will *you* get home?" Abby asked.

Surprised, Mac said, "In *your* car, of course."

"Mac!" Her voice dropped to a whisper. "We have to talk."

"I've got some information for Stan. You go on ahead. I won't be long."

Stan frowned. "You said you weren't here. What information?"

"I spent a good part of last night tailing Bennet. I also spent part of the night in your jail. Or at least in Almeir's office. And this morning I had a run-in with Bennet's girlfriend. Interested?"

126

"You stay."

The rain had diminished to a fine drizzle but Mac remained in the booth watching the police activity. He wondered why Abby had insisted on talking to him alone? It had been impossible with police hovering over them. What was it Stan couldn't be told? Unless it involved Daugherty. Since he was a client she might feel Mac should have the information first. Of course Daugherty had a perfect alibi. He was in jail.

At Stan's request Almeir set his men to searching the area but otherwise took no part in proceedings. He stood on the sidelines for a while, probably watching for Stan to make a mistake that could be reported to the chief. Then he disappeared.

After Sgt. Henderson, who doubled as Sarahville's evidence technician, had finished with the tent and the body had been removed Stan motioned Mac to come with him.

He entered the tent. "Bennet was slumped forward over the table. Somebody came up behind him and hit him. Hard."

"With what?"

"Don't know. But here's the funny part. He had a knife in his back. No bleeding to speak of, which is why I'm guessing the blow to the head did the job."

"Well, Sherlock, what do you deduce?"

"Same as you, Watson. Not a damn thing."

"Sitting there, he'd see anyone coming in."

"Right. So when the person came around behind him, he wasn't alarmed. He didn't turn his head."

"Abby can probably tell you who came and went the front way, but she wouldn't know about the backdoor."

Stan lifted the rear flap. "To make matters worse, the tent backs up on the hedge that borders the park. There're a number of gaps in the hedge; people are always taking shortcuts through it. One of the gaps is right here."

"So if you didn't want to be seen, you'd approach from the other side of the hedge. But why pitch the tent so close to the hedge in the first place? Why not closer to the path?"

"Maybe she expected customers to line up out front and didn't want to block the path." Stan stepped through the exit and the gap. "Don't worry about footprints. The heavy rain washed out just about everything. And that genius Almeir admits he came out here expecting to shoot down a fleeing suspect. His size fourteens are over the top of everything else."

Mac jumped the muddy area between the tent and the grass beyond. Village maintenance had mowed a ten-foot strip along the hedge to keep the weeds from invading the parkland. Beyond the cleared strip staghorn sumac grew thickly and second growth trees rose above those.

He followed Stan south along the hedge to where it curved west, following the blacktop path inside the park. There, where Abby's view would be blocked by other exhibitor's booths, there was another gap in the hedge. This gap was wider and had been mulched with pine bark. No chance of footprints.

"Get the picture?" Stan asked.

Mac sighed. "Sure. Anyone could go through the back of the tent, come back on the path at this point, and nobody would know where they had come from."

"The whole world could go in and out of that tent and nobody would be the wiser."

"Good luck, Officer."

"Let's go over to the food tent. They're closed down, but we can sit a while without Almeir hanging over my shoulder."

"Where'd he disappear to?"

Stan shrugged. Clearly, he counted Almeir's absence as a plus.

The tent was deserted and they sat at the first table they came to. "You want to know why I was following Bennet," Mac said.

"I suppose it has something to do with Abby's problem with the inspector."

Shaking his head, Mac said, "No. I was trying to keep him from falsifying evidence in a felony." He briefly described the case against Daugherty and subsequent events, including Almeir's role.

"Don't surprise me," Stan said. "Almeir is Bennet's man. With Bennet gone I don't think Almeir will last long."

"How come Chief Venlow puts up with it?"

"The Chief's been wanting to retire for at least the last two years. The only reason he hasn't is, he's afraid Almeir will get his job. Meantime he can't buck the mayor if he wants his budgets approved." Stan pulled out a second chair and put his muddy feet on it. "This morning is going to change a lot of things."

"With that assault charge against Daugherty, I guess he's lucky to be in jail. Otherwise he'd be at the top of your list."

"Right. Can't beat a jail cell for an alibi."

"Now I'll tell you what happened this morning when I staked out the gravel pit." He recounted his encounter with Maggy Kazmierski.

Stan took his time lighting a cigarette, wished for a thermos of coffee, and drummed his fingers on the table. Finally he said, "Obviously, Bennet stashed something in the shack. His girlfriend knows what it is, but not where it is. She followed him and knows he went into the shack. Came back to get it in daylight, but it wasn't there. You were. Which leaves two questions. What is it? And where is it?"

129

"Care to guess what it is?"

"Graft he's hiding from the IRS. Judging from the way he's been rushing around, he was getting ready to skip with his little retirement fund."

Mac nodded. "That was my idea too. He hired his nephew to increase the take, and got him to put the arm on every new business in the village in just two weeks. That's got to be a record. And if anybody put up any resistance, he backed off real quick. Bennet didn't want any hassles."

"Can't complain about lack of leads," Stan said. "I'll have to check those two banks you mentioned, haul in the Lady Kazmierski for questioning, not to mention interviewing all the exhibitors. And Gladys the fortune-teller, of course. Why was Bennet in her tent, and where was she? Come to think of it, where is she now?" He started to get up. "I better have somebody track her down."

"Any chance of nailing Almeir with any of Bennet's graft?"

Stan shrugged. "Not if—speak of the devil!"

A grim-faced Almeir strode toward Stan. "Pawlowski, you've screwed around long enough. I just collared Daugherty. It's open and shut."

"I understood he was in jail."

"Bennet dropped the charges and he was released this morning."

Mac suppressed a most sincere oath.

Almeir leaned across the table, grinning. "And—the knife in Bennet belongs to Daugherty!"

130

# Chapter Thirteen

Abby headed for home, the shock of Bennet's murder fading as other emotions rose to the surface. Good girl, Abby! Now let the grown-ups take over. Serve Stan right if she kept what she knew to herself. She hit the brakes at the Harper Road traffic light and nearly skidded through on the wet pavement.

Of course, leaving let her avoid questions she didn't want to answer. At least not until she'd talked to Mac.

And Mac! Leaving her in a rainstorm. Not giving her a chance for a private talk. He could have found *some* way to manage it. But no! Had to get with his buddy, doing man's work!

Well, he was in the dark, too. And if he thought he was coming home to a pot of coffee and a hot lunch, it would be a cold day in hell. About to turn into Twilly Place, she caught sight of the Kurtz Bakery sign a block down Old Main.

Where was Gladys? In the tent to put on her costume. Then left by the rear exit. But why? The whole point of the second door was so no one would see her on the grounds dressed as a gypsy. And did she leave before or after Bennet got there? Abby drove on and parked in front of the bakery.

Later Gladys came back through the front. Then what? Calmly remove black dress and wig in the presence of a corpse and leave quietly? Unlikely.

Abby approached the door next to the bakery and read a sign in the curtained door window. MADAME GLADYS. READINGS BY APPOINTMENT.

The door was unlocked. Appointment notwithstanding, Abby went in. The smell of baked goods was strong and the light weak in the small hallway. Both grew weaker as she mounted the creaking stairs. She knocked at the door on the second floor landing and waited, wondering if she was wasting her time.

Abby could hear movement inside. She was about to knock again when Gladys opened the door. "Well, this is a surprise!" Gladys said. "What brings *you* to my dark and dreary cave?"

The doorway opened directly into the front room. The cloudy day, combined with heavy curtains at the windows overlooking the street, did indeed make a dim scene. Abby noted that Gladys had changed from shorts to jeans and a knit top. "I wondered where you disappeared to," Abby said. "You went into your tent and never came out again."

Gladys motioned Abby to a seat on a sagging couch and took a swivel rocker for herself. With her back to the window she was a featureless silhouette. "I left the back way. Felt the need for a beer. Then the monsoon started and there didn't seem much point in going back."

"But you took off your costume and left it in the tent."

"Costume? No. I never put it on. Where'd you get that idea?"

Abby frowned. The answer made no sense. Gladys must be aware that Abby and Goose had both seen her. "Gladys, I think you better tell me what *really* happened when you found Bennet."

Gladys was silent for a moment. Then she sighed. "I

guess you're right. Not much point in keeping it a secret. I don't know what you mean by 'found Bennet.' More like he found me." She reached over and snapped on a lamp next to her chair.

Abby gasped. Gladys's left eye and part of her cheek was marked by a dark bruise. The edges were beginning to take on a sickly yellow color. "My God! What happened?"

Gladys's grin quickly turned to a grimace, the movement of her jaw apparently causing pain. "Bennet happened, the son of a bitch! Really rung my bell. When my head cleared I picked myself up and left before he could do it again."

"Shouldn't you see a doctor? You might have a concussion."

"I've taken worse. And you don't get Blue Cross in my business, you know."

"Why didn't you go to the police?"

Gladys snorted. "An ex-carny fortune-teller complaining about the mayor? I'd laugh if it didn't hurt."

Questions rushed in Abby's mind and she took some time to sort through them. Gladys got up and left the room without explanation, returning in a few minutes with an ice bag. She sat down and gingerly applied the bag to her face.

"Why did you go back to the tent with Bennet still there? Why not just leave in your costume?"

"That's the second time you mentioned that. I told you. I never had the gypsy rig on."

Abby shook her head in confusion. "All right. So what happened? Starting when you left me to get ready."

"Why are you so interested? I know I've got you chasing Bennet, but that's for the girls. I'm not your

133

client, and this"—she pointed to her face—"is a personal matter."

"You'll have to explain it to the police, Gladys." Abby paused. "Bennet is dead. Murdered in your tent."

Gladys rose from her seat. "Damn!" She began pacing the room. "Not that he didn't deserve it. But why drag *me* in? Why couldn't he get himself killed somewhere else?"

Abby leaned back, watching the performance with a critical eye. "Very inconsiderate of him."

"This makes me number one suspect doesn't it?" Gladys stopped in front of Abby. "No way the cops are going to buy my story, are they?"

"I don't know. I haven't heard your story yet."

"Okay." Gladys returned to her chair. "Okay. I no sooner got to the tent when Bennet came storming in. I'm surprised it didn't happen sooner. I gave my real name when I registered with the county. You know. Doing business as Madame Gladys. And then I had to get a license from the village. He must have had a lot on his mind not to tumble sooner."

"You knew Bennet before?"

"Yeah. When I was Gertrude Brettmacher. How's that for a handle?"

"How did you come to know him?"

"From the old neighborhood. I was just a kid, so I suppose he didn't know I was around. I skipped when I was fifteen. Joined the carnival." Gladys turned the swivel rocker toward the window and parted the curtains. She was silent for a time, then said, "Look at that street. The old tavern down on the corner, old houses with curlicues and doodads around the top. Even the street lights rigged to look like gaslights."

Abby came to the window. The street was deserted,

134

but her imagination peopled it with characters taken from turn of the century woodcuts.

"Looks like a postcard, don't it?" Gladys asked. "But out there you find the same bastards pulling the same crap they do everywhere. Play a few small towns as a carny and you learn that pretty quick."

"Didn't your family look for you?"

Gladys shrugged and turned her chair. "Maybe. If they stayed sober long enough to remember they had a kid."

Abby touched her shoulder. "Did you ever go back?"

"I kept in touch with what was going on through a friend. When my mother died I went for the funeral. The old man wanted me to stay, but that was mostly so I could support him. I split again."

"And since then?"

"He died a couple of years later. I missed the funeral."

Gladys fell silent and the ticking of a clock took over until Abby, clearing her throat, said, "It doesn't sound like you knew Bennet very well. Why would he do this to you?"

"Oh, I knew the bastard all right. The carnival played Libertyville one season and it turned out he was working for an insurance agency there. I ran into him and introduced myself. He pretended to remember me." Gladys tried to grin, then touched her jaw. "One thing led to another, you know? The guy could turn on the charm. Well, to cut through all the crap, I got pregnant. Stupid, right?"

"From what I've learned about his honor, the mayor, I don't suppose he offered to stand by you?"

"It gets better," Gladys said. "Turned out I wasn't the only horse in his barn. The other mare had money, and no kid on the way. He disappeared like a puff of smoke, along with her."

"Did you—the baby—"

Gladys turned back to the window. "Stillborn. Full term."

"Oh."

"Well, that's life, right?" She got up and gestured to the couch. "Take a load off and I'll get us a beer."

Alone in the room Abby looked at the rose-patterned wallpaper, then the card table, covered with a fringed cloth, at one side of the room. The same setup, including a card deck and two folding chairs, that she had seen in the tent.

Gladys was tough. A survivor. But tough enough, and bitter enough, to drive a knife into a man's back?

Gladys returned with a quart bottle of beer and two glasses. She filled the glasses and set the bottle on the table. "Okay. Let's get this over. I don't know what was eating at Larry when he busted into my tent. But he must have been under a lot of pressure lately." She took a swig of beer and returned to the seat by the window. "His wife was divorcing him and was out to get everything he had. I hear there was no chance he'd get re-elected, and with the deals he's pulled, he must have been hearing footsteps. Then I turn up out of his past, and he has to worry about what I'm doing here."

That was a question that had also occurred to Abby. There were entirely too many coincidences.

"With all that," Gladys continued, "he was ready for a warm climate and early retirement."

"Did he tell you that?"

Gladys, holding her glass in two hands, close to her chest, said, "Not exactly. But I had it figured anyway. I'd bet those annuities he's been peddling were phony. And that's a scam with a limited life. Sooner or later somebody dies, somebody writes to the insurance company, anything like that and it blows up in his face. So he was building a pot he'd have to cash in before long."

"But he said something to confirm your suspicions." Abby put her glass, untouched, on the card table and returned to the couch. "What was it?"

"He busted in raising hell. Why did I come here? What was I doing to him? I turned his wife against him. Did I put the McKenzies onto him? How did I find the money? Where was it?"

"The money?"

"Yeah. I said I didn't know what he was talking about and he belted me. I didn't give him a chance to do it a second time"

"What did he mean about the money?"

"Don't you get it?" Gladys stirred restlessly. "A hell of a time to run out of cigarettes. You don't smoke, do you?" She swallowed the rest of her beer and set the glass on the floor. "He must have been stashing his money somewhere."

"Why not a bank?"

"Money in the bank leaves tracks. He had to worry the account would be frozen. His wife, the IRS, or if the scam folded, the cops. So it was in cash. And he was hijacked. He must have figured it was me."

"Was it?"

"No. But then I wouldn't tell you if it was."

Abby sighed. "No, I don't suppose so. Where did you go when you ran from him?"

"I went to the beer tent to cool off. They had one of those mirrors with a can of Hamm's sitting under a waterfall on it. One look at my mug and I could see business was over for the day. The bastard probably put me on the bench for at least a week." She touched her eye. "Maybe I could work in a veil. Think so?"

Abby walked into her kitchen to find Mac sitting at the table staring into a cup of coffee. He jumped up as she entered and put his arm around her.

"I was worried about you. Where have you been?"

Glancing at the table littered with sandwich makings she said, "Just as long as worry didn't interfere with your appetite." She removed his arm and sat down.

"Can I get you something?"

"Stop hovering over me!"

"Sure." He put a hand on her shoulder. "Must have been a shock, finding Bennet like that. Want to talk about it?"

She sighed and leaned her head against him. "I have a lot to tell you. And you're not going to like any of it."

"You need coffee." He brought her a mug with a Chicago Bears helmet on the side and sat down across the table. "Okay. Tell me."

Abby sipped slowly, searching for the right place to begin. "Mac, I lied about finding the body."

"You what!?"

"Kim found him."

"Oh." Mac shoved his cup aside and leaned forward. "Then don't worry about it. I don't see any reason to get her involved." He sighed. "The poor kid has enough trouble facing her."

"Trouble? What trouble?"

"Roy Daugherty has been arrested for Bennet's murder."

Shocked, Abby asked, "Why Daugherty? I didn't tell anyone he'd been in the tent. Unless Goose—did Stan question Goose Quill already?"

"Who the hell is Goose Quill?"

"That's right, you don't know about her. But why Daugherty?"

138

"The knife in Bennet's back has been identified. When he was arrested his personal effects were taken and inventoried. Daugherty signed the inventory as correct. When he was released, he got everything back and signed again."

"And the knife was on the list?"

Mac nodded. "Unfortunately, it's easy to identify. Daugherty burned his initials into the handle."

"Poor Kim. So it must have been her father."

"Not a chance."

Abby's face brightened. "You don't think so?"

"No. And Stan isn't sold on it either. But Almeir arrested him and with the evidence—well, they have to hold him."

"Okay, Sherlock. What am I missing? I mean, I prefer to believe he's innocent, but I'm sure you two cold-blooded bloodhounds—"

"Bloodhounds aren't cold-blooded, they have cold noses. Look. If you had found Bennet on the ground with his head against a rock, I'd buy it. Daugherty has a short fuse and tends to come out swinging. But Bennet was killed by a blow to the head while he was sitting. Then, somebody stabbed the corpse and left an easily identified weapon behind. I can't make any of that fit Daugherty."

"So, if Stan thinks the same way, Daugherty has nothing to worry about."

"The decision to prosecute isn't up to Stan. Add your statement that Daugherty was in the tent—the State's Attorney is going to move on this one. It's about as solid a case as you can get." Mac leaned back and stared at the ceiling. "I think I better run down this Madame Gladys, whoever she is."

Not anxious to jump into the rest of her confession,

Abby asked, "What about quitting the detective business?"

"Oh. Yeah." Mac avoided her eyes. "I meant to tell you. The more I think about it—I'm not cut out for clerking in a store. Well, you probably know that." He leaned forward earnestly. "I can still help out when you need me. Repairs, the heavy stuff so you don't have to hire somebody."

"I'll manage." Abby smiled with relief.

"You don't mind?"

"Besides, you have too many clients right now."

"Just Daugherty." Mac looked at Abby, who looked away, and his eyebrows climbed. "Abby? What have you been up to?"

"Well—you told me I could look into this inspector graft, and one thing led to another, and—" She took a deep breath. "I better tell you from the beginning."

By the time she had finished, Mac was leaning on the table with his eyes closed. He opened them slowly. "In other words, you've signed up practically the entire list of suspects. Not only that—"

"What about the Kazmierskis? Or this mysterious Charles Ingram?"

"Okay. There are a few left out. If you hurry you can sign them up this afternoon."

"And then there's Gladys."

"What about Gladys? Besides her refusal to admit she went into the tent dressed in her fortune-telling outfit?"

"She's scared. And I sort of promised we'd—"

"Not another one!"

"—I didn't say positively. Mac, she swears that costume never left the tent."

"The dress was wet." Mac said. "I felt it." He folded

140

his arms and leaned back, tilting the chair on two legs. "Let me think a minute."

Abby got the pot and refilled her cup. Mac hadn't touched his. "None of these people killed Bennet," she said. "I'm sure of it. Well—pretty sure."

"Okay," Mac said. "It's not as bad as it looks. We were to find Bennet's loot for Mrs. Bennet. But that wouldn't help her now. If it's ever found, what the IRS doesn't get, Bennet's victims will. So we tell her case closed, no bill. These two ladies, Quill and Prestwick. Stan will check into the fraud angle and then, if there's any money, they can put in a claim. Maybe they'll get some back. No bill. As for Elmer, the point is moot. He'll probably run unopposed now. Think I'll send him a bill anyway."

"What about Gladys?"

"I'll put it to her straight. Daugherty's my client and she's an alternative suspect. She didn't give you any money, did she?"

"None of them did. But Mac, she had no idea Bennet was dead. I'm sure of it."

"The woman is a con artist. That's how she makes her living."

"I'm an expert on con artists, remember," Abby said, referring to her former husband. "She's telling the truth."

Mac smiled. "Okay. Tell me this. Does it strike you there are a few too many coincidences in this case?"

"You mean Gladys coming here, where Bennet was living?" Abby sighed. "Yes. It occurred to me."

"Not just that. Daugherty too. And he knows Gladys *and* Bennet from the old neighborhood. And who sent you all these women who had the knife out for Bennet?"

"An unfortunate figure of speech." Abby stared

141

moodily into her cup. "I should have asked Gladys a few more questions."

"You did fine. I'm sure she told you a lot more than she would have told me—or Stan." He came around the table. "Gladys is stage-managing a lot of what's been going on." He lifted her chin and kissed her. "Roy Daugherty has to be my main concern. The rest will just have to sort itself out."

"Where are you going?"

"Ingram went into the tent after Daugherty. If Bennet was dead—why didn't he call for the cops?"

"He sounds so strange. I suppose it's possible he just didn't think it was any of his business."

"It's also possible he placed a fatal curse on Bennet. With a rock."

# Chapter Fourteen

Mac knocked at Charles Ingram's door for the third time with diminishing expectations. No answer.

The temperature was climbing again now that the rain had passed, and the humidity was worse than ever. Might as well see if the people in the house knew anything. On his way he glanced through the garage window. There were no cars inside. He gave the doorbell of the house a halfhearted punch, expecting no response. He got none.

Halfway to his car he looked back at the garage and wondered what he might find inside. The lock picks were in the glove compartment and no one was about. On the other hand, although he had seen a lock like that opened in under ninety seconds, he had never managed it in less than fifteen minutes himself. Not the kind of skill careers are built on. Reluctantly, he gave up the idea.

He sat in the car for awhile listening to the buzzing of cicadas and considering his next move. Search out Ingram in the pit? If he was there, and didn't want to be found, it would be a waste of time. He could stop by the Daugherty place. That was close by. Poor Kim was probably taking her father's arrest hard and needed reassurance. Could he, in honesty, give her hope? He shrugged aside his doubts. Kim needed her father. She would have him.

It took only five minutes to drive to the Daugherty house. The missing front stoop, muddy drive and barnyard, the barn door standing open, gave the place a desolate look. It was as though Roy Daugherty's absence had given the place permission to fall into decay.

The screen door was unhooked. He let himself onto the porch and knocked on the kitchen door. There was no response.

What now? Fran and Kim were probably at the jail, or Metlaff's office. What about the one known as Goose? She had been with Abby this morning and might have seen something Abby missed. Not that Abby missed much. He grinned as he suddenly made the connection. Based on Abby's description he must have seen Goose Quill as he entered the fair grounds. The Great White Hunter. And the bedraggled woman with her must have been Estelle Prestwick. He should have asked Abby where they lived.

He turned to leave. Who else? Gladys and Mrs. Bennet. And the Kazmierskis. He'd certainly like a word with Maggy Kazmierski. Mrs. Bennet would know where they lived, so he'd better see her next.

He glanced through the kitchen window as he passed, then turned back for another look. Something odd. He shielded his eyes with cupped hands to cut out reflections and peered through the glass. The freezer compartment of the refrigerator stood open. That's what had attracted his attention. And the canisters lined up on a kitchen counter had been dumped.

He pulled out his shirttail and used it to avoid leaving fingerprints on the doorknob. The door swung open easily. He stepped inside, glancing through the gap at the hinged door edge as he did so. No one in the kitchen. He listened. No sound.

Skirting the flour, sugar, and coffee spilled across the

144

tile floor, he checked out the other ground floor rooms. He stopped at the foot of the stairs. Why take a chance on the burglar being up there? He could call Stan and wait in the car until help arrived.

He had to know if Fran and Kim were in the house. Probably not. He hoped not.

Mac set foot on the stairs, close to the wall to minimize creaking, and slowly climbed to the second floor hallway. Still no sound. So the house was empty. Or the burglar was aware of him and keeping quiet. Either way, no point in pussyfooting around. He moved rapidly from room to room, shoving doors hard against walls, ducking low as he went through. Nothing.

All the drawers and closets on the second floor had been turned out. A jewel box, on what he assumed was Fran's dresser, stood open. It contained cheap costume jewelry. It also contained three ten-dollar bills.

Finally, after checking the cellar, he called the police and settled down in his car to wait.


It took over an hour before Mac was free to leave the Daugherty place and head for Bennet's. On arriving he was surprised to find Almeir's car in the drive. He parked on the street and rang the doorbell. Almeir opened the door and came out, shutting it behind him.

"I seem to run into you everywhere I go, McKenzie. Why is that?"

"Just came by to give my condolences to the grieving widow. You too?"

"Stick around, McKenzie. Somebody will be along to talk to you in a minute." Almeir walked to his car and leaned on the fender, pointedly ignoring Mac.

Less than a minute passed, during which Mac imagined six reasons for Almeir's strange behavior, before Sgt. Bob Henderson arrived. He glanced toward Mac, obviously surprised, but directed his attention to Almeir.

"What happened, Captain?"

Almeir spoke softly, but Mac had moved closer and had no trouble hearing his reply.

"Came by to see how Mrs. Bennet was holding up. Nobody answered at the front, so I went around back, in case she was in the yard. Noticed the glass in the back door was broken. I went in and checked it out. The place is empty, but somebody tossed it. Can't tell what's missing."

Henderson nodded. "I'll get on it. Are you staying, Captain?"

"No. I'll try to find Mrs. Bennet." Almeir pointed toward Mac. "You be sure to find out what he's doing here before you let him go."

As soon as Almeir left, Henderson gestured to Mac to follow him. They went around to the back. Before they entered Henderson asked, "You know anything I should know?"

Mac shook his head. "I punched the button and Almeir popped out. That's about it."

The inside, except for being expensively furnished, looked much like the Daugherty place: trashed.

"Sarahville seems to have a crime wave," Henderson said.

"Might not hurt to send a man around to the Kazmierski place. And that fortune-teller's—Gladys something."

"I'm ahead of you," Henderson said. "We get about two burglaries a month. Don't take a genius to figure the odds on this being a coincidence." He glanced at his watch. "They should all be covered by now."

Mac grinned. "Okay, Bob. I'll keep my amateur suggestions to myself."

146

"Stop by the office. Stan wants to see you."

On his way to see Stan it occurred to Mac that it might be best to postpone their meeting. Abby had made a commitment, however ambiguously, to Gladys. Maybe Gladys was entitled to know the deal was off before she found herself lying to the police. Also, he had to think about how much of what had been told to Abby in confidence he could hold back. He had his license to consider. And his friendship with Stan.

Best talk it over with Abby. Then visit Gladys before going on to Stan's office.

Turning onto Twilly Place he was surprised to see his driveway filled with cars. He parked on the street and peered through the bay window from the porch before going in.

Abby stood behind the glass-fronted counter. The various merchandise displays limited floor space and kept the people that faced her bunched tightly together. They all seemed to be talking at once.

When Abby raised her eyes to the ceiling Mac could read the exasperation in her face.

She smiled with relief as Mac came through the screen door. "Mac, get in here and speak to these people. I'm beginning to think they don't understand English."

At her words the group, responding like a school of fish to some mysterious signal, wheeled in unison to face him. Smiling, he asked, "You having a closeout sale before you've opened the store, Abby?"

Abby ignored this and said, "Mac, you know some of these people. I'll introduce—"

"That's okay. I can sort them out." He advanced toward the group, and again acting in concert, they

147

spread out at his approach. Only Fran and Kim Daugherty remained where they were. Mac smiled reassuringly at Fran and placed his hand on Kim's head. "I'm sure everything will turn out all right."

"Are you gonna make them let Daddy go?"

"Yes, Kim. We won't let anything happen to your Daddy."

Fran Daugherty's lip trembled. "We don't have much money. It's cost a lot for the lawyer already and with Roy not able to work because he's in—because of what happened."

Seeing Fran was about to cry he turned hastily toward Elmer Johnson, who had drifted to the far side of the room and leaned on an old oak bookcase now used to display macrame kits.

"I suppose you're here to get your money's worth, Elmer?"

"Something like that." Elmer struggled to look sad. "Of course I'm shocked at what happened to Mayor Bennet. I intended to run against him in the next election, that's no secret. But it grieves me to run unopposed under such tragic circumstances."

"I can see you'll be a great success as a politician, Elmer."

Elmer was unable to keep his habitual half-smile from returning.

Mac turned, his back to Abby and the counter. He found himself facing Charles Ingram, who stood erect, hands at his sides, unmoving. "Mr. Ingram. We've met, if you recall."

Ingram nodded. Mac held out his hand. Ingram grasped it firmly, pumped it twice, and let go. His lips twitched, but he said nothing.

Goose and Estelle had moved to the left end of the counter. They stood close together, Estelle nervously playing with the clasp of her purse. "And I can guess who these two ladies are," Mac continued. "Miss Prestwick and Miss Quill."

Estelle Prestwick smiled faintly and nodded.

Irene Quill thrust out her hand. "Glad to meet you at last, McKenzie. Everyone calls me Goose. Can't think why."

Mac shook her hand. "I'm glad you're here. I've been wanting to talk to you." Turning back to Abby, he said, "The lady leaning on the counter to your left is an easy guess." He smiled and said, "You've done a good job with the makeup, Madame Gladys, but I'm afraid your memento from the late mayor will be with you for a while."

Gladys's expression remained grim. "You got it, McKenzie."

Turning to the remaining woman, he said, "And you must be Mrs. Bennet." Although she gave no indication of being grief-stricken he added, "Sorry about your husband."

"Not many are sorry, Mr. McKenzie." She wore a dark blue dress, suitably subdued in keeping with her widowhood. "And yesterday I wouldn't have believed I would be either. But now — well — I did love him once."

Mac nodded. "Sure. And sentiment aside, you'd like to know what happened to his money." Turning to the group, he said, "Except for the Daughertys, and Elmer — maybe including Elmer — that's what you'd all like to know, right?"

No one rushed to answer.

Mac walked around the counter and stood beside Abby. Her lips silently formed the words. "Show-off."

The group began a slow drift in Mac's direction. "Let's get a few things straight right away," he said. "Whatever commitments Abby made to any of you are

149

now moot. Bennet's murder took care of that. His assets, any fraud—that's all part of the police investigation now. Naturally you won't be billed." He grinned at Elmer. "Except you. You'll be billed for the time Abby spent."

Elmer's right brow rose to join the normally raised left. "How'd I get so honored?"

"You wanted information on Bennet. She's prepared to give it. The fact that it's no longer of use to you is your problem."

Elmer chuckled. "Fair enough. And don't be so sure I can't use it."

Mac decided not to pursue that remark. Scanning the faces of Ingram, Goose, Estelle, and lingering a bit when he came to Gladys, he asked, "Anyone here that's not a treasure hunter?"

"Yeah," Gladys said. "At least not directly. I want the people he screwed to get what's coming to them, and that ain't going to happen until the money's found."

"And maybe not then," Mac said. "Are you sure that's all you're interested in?"

"I hope you get Roy Daugherty off." Gladys was silent for a moment, then came around to stand before Mac. "But if you do, guess who goes to the top of the list?" She touched the bruise on her face. "He was killed in my tent. And—has Abby told you the rest of the story?"

Mac nodded. "She told me what she knows. We'll have to talk about that some more."

"I know cops. They go for the easy mark every time." She shrugged. "I'd like somebody on my side when it happens."

"But you see my problem, Gladys. I'm supposed to prove Roy Daugherty's innocent. That might mean

150

proving you're guilty." He looked over her head at the rest of the group. "Or one of you. We seem to have a large percentage of the suspect list gathered right here."

"Quite right, old man," Goose said. "However, since none of us gave Bennet the push, anything you can do is bound to be to our advantage. I intend to work on the case myself, but freely admit the help of a professional would be welcome."

Mac laughed. "I wouldn't get too much into playing Miss Marple, Goose. Captain Pawlowski won't like it."

"Think of myself as more the Peter Whimsey type. And a bit of Bulldog Drummond, perhaps. Lord Peter can be a touch too cerebral."

Mac noticed Mrs. Bennet looking at Goose with open contempt. "How about you, Mrs. Bennet? What do you imagine I can do for you?"

"The police aren't going to focus much attention on the money," Mrs. B said. "If they find it, it'll be by accident."

"Sorry I can't help you."

Abby grasped his arm. She was frowning. "Why not?"

"I just explained—"

"I don't see the problem. As long as everybody understands you're not going to keep information from the police. And Mrs. Bennet has a point about the money."

"But—"

Abby leaned toward him and whispered. "And Fran can't pay for Roy's defense."

"Oh" Mac took a moment to digest a new idea. Then said, "Okay. Here's the deal. Take it or leave it. I'll take you on as clients to find the money. But no special treatment as far as the police are concerned. You all agree?"

A variety of nods, grunts, and other indications seemed to signify a unanimous aye vote.

"And the second condition. You each pay my full fee."

Judging from the reaction, Elmer seemed to speak for them all. "That's a mite steep, ain't it, Mac?"

"Consider it a contribution to the Roy Daugherty defense fund."

# Chapter Fifteen

After agreeing to Mac's terms the group seemed to lose focus and drift apart. Abby wondered if the various motives that had converged briefly to bring them here were now driving them in different directions.

Goose stood with one foot on the stairs that led to the McKenzie living quarters. She leaned forward, whispering to Estelle seated on the third step, then straightened up. "Well, I suppose that's that. I believe Estelle and I will take ourselves off and let the McKenzie's get on with it."

Goose leaving while the game was afoot? That seemed a bit out of character. And surely Mac would insist on the answers to a few questions. If he didn't, Abby certainly would.

As if echoing Abby's thought, Gladys said, "I don't think we'll get out of here that easy, Goose."

Estelle hadn't said a word since she first arrived, letting Goose speak for them both. Now she stood up, smoothed her skirt, and spoke in a soft, barely audible voice. "Before we leave, I just want you to know that Madame Gladys had nothing to do with the—with what happened. I was in the food tent, staying out of the rain until Goose came for me. And I could see her the whole time."

Abby glanced at Gladys in surprise.

Gladys seemed equally startled. She took a step away from the counter. "You saw me at the beer tent?"

"Yes."

Abby looked at Mac, expecting him to challenge Estelle. He returned her look and nodded.

"When did you first see her, Estelle?"

"Oh, I didn't look at my watch."

"Was it raining hard?"

"No. I remember that. It hadn't started yet."

"And when did she leave?"

Estelle looked at Goose. "Do you remember when we left?"

"As to the time? No. But we sheltered there during the cloudburst. Thought it was time to man the boats!"

"Yes, wasn't that awful?" Estelle nodded decisively. "Madame Gladys was still there when we left."

Abby looked at Mac again, but he remained silent. She continued. "How about you, Goose? Did you see Gladys there?"

"No, not actually. Estelle mentioned it, I suppose. I was watching the weather. Hoped it would let up so we could break for the car."

Abby was about to ask Gladys to explain why her story and Estelle's differed when Mrs. Bennet, who had been wandering around the shop, spoke.

"It occurs to me our deal with you is a little one-sided, Mr. McKenzie." She turned from a rack of needleworker's gadgets. "There's one condition I'd like to impose. If you find the money, you report to me first. I mean, before the police."

"The money, if it's found, will be impounded anyway," Mac said. "I don't see that it matters who hears first."

154

"I want to inform my attorney as soon as possible. There might be something he can do to protect my interest."

"Fair enough. Now I'm afraid I have—"

The deep, solemn tones of Charles Ingram caught everyone's attention. "The money will reappear when it has been cleansed of evil." He had been as unmoving as an ancient oak. Now he strode with measured tread to the counter and stared directly into Mac's face. "The death of Lawrence Bennet was the result of his own evil actions. Justice has been done."

Ingram's face was set in grim lines and his gray eyes seemed alight with some inner passion. Uneasy, Abby backed away from the counter and turned to Mac. He showed only polite interest in Ingram's words.

"Charles! Stop that talk!" Goose said. "I'm sure the police won't agree justice has been done. Not yet, anyway."

Another surprise—Estelle came to Ingram's side and took his arm. "We must be going, Charles," she said.

Ingram's face relaxed into its usual impassive mask. He turned away.

"I'd appreciate it if you would all remain just a little longer," Mac said.

Estelle and Ingram stopped.

"Thank you. I'm sorry to break it like this, but I have some bad news. Mrs. Bennet, your home was broken into this afternoon."

She grasped her broach. "My jewels! They stole my jewels?"

Mac shrugged. "The police won't know until you take an inventory."

Fran sat in a folding metal chair, a garage sale acquisition, with the words HANNIGAN'S FUNERAL HOME stenciled on the back. She nervously chewed her lower

155

lip. Kim leaned against her mother and stared at Ingram, her expression half afraid, half fascinated. Mac came to Fran and touched her shoulder.

"I'm sorry to add to your troubles, but your place was hit too."

She clutched Kim. "My house?" She seemed confused, overwhelmed by still another disaster.

"I don't think anything was taken."

"Then why—"

Goose drew near. "Can't be coincidence. You agree, McKenzie? First Mrs. Bennet, then Mrs. Daugherty? Same day Mr. Bennet is murdered? The murderer, of course."

"Whether it's the murderer or not," Mac said, "it's pretty certain to be a treasure hunter."

Elmer, still leaning on the bookcase he had made his home, looked as Elmer always did. Slightly amused, an observer of the follies of the world. "We seem to have a room full of those."

"Good point, Elmer. Fran, what time did you leave home?"

"When? Oh, I don't—maybe two-thirty. As soon as they told me about Roy."

"And you, Mrs. Bennet?"

"Sorry. I don't really know. Late afternoon at any rate. I went to that Captain Pawlowski's office, to make funeral arrangements, that sort of thing. Then I went to Madame Gladys."

"Why?"

"For advice. As I often do."

"Advice about what?"

"I set Lawrence Bennet up in business. I furnished a large down payment for the house. With one thing and another, I had a considerable investment in him. I want what is mine."

156

"And did Madame Gladys tell you how to get it?"

"It was her advice to come here."

"Thank you," Mac said. "Now, if you all wouldn't mind, I'd like to know where each of you were today, say from two-thirty on."

Leaving Estelle with Ingram, Goose stepped forward. "I can account for the three of us, McKenzie. Estelle and I went directly home from the fair. Required dry clothing, that sort of thing. Took the opportunity for a quick bite as well. Then collected Charles and went on to Madame's place. Can't say I paid much attention to the clock. Expect we arrived home about eleven-thirty. Allowing for the time required to dry out and eat, left again perhaps as early as two o'clock."

"I can tell you about the time," Gladys said. "Abby there was at my place until about two-thirty. She no sooner left than they arrived, like Goose said. Fran Daugherty came about three-thirty, maybe four. Mrs. Bennet sometime later. The bunch of us noodled around—another hour?" She looked around at the others and several nodded. "And came over here—" She looked to Abby.

"Ten minutes before you got home, Mac," Abby said. "About seven."

"That seems to take care of that. How did you get inducted into this group, Elmer?"

"Came on my own. Got here just before they did."

"Okay," Mac said. "While I've got you all here we might as well clear up one other thing. Abby was in a position to watch the front of the tent all morning. Why don't you tell them who went in and when."

"Yes, well Gladys, of course. That was before the rain started. Mrs. Bennet was with me when Lawrence Bennet showed up. She left and he went

157

into the tent. As far as I know he never came out."

"And as far as you know, neither did Gladys. She says she left the back way, but you can't swear to that."

"That's right. Then Goose came along and stayed with me, so she can corroborate that Mr. Ingram was next."

"That's true," Goose said, "but Charles barely poked his head in."

"No, he entered the tent, but I don't believe he was there more than two minutes. By then the rain was getting heavier. He ignored that and continued down the path in the direction he was originally going."

"How about it, Mr. Ingram? What did you see?"

"Nothing."

"Bennet?"

"No."

"Cards on the table?"

"The Tarot was on the table."

"Not on the ground?"

"No."

"Thank you. That's most helpful."

Abby nodded. "Then Roy Daugherty came. He went in and came back out very quickly."

"Unfortunately we can't ask him what he saw," Mac said.

"I talked to the lawyer," Fran said. "The tent was empty."

"You're sure that's your husband's story?" Abby asked. "Bennet wasn't there?"

"That's what the lawyer said."

"Any more visitors, Abby?" Mac asked.

"The next visitor to the tent was—well, I thought at the time it was Gladys. In costume."

"Not me. I told you. I never had the costume

158

on. Never came back after I went to the beer tent."

"Whoever it was, she never came out. Or rather, must have left the back way."

"And that was the last one, right?"

"Yes. Well, Maggy Kazmierski. She had been in the vicinity earlier, then I lost track of her. She reappeared out of the rain and stopped in my booth, chatted with Goose and me, then left."

"Unfriendly woman," Goose said. "Looked like a drowned rat."

"True," Abby agreed. "Then Goose left, and I was alone until Fran and Kim came."

Elmer, chuckling, left his leaning post. "So what you got is this. Bennet and Gladys went into the tent. She leaves the back way. Bennet becomes invisible. Two witnesses go into the tent and can't see him. Then a spook in a gypsy dress goes in. Waves a bunch of garlic to make him visible and kills him. She never comes out either. Is that right?"

Mac grinned. "If everybody can be believed."

"There's something I'd like to know," Abby said. "Gladys, where do you usually sit? In the tent, I mean."

"To the left as you go in."

"So Bennet was sitting where the questioner sits. There were two cards dealt. Relative to where you sit, The Fool was reversed. Now when you deal the next card does it matter which end is up?"

"Different strokes, folks. Not to me, because the next card goes on top of the first card. It has to be interpreted in relation to that card."

"Which way do you place that card? Head left or right?"

Gladys paused for a moment. "Head left."

"Would everybody do it that way?"

159

Gladys shrugged. "Seems more natural that way. Maybe because I'm right-handed."

"Assuming that's true, then the cards were dealt from Bennet's side of the table. And The Fool was not reversed. What would you make of The Fool crossed by a tower with people falling off of it?"

"Bad news. People usually think of Death as the bad news card. But in some cases Death can mean an end and a new beginning. But there's no up side to The Tower."

She took a deck from her purse and riffled through them, drawing two cards. She laid them on the counter as Abby had indicated. "The Fool. I'd say someone starting a new venture or —" She closed her eyes. "No. A new life. The Tower. Everything ends in disaster." Her eyes flew open. "Bennet was about to take the money and skip. He was feeling pressure. Everything was falling apart. And — he died."

Mac smiled. "Very good. Do the cards reveal how he died?"

"According to Mrs. Bennet he was knifed."

Mrs. Bennet crossed her arms self-protectively. "That's what the police told me. He was hit on the head and then —"

"No more information from the cards?" Mac asked Gladys. "Can't they tell you who did it?"

Gladys grinned. "If I knew the order of the rest of that deck, I might be able to tell you."

Abby noticed that while this exchange was going on Kim had left her mother and come around behind the counter to look at the cards. Seeing her curiosity, Gladys pushed the cards toward her.

Kim picked up The Fool, pictured with a dog snapping at his heels. "Fidget!" She turned to Mac. "Where's Fidget?"

Abby put her arm around Kim. Oh, Lord! No one had thought about the dog. "Mac? Fidget's all right, isn't she?"

"Damn! It never crossed my mind." He picked up the phone on the counter and dialed quickly. "Sergeant Henderson, please." While waiting he picked up the Tower card and tapped it impatiently on the counter. "Bob? Listen, did you find a dog at the Daugherty's? Yeah, that's the one. Okay, thanks."

Mac hung up and said, "Fidget's safe. The police opened the door to that building behind the house and she came running out."

"See, Kim," Fran said. "Nothing to worry about. We'll pick her up at the police station."

"They couldn't catch her," Mac said. "She ran off." Kim was about to cry and he hastily added, "She's probably hanging around the house waiting for you."

Kim tugged at her mother's arm. "We have to go find her!"

"Yes, I guess we better."

"Why don't you and Kim stay here tonight?" Abby suggested. "Your house is a mess and you don't want to tackle the cleanup right now. Mac can check on the dog."

But Kim was adamant and Fran gave in. Mother and daughter departed, hand in hand, Fran trailing, Kim urging greater speed.

After this final bit of excitement the rest of the group followed the Daughertys. They all left in silence, except for Elmer who cheerfully wished them a good night.

"I hope Fran's house isn't too much of a mess," Abby said, watching the last car turn the corner onto Main.

Mac put his arms around her and drew her close.

161

"It's pretty bad. Whoever searched the place was in a hurry. No time wasted on finesse."

"Could it have been a random burglary?"

Mac shook his head. "A jewel box had been opened. There was money in it, in plain sight."

"Bennet's is an obvious place to look for the money, but why the Daugherty house?"

"Roy Daugherty and Bennet were known to be enemies. Daugherty's place backs on the pit. It's logical to assume he's been down there. He might have seen Bennet put something in his hideaway."

"Okay, Hawkshaw. Why wasn't anyone else burgled? I should think Gladys and the Kazmierski's would be logical candidates. Gladys because Bennet came to her tent, and we know now it was because he suspected her of stealing his money. And of course Maggy, as his mistress would be thought to know his plans."

"Sergeant Henderson was too quick. As soon as he heard about the second break-in he sent men to cover them both."

Abby led the way to the kitchen. "I don't know about you, but I'm starved. I'll scramble the eggs, if you make coffee." She took eggs from the refrigerator. "You notice Mrs. Bennet reeled off her alibi before you asked? Like she was all prepared?"

"That *was* interesting. And how about the alibi Estelle gave Gladys? That even surprised Gladys."

"Why do you suppose she did it?"

"Did you notice that Estelle is almost as short as Gladys? And no other woman in the case is?"

Abby dropped an egg in a bowl. "Damn!" She began fishing out bits of broken shell with a fork. "You really think it was Estelle in the gypsy costume? Why would she do that?"

Mac shrugged. "How about some pork sausage with

those eggs?" He took a package of links from the refrigerator.

Whipping the eggs briskly, Abby said, "Goose told me Estelle had an umbrella. But you saw her in the parking lot, soaking wet. Right? She might have mislaid it while getting in and out of costume."

"Good point. I'll ask Stan if he found it." Mac put bread in the toaster. "So maybe she gave Gladys an alibi because it would also give *her* one."

"Or, she had made Gladys a leading suspect and wanted to square things. Assuming Estelle *was* the gypsy." Abby placed four links in the skillet. "Are you going to make that coffee or aren't you?"

Mac filled the pot with water. "I'm sorry Kim didn't stay the night. I'd like a child's unbiased account of this afternoon's seance." He put dishes and silver on the table. "What was that business with the cards? You're not starting to fall for this fortune-telling scam, are you?"

"Of course not. But now we know that either Bennet dealt the cards himself—"

"Psychic solitaire?"

"Or someone did it while leaning over the corpse. In which case it was a message." Abby poured the eggs from bowl to skillet. "Or a warning. For who, I don't know."

"I can't think of one rational reason for either."

"I'd also like to know if the meeting at Gladys's included card readings and what they showed."

"You said you didn't believe—"

"But a lot of people do. Goose, Estelle, Mrs. B, Fran. Well, suppose *you* believed. And Gladys said you might be run over by a bus. What would you do?"

"Take a taxi?"

163

"Right. So if we knew what they've been told by the cards we might have a better idea of what they might do—or have done."

Mac drew her close and kissed her. "You're pretty smart for a girl."

She punched him in the stomach.

# Chapter Sixteen

It was difficult for both Mac and Abby to squeeze into Stan Pawlowski's office. Abby got to sit in the visitor's chair and bang her knees against the desk. Mac leaned on the bookcase and led off with an account of his actions from the time he'd signed on to follow Bennet. Abby followed with her story of the comings and goings at the fair.

They committed only two crimes of omission: Kim was not mentioned, and they refused to speculate on who the gypsy might be.

Stan listened, took a few notes, and then settled back in his chair. "Sure you don't want coffee? It's only an hour old."

"No we don't," Mac said. "We had a good breakfast. Why ruin it?"

"You got a point." Stan sipped from his and made a face. "Well, you've given me a lot of good leads, but right now I'm not sure what to do with all this."

"Why?" Abby asked. "There's the missing money, that weird Ingram going into the tent, and my personal favorites, the Kazmierskis. They were both acting suspicious, and either one could have gone in the back way."

"And a little domestic strife is always my first choice as a motive," Stan said. "But I've got a perfectly good suspect in jail, courtesy of John Almeir, may his feet have fungus."

"He's an overbearing fool," Abby said.

Mac grinned. "I'd put it a little stronger. What's with him anyway?"

Stan craned his neck to look through the glass in the door. "I'll fill you in on a little office politics, but keep it to yourself." He lit a cigarette and blew the smoke toward the window propped up with a two-by-four. "See, the chief—Pete Venlow—started this police force back when it was just him and two other volunteers. As the population went up, he expanded. Took night courses. Turned himself into a pretty good cop. When I started here he had Fred Zimmer running the blue suits and the chief handled investigations along with his other duties."

"Must have been glad to have you take part of the load," Mac said.

"Sure. Now he could concentrate on administration and dealing with the village board, which meant mainly dealing with Bennet. And in the back of his mind was retirement. So when Bennet suggested moving Zimmer up to deputy and bringing in an experienced cop to take his spot, the Chief jumped at it."

"Don't tell me," Abby said. "Bennet brought in Almeir."

Stan stood and reached over Mac's shoulder for the coffeepot. "Seemed okay at the time. Almeir had been around. Knew the ropes. Then Bennet started finding fault with Zimmer. My guess is he was harassing him into quitting."

"So Almeir could take his place?" Abby asked.

"What else? The last straw was when Bennet's hand-picked committee decided to reorganize the department and made Almeir and me captains, same rank as Zim-

166

mer. He quit last month and took a job as chief up in Michigan. Little place. Population five hundred and a good fishing lake."

"What's Venlow's position in all this?"

"This is why he hasn't retired yet. He's afraid Almeir will get his job."

"Sounds like Almeir should tread carefully, now that Bennet's gone."

"Yes," Abby said. "Instead he's running around like a bull moose."

Stan laughed. "I always figured him for an ox. Him and me, we've gored each other a couple of times. And he hates your guts, Mac, ever since you made a fool of him last spring."

"That was an accident."

"Tell it to Almeir. Anyway, without his political clout his only way up is to play the hero on this one, and make *me* look like a fool. So far he's doing pretty good."

"I don't see that he's done anything so great," Abby said. "All he's done is arrest the wrong man."

"The case against Daugherty is rock solid. And Almeir's already taken full credit. Seen the paper this morning?"

They shook their heads. "Not yet," Abby said.

"He comes off like a combination J. Edgar and Wyatt Earp. So if you see a lot of Almeir on this one, you know why. He ain't going to let Daugherty get off the hook and spoil his big triumph."

"You buy Daugherty as the killer?"

Stan shrugged. "I admit there are a lot of loose ends, and the crime is out of character, but you can't get around that knife."

"Someone could have stolen it," Abby said.

"No chance. When Daugherty was released on the

first charge, the knife was returned to him. He signed for it. He went pretty much straight to the tent."

"A pickpocket could have taken it," Abby insisted. "Does he remember getting bumped going through the fair grounds?"

"I wouldn't know. The lawyer won't let me talk to him. Maybe your old man here can find out."

"Get me in to see him," Mac said.

Stan stood up and patted Mac's shoulder. "Almeir runs the jail. Care to ask him?"

"I guess not." Mac straightened up and stretched his back, which was beginning to ache. "But he can't keep Metlaff out."

"Wish you luck. I'm going to keep a low profile on this one and hope Almeir screws up. If not now, then later."

Surprised, Mac asked, "You're not dropping the case altogether, are you?"

"No. We'll be taking statements and doing backgrounds on everybody. The State's Attorney expects it. But I'll have to leave the loose ends to you."

"I suppose it's too early for anything on the backgrounds?"

"It's Sunday. What d'you want?" Stan tapped the top of the telephone. "But I might have something on Ingram today."

"That's quick."

"I said maybe. The name sounded familiar, and when you told me you thought that witchcraft book was his, it came together. Back when I was still on the Chicago cops there was a looney named Ingram tried to do a number on the summer solstice under the Picasso at the Daley Center."

"Considering some of the stuff that goes on there I'd think he'd fit right in."

"He didn't have a permit. Anyway, I called a guy owes me a favor. He says he can get the record on Ingram, maybe today. Check back later."

Mac nodded and held the door for Abby. "I'll be at Metlaff's, then Quill, Prestwick, and Ingram, in that order."

"One other thing," Stan said. "An insurance investigator stopped by. Seems he's had an eye on Bennet for the last month. You were right about the annuities scam."

"Could he tell you anything new?"

"Pretty much confirms what you two found. He was about to blow the whistle when Bennet got himself killed. Now he's worried the company will get sued because Bennet acted as their agent."

Mac and Abby spent a few minutes in the parking lot discussing how they would split the tasks at hand. Then Mac dropped Abby at home where she could pick up her own car, and he went on to Metlaff's home and office.

Metlaff answered the doorbell in paint-stained pants and a ragged sweatshirt. The only remnant of his usual lawyer's costume was a two-inch stub of cigar clamped between his teeth.

"I've been expecting you." Instead of leading the way to his office Metlaff headed for the kitchen at the back of the house. "I was eating lunch. Are you hungry?"

Mac looked at the paper plate of canned tuna mixed with chopped onion and ketchup. "No thanks. Had a late breakfast."

Metlaff laid his cigar in a saucer and bit into a cracker. "Can you explain how the knife got into Bennet's back by some agency other than Roy Daugherty's hand?"

"No. But I've got a long and interesting list of suspects."

Scowling, Metlaff lifted a fork laden with tuna. "If you can't explain the knife, there *are* no other suspects."

"Yeah." Mac picked up a cracker and looked at it as though it might provide a clue. "What does Daugherty have to say for himself?"

"It's a good thing I kept him from making a statement. He admits the knife was in his possession. He went directly to the fortune-teller's tent, meeting no one on the way. Or more precisely, he interacted with no one. There were many fairgoers leaving the grounds at the time."

"Why Gladys? I'd think he'd be anxious to call his wife at that point."

Metlaff nodded. "He said he was looking for change." He shoved the plate aside and relit his cigar. "I found his story, at every point, to be unbelievable. More importantly, a jury will find it unbelievable." He maneuvered the cigar to one corner of his mouth and folded his hands across his stomach. "If I required every client to be innocent, I would soon run out of the price of cigars. But I do insist they be honest with me. I was tempted to tell him to get another attorney. I may yet do that."

"I don't think he can afford another lawyer."

Metlaff glared at him. "Do you imagine I work at cut-rate?"

"No, but I thought you might settle for whatever is in the Daugherty defense fund."

"The what fund?"

Mac explained the deal he had made the night before, ignoring Metlaff's growing air of disbelief.

"You are an ass." Metlaff stubbed out his cigar. "If

by some miracle you should manage to divert suspicion from Daugherty, you will open yourself to conflict of interest charges. And in any case, with the funds flowing through McKenzie Associates, you will be liable for taxes."

"I figured you could find a way around that."

"Well—perhaps. Can you trust them to pay?"

Mac shrugged. "I can but lean on them."

"Send no bills. Tell them to make their checks payable to the fund, not to you. I'll set up an escrow account."

"Then you'll defend him for whatever we collect?"

"What makes you so sure he's innocent?"

"I told his kid he was. So he must be."


"I appreciate the offer, Abby," Fran said, "but I'm about done down here." She pulled the plug on the vacuum cleaner and began rolling up the cord. "Besides, the work takes my mind off other things."

Abby nodded. "Did you find anything missing?"

"No. Seems as if somebody just went through the place out of meanness." Fran left the vacuum in the middle of the room and sat on the couch. "Dumped every drawer, every bed, everything." She slumped back against the cushions. "And my best dishes. I had them put away in a box, because we don't use them except the big holidays, you know? They were dumped out and about half broke or got chipped."

It was apparent to Abby that Fran was emotionally and physically exhausted. "Why don't I make coffee? Later I'll give you a hand upstairs."

"Coffee would be nice." Fran lifted herself from the couch. "I'll get it." Ignoring Abby's protest, she went to the kitchen.

Following along, Abby said, "I know you want to keep busy, Fran. But it's not going to help if you're too beat to think straight." She took the coffeepot from Fran's hand. "By the way, where's Kim?"

"Kim? Out hunting for Fidget, I guess." She sat at the kitchen table. "The dog never did come home." She stirred uneasily in her seat. "Guess I should be more worried about that."

"You've got a lot on your mind."

"But it's important to Kim, and worried as she is about her Daddy the dog's kind of a last straw." She started to get up. "Maybe I should go look for her."

"Sit. What you need is coffee. I'll check up on Kim in a bit." Abby managed to maneuver a mug under the still running coffee maker while removing the pot. Only a few drops spilled. "You relax and—when did you eat last?"

"Breakfast."

"What?"

"Piece of toast. I'm not really hungry."

Abby rummaged in the refrigerator and came up with summer sausage, lettuce, and mayonnaise. The bread on the counter was beginning to dry out, but would have to do. "Has Kim been gone long?"

"She left after breakfast, came back for cookies and some dog biscuits—I guess about an hour this last time." Fran accepted the sandwich from Abby. "Why don't you have something?"

"Just coffee, thanks." Abby sipped from her mug and watched Fran begin to eat. "How did you come to live here, Fran? I mean, it's quite a coincidence, you, Bennet, and Gladys all winding up in the same small town."

"Yeah, it is. I said that to Roy the other day."

"Bennet came here first. Then who?"

172

Fran was making good progress with her food, and looked more relaxed. "We came next. Roy always wanted to go in business for himself, and figured out this way was where new homes would be going up."

"But why Sarahville, especially?"

"Gladys found this place. One of the ladies she did readings for told her about it. It's really ideal. The house is well-built, the barns are good for Roy's business, and the price was what we could afford."

"So Gladys steered you here. And then moved here herself."

"She visited us a few times and seemed to like the area."

"And Mrs. Bennet is one of Gladys's clients."

Fran swallowed the last of her sandwich and rose to get more coffee. "Now that *was* a coincidence, her knowing Larry and all."

"Do you know how Gladys came to know Bennet?"

"From the old neighborhood, same as Roy. Of course, she was just a kid then."

"Did you know them all in the old neighborhood?"

"No, not really. I lived near Ashland and Milwaukee Avenue, you know where that is? I didn't meet Roy until he got out of the Army." With obvious pride, she said, "He got a Purple Heart and a Bronze Star."

"Really? Well, thank God he came home in good health." Abby toyed with her cup. "I was wondering about this feud with Bennet. Do you know what started it?"

Fran half-turned and stared out the window. She nodded. "But Roy doesn't want me talking about that."

"Fran, we need to know. If the police find out, and your lawyer isn't prepared, well, lawyers don't like surprises in court."

Fran turned back to Abby and tears began to

173

gather. "He'll really have to go on trial, won't he?"

"We'll do our best to keep that from happening, but it won't be easy. So you see, we have to know everything, even though you may not think it's important." Abby reached across the table and touched Fran's hand. "You *do* see that, don't you?"

"I guess you're right." She wiped at her eyes and straightened her shoulders. "Roy's sister, Mary. She went with Bennet. Mary was just a kid. Seventeen I think. Bennet was a lot older and Roy never liked him. Mary's father didn't know about it." Fran hesitated. "Well, Mary got pregnant. I guess she didn't feel like she could talk to anybody, you know, like her father. Then Bennet ran out on her."

"I see. Bennet seems to have been good at running. I can see why Roy disliked him."

"Dislike? Roy hated him. Mary committed suicide."

Goose Quill, dressed in Army fatigues and bearing Staff Sergeant's chevrons, led Mac into the living room. "Glad you came by, McKenzie. I was about to call."

Mac, pointing to Goose's sleeve said, "Should I address you as Sergeant Quill?"

"Surprised, eh?" She chuckled. "You might say I've had a varied career. Army from '45 to '58. But you didn't come here to trade war stories."

"You said you were going to call me?"

"Coordinate our efforts. Unless you have some other assignment in mind for me, thought I'd climb down in that pit behind the garage. See what all the traffic's about."

This Dr. Watson business had to stop. "Miss Quill—Goose—I work alone and—oh, hello Miss Prestwick."

Estelle, dressed in a summery cotton print dress, had

slipped quietly into the room. She nodded to Mac and sat at the far end of the couch.

"McKenzie's come by to chat about the case, Estelle." Turning back to Mac she said, "Quite understand your point, McKenzie."

Well, that had been easier than he'd expected.

"You're the professional. Just consider me the gifted amateur. Help where I can. Just say the word."

Mac sighed. "Did you say something was going on in the pit?"

"Great amount of traffic. Been watching all morning. Police, that Kazmierski woman and her husband—not together mind you. Believe he was following her. What do you suppose it's all about?"

"The Kazmierski's are after Bennet's money. The police, the same thing plus whatever they can find that relates to the case."

"Why are they looking down there for the money?" Estelle asked. "What made them think it might be there?"

"It *was* there at one time. But either Bennet moved it, or it was stolen. If he moved it himself, then it may be somewhere down there."

"What do *you* think, McKenzie?"

"It was hijacked. Could be anywhere by now."

"Still—worth a look, don't you think?"

Mac shrugged. "Maybe." Then it struck him that this might be a good assignment for the gifted amateur. "It should be checked out, but I won't have time. Do you think you could handle that, Goose?"

"Will do. If it's there, I'll find it."

"That'll be a big help." While she was busy combing a hole in the ground she wouldn't have time to mess up his investigation. "And while you're doing that, I've got a few questions for Miss Prestwick."

175

"Oh, well. No hurry." Goose sat in a lounge chair opposite Estelle.

"Miss Prestwick, could you go over your movements at the fair for me? I'm trying to get a picture of where everyone was and what they might have seen."

"I'm sure I didn't see anything. Connected with the murder, I mean."

"You already told us about seeing Gladys. That was connected."

"He's quite right, Estelle. Mustn't leave anything out."

Estelle brought her hands together and placed them under her chin. After a moment she said, "I'm trying to think back. I know it was only yesterday, but it seems long ago. So much has happened."

"Take your time," Mac said.

"We went along the path on the right, I remember. Not all the booths were open yet. I had heard a dealer in paperweights would be there. That's a hobby of mine. Collecting. The weather was threatening and I wanted to be sure of seeing his booth, if no other."

"I understand you had the foresight to bring an umbrella."

"Did I?" She looked at Goose.

"Believe you did. Yes."

"So you were looking for this dealer—"

"Yes. We located him about halfway around the circle. Goose is easily bored by that sort of thing and she took off on her own."

"Did you see anyone you recognized? Up to that point, I mean?"

Estelle considered the question. "No, no one that I noticed. Of course, once I found the booth I didn't really pay attention."

"How long did you stay with the paperweights?"

176

"I lost track of time. But then a light rain started and the man began covering his display with a plastic sheet, so I left."

Mac noticed Goose had been following Estelle's story intently. "How about you, Goose? Where did you go when you left Miss Prestwick?"

"Estelle, please," Estelle said. "We *are* friends, aren't we?"

Mac smiled, then turned his attention back to Goose.

"Continued around the circle, scanning the booths as I went. Made note of one or two I might come back to. Ran into your wife and stopped to chat. Expect you know all about that."

Mac nodded. "What did you do when the rain started, Estelle?"

"Went directly to the food tent for shelter."

"Didn't rely on your umbrella?"

"We'd arranged to meet there," Goose said.

"I see. So you remained snug and dry. And that's where you saw Gladys."

Estelle nodded. "And I stayed there until Goose came for me. I didn't see anyone else I recognized."

The moment had arrived to begin picking Estelle's story apart, starting with the umbrella, and ending with an accusation that she was the gypsy. If she was the gypsy, he felt fairly sure she'd crumble. Although that would be more likely if Goose hadn't decided to stay.

"I say, Estelle," Goose said. "It just occurred to me you have an appointment at the hairdresser. You'll have to hurry if you're to make it."

"On Sunday?" Mac asked.

"Woman does this in her home. Weekends only. Gets quite testy if you fail to arrive on time."

Estelle was already up and moving toward the door, murmuring an apology.

177

"I just have one or two more questions," Mac said.

"I'm sorry. Where did I put my purse, Goose? Oh, here it is."

Mac was about to follow Estelle to her car, questioning along the way, when the phone rang.

"It's for you, McKenzie."

As Mac took the phone, Estelle disappeared through the door. Mac cursed under his breath as he heard Stan's voice.

"Got a line on Ingram. I'll give you the details later, but he made some threats at the time he was arrested, so they did a thorough check on him. Seems he had a rough war. OSS. Dropped into France two months before the invasion."

"Really? Coordinating with the resistance?"

"No. He had a list of three collaborators to get rid of before the balloon went up. He got to all three in record time."

There was silence as Mac absorbed this information.

"Anyway," Stan said, "if you decide to question him, be prepared."

# Chapter Seventeen

Mac sat in his station wagon and watched Goose cross the back yard heading for the path to Ingram's ladder. He had intended to follow Estelle, but Stan's phone call had delayed him too long.

What next, then? Ingram was probably stirring a bubbling cauldron somewhere. The Kazmierski's? Why not. He reached for the ignition, but stopped as Goose turned toward Ingram's apartment.

Estelle and Goose had taken charge of the man yesterday and steered him away from—from what? Talking too much? And today Goose had assured him that Ingram was not home. So why was she climbing his stairs?

Ingram's record invited caution. Should he go home and pick up a weapon? Would Ingram leave before he got back? Anyway, it was broad daylight. And he was fifteen years younger than Ingram. Maybe twenty. Stop dithering, McKenzie.

The curtains parted at his knock and Goose peered out at him. She opened the door.

"Glad you're here, McKenzie. Seems to have been a break-in."

At first glance the kitchen seemed reasonably neat compared to the burglaries he'd seen yesterday. But then he realized that was because there was so little to trash.

A card table and two chairs, a refrigerator, and one cabinet over the sink. That was all. The cabinet doors were open and he could see a few cleaning supplies had been dumped and spilled. Dishes consisted of two plates, a bowl, and a mug sitting on the drainboard.

"Have you touched anything?"

"Of course not!"

"Sorry." Mac opened the refrigerator using his pen hooked through the handle. Nothing but milk, cheese, and a loaf of bread. Ice cubes in the freezer.

The bathroom with shower stall had a mirrored medicine cabinet containing a straight razor, shaving mug, and soap. A razor strop was fastened to the wall above the sink. Not even a bottle of aspirin. Apparently Charles never got headaches.

Goose followed Mac, saying nothing.

The roomy bedroom was more interesting, and it was here the search had focused. The mattress on the narrow cot had been dumped on the floor and ripped open. The drawers of an old and scarred dresser were on the floor and the few articles of clothing thrown about.

Goose remained in the doorway, hands in pockets. "Strikes me as pure vandalism," she said.

"Treasure," Mac said. "Somebody has treasure fever." A number of small bottles containing powders, leaves, and other, less recognizable, substances were intermixed with the clothes. Each was neatly labelled in Latin. Two were broken. "What's all that stuff?"

"Witchcraft nonsense. No idea."

Mac smiled briefly. Henderson would love this!

An oak bookcase had once held a number of works on the occult, astrology, water divining, and witchcraft. The books were scattered across the floor. A photograph, apparently fallen from one of them, pictured a young man sitting on a porch swing next to a young girl. From the clothes Mac put the date somewhere in the thirties. "Recognize them?"

Goose inspected the picture briefly. "Charles as a young man, I should think. Can't say more than that."

Ingram's closet held three white shirts on hangers and a black suit that had been thrown on the floor. Mac picked up the coat and found a fringed pillow with the embroidered phrase, WELCOME TO HOT SPRINGS, ARKANSAS under it. The trousers covered a dog's feeding dish and water bowl. There was water in the bowl.

"Ingram has a dog?"

"Apparently. But no, I wasn't aware of any pets." She paused. "Well, he had some sort of lizard for a while. Tiny thing with a colorful tail. Quite useful; Ate flies. Don't know what became of it."

They left the bedroom and Mac pointed to a door just to the left. "Where does that go?"

"Garage. Must have two exits, you know. Fire regulations."

"Looks like tool marks here." Mac used his shirttail to turn the knob. "Lock's been broken."

They descended the stairs and it was immediately obvious that the burglar had gained entry through a broken window.

"Who would know about the entrance through the garage?"

"Charles never had visitors. Can't remember Estelle or I ever pointing it out to anyone." Mac started back up the stairs and she followed. "Been various people about over the years. Had the roof repaired, for example. And a man from the garage when the car refused to start last winter. With one thing and another I suppose quite a few might know of it."

"Anybody in here recently?"

181

"Just a policeman. Questioned Charles and went off muttering to himself. Charles has that effect on some people."

"Can't imagine why," Mac said. "No phone in here?"

"Charles doesn't feel the need."

"We'll have to call this in from your place."

As they descended the outside stairs Mac asked, "Why did you come here? You told me Ingram was gone."

"Right. Early riser myself. I'd just come down to get the morning tea. Barely light, sun not up as yet. I saw Charles leave going toward the pit."

"Was that unusual?"

"Can't say that it was. Thought he might have come back while we were talking. Decided to check before going down into the pit. Knocked, got no answer Looked through the gap in the curtains, in case he was on his way to the door. Just about to leave when I realized something was amiss."

"How did you know?"

"Saw the cupboard open and things knocked about. Charles is very neat."

"How did you get in?"

"I have a key. After all, it *is* rental property."


Abby was ready to get on with the cleanup, but Fran had started to fret about Kim again. "You rest a bit more," Abby said. "Have another coffee. I'll find Kim."

Before Fran could object, Abby left. The yard, as far as she could see, was empty of life. Calling brought no answer. She tried the steel pole building first. It was locked. Circling the building she found a broken window, no doubt used by the burglar to gain entry. Peering into the interior gloom, she could make out a truck with its hood raised and the front wheels jacked off the ground. She called again on the off chance that Kim had climbed through the window. No response.

Abby walked slowly toward the wooden barn, trying to visualize how the burglar would have searched the steel building with Fidget inside, probably barking frantically.

By contrast with the sun-baked yard, the barn seemed almost cool and, until her eyes adapted, quite dark. Even here there were signs of a hasty search. Sacks of mortar that should have been stacked against the wall were scattered over the floor. A tool box lay up side down, trowels, chalk line, and mason's hammer spilled.

She found Kim's "office," recognizing the crate that served as desk from Mac's description. There was a cardboard box on the crate labelled CLUES in red crayon. It contained a conglomeration of junk that looked as if it might have been collected from any roadside. She was about to leave when the small door at the rear of the barn opened and Kim entered.

"Hi, Mrs. McKenzie." The child seemed unsurprised by Abby's presence.

"Hi, Kim." Pointing to the box Abby said, "I'll have to get one of these for Mr. McKenzie. He leaves clues scattered all over the house." This failed to get a smile from Kim.

"Is my daddy coming home?"

Abby put her arm around Kim. "Not yet, honey. But I'm sure it won't be long."

Kim sat on the crate and, staring at the ground, began rhythmically kicking its side.

"No luck finding Fidget?"

Kim shook her head. "Did you know that Mr. Ingram is a war—war something? He does black magic."

"Warlock?"

183

Kim nodded.

"How do you know?"

"Mom said so. She knows about that stuff and besides"—Kim reached into the clue box and took out a stub of black candle—"this is his and it's magic."

"Where did you get that?"

"Oh—" She waved her hand in the direction of outdoors. "I found it."

Abby shook her head. "Kim, you've been down in that pit again. You promised you wouldn't."

"Only once, honest. I had to. Fidget was barking!"

"You heard her bark?"

"Uh huh." Kim looked at Abby, who raised a skeptical eyebrow. "It could have been!"

"But you didn't find her."

Kim stared at the ground and resumed her rhythmic kicking. "I bet that warlock's got her. He prob'ly killed Mr. Bennet too and blamed it on my daddy."

"We don't know who killed Mr. Bennet. But we'll find out. And we'll find Fidget too." Abby placed her hands on Kim's shoulders and looked directly into her eyes. "But you *must* stay out of that pit. What if you fell and broke a leg? You wouldn't be able to climb out and no one would know where you were."

Kim didn't respond and Abby could see this argument was not entirely convincing. "And don't forget, the warlock is down there."

Kim drew her arms close to her body as though to shrink into a less noticeable bundle.

Abby regretted her words. The child felt badly enough without being frightened as well. After all, at Kim's age she had persisted in climbing the bluffs along Lake Michigan and swimming at unguarded beaches. If there had been an abandoned gravel pit near her home, no doubt she would have been the first to explore it.

But once grown up it became your duty to take the fun out of life.

She drew Kim close. "I don't want to frighten you, but the pit *can* be a dangerous place. You never know who might be down there or when you might have an accident. Understand?"

Kim nodded, but Abby wasn't entirely sure that she did. "For instance. You remember telling me about the argument between Mr. Bennet and Mr. Kazmierski?"

Kim nodded.

"Well, suppose they had seen you. And suppose then Mr. Kazmierski had gotten mad at *you?*"

Kim shook her head. "Mr. Bennet is the one that was *really* mad."

Puzzled, Abby asked, "Didn't Mr. Kazmierski threaten Mr. Bennet?"

"Uh huh. And then Mr. Bennet threw down his fishing pole and he said, 'Just you remember, Kaz.' That's what he called him for short. 'Just you remember, Kaz. I've got you down in my little book.' And then Mr. Kazmierski didn't say anything and he went away. Mr. Bennet kicked his tackle box and it went in the water. I almost laughed."


Abby watched Mac take the last slice of pizza and wondered how he managed to keep his weight under control. He claimed it was the result of hard work and exercise, but she'd seen little evidence of either.

"I suppose after gorging yourself you'll suggest a short walk and an ice cream cone."

"You know how it is with Italian food. An hour later and—"

"If you can talk with your mouth full, tell me where we are with this case. It seems to me that after a day

185

of running around in the heat we're exactly nowhere."

Mac wiped tomato sauce from the corner of his mouth and shoved his paper plate aside. "Well, we know the treasure hunter hasn't found what he's looking for. Unless it was in Ingram's apartment. Only now we're not sure if the main object of the hunt is money or Bennet's little book. Assuming there *is* a book."

"I think there must be some kind of record, don't you? Keeping track of who made payoffs over the years would give Bennet some leverage in case anyone was inclined to give him trouble." Abby ran a finger down the side of her iced-tea glass causing condensed moisture to form a rivulet and run onto the table. "As in the case of Kaz."

"Maybe. Keeping a record is dangerous, but a lot of people have made that mistake. It's usually done when there's a need to split with someone else and they want an accounting."

"Who would he split with?"

"A main source of graft in places like Sarahville comes from zoning and the approval of development plans." Mac put ice cubes in a glass and filled it with tap water. "For instance, letting a builder get away with filling in wetlands, as happened on Running Fox Creek. But the Mayor can't do it alone. He needs votes."

"You mean the whole village board?"

"No. But Bennet controlled committee assignments. He'd appointment people too dumb to ask questions Lord knows he'd have no trouble finding them on *our* board of trustees. But one or two would probably know what he was doing and demand a cut."

"That could be the answer to this string of burglaries," Abby said. "But even if it's a trustee anxious to cover up, it doesn't help us. I mean, someone threatened by the book is unlikely to kill Bennet without

186

knowing where to find it."

"Unless they thought they knew where it was and—but then why not get the book first?"

Abby nodded. "It seems more likely the threat arose as a result of Bennet's death. Unless—do you suppose Bennet tried blackmail as a last act before leaving? At that point he could reasonably say he had nothing to lose by sending the book to the police. He wouldn't be around to take the consequences."

"Possible. And someone might react in panic."

Abby fanned herself with a napkin. "Do you suppose we can ever get this place air-conditioned?"

"With twelve-foot ceilings, plaster walls, and under-sized ducts? Cost a fortune. Maybe a window unit here in the kitchen." He got up. "Let's try the back porch. Maybe there's a breeze."

There was no breeze, but the temperature had dropped a few degrees since sundown. Abby settled into a wicker chair. "When Stan came to investigate at Ingram's, did he have anything new to say?"

"Preliminary autopsy results. The cause of death was a blow to the head. He was dead before he was stabbed. Even if he hadn't been, the stab wound missed anything vital."

"Then why stab him?"

"To incriminate Daugherty. That's the only explanation that makes sense. Of course, it may be hard to convince a jury of that."

"What's Stan's opinion?"

"Chief Venlow has assigned this case to Almeir as arresting officer. Officially, it's none of Stan's business."

"Unofficially?"

"He'd like nothing better than having Almeir fall on his face." Mac walked to the porch screen and stared

187

into the gathering dusk. "But there's no way around that knife."

Abby joined him and linked her arm through his. "There must be a way. Fran is close to falling apart, and I can't imagine the effect this is having on Kim. For the moment she's displaced her anxiety to her missing dog. I don't know what she'll do, if something's happened to Fidget."

"I'm sure Ingram has the dog. If I can ever find him—"

"The Phantom of the Pit of Hell."

Mac laughed. "Pretty solid phantom. He sounds like the voice of doom and walks like implacable nemesis." He sobered quickly. "Which reminds me. We need to talk about Ingram."

"We were. Anyway, I don't see how *he* could have gotten the knife."

"Magic. No, that's not—"

"But then, I don't see how anyone could have. Does Stan have any ideas?"

"No. When you're arrested, your personal belongings, weapons, contraband, that's all inventoried and bagged. Then the sheet's signed by you and the arresting officer and everything is placed in a locker. When you're released, the stuff comes out of the locker, you check that it's all there, and sign again."

"So Roy Daugherty left jail with all his possessions—"

"Right down to his pocket lint."

"—including the knife, and went straight to Gladys's tent. That *is* what he did, isn't it?"

"Far as I know."

Abby turned to face Mac. "Why did he do that? Go to the tent?"

"According to Metlaff, looking for change to make a

phone call."

"There were lots of places to get change before he got to the tent. He could have made a call from the police station. He could have gotten change from the carnival rides, or from me, for that matter."

Mac put his arms around her. "Sorry, Madame Prosecutor. It's the only answer we have right now."

"What happens next?" Abby lay her head against his chest and listened to the slow beat of his heart. "Can he get out on bail?"

"It'll be high."

"And if he doesn't have the money?"

"He'll be transferred to the Cook County lockup."

Abby sighed. "The window air-conditioner in our bedroom has been on all day. Why don't we go cool off and forget all this for a while."

"Yeah. Good idea." Mac separated himself from Abby. "But first—there's something else."

Alerted by his hesitant tone, Abby stepped back. "What's wrong, Mac?"

He told her of Ingram's career as assassin.

"But that was war. And a long time ago."

"The potential for violence is there. And you have to admit this guy's not driving with a full tank."

Abby nodded. "Okay. I'll be careful." She moved back into his arms. "And you be careful too. Don't go searching for him down in his pit. If you have to question him do it where there are people around."

"It's not just Ingram. Unless we're wrong about Daugherty, one of these people is a killer. And a very cool and dangerous one. It took a lot of nerve to pull off a murder in the middle of a fair. Anyone could have walked in on him."

Abby began to suspect where the conversation was

leading. She stepped away. "Go on."

"Well, under the circumstances—"

"I should mind the store and stay out of the case."

"Yeah. That's about it."

"Mac, don't be silly. I'm not going to do anything foolish. And if it'll make you happy, I'll just talk to the women."

"Who may be deadlier than the male."

"You certainly don't think Goose or Estelle are killers?"

"I don't know who is what in this mess. I know they're hiding something. I think Estelle is the gypsy. I think Maggy Kazmierski is dangerous and I *know* she carries a gun."

"Well, I'm certainly not going to let you see *her* alone, even without her gun."

"And your friend the fortune-teller has a lot of questions to answer. She's the one who brought all Bennet's enemies together, maybe to create an explosive situation, and maybe for cover when she lit the fuse herself."

"All right, all right. But I'm going to see Fran tomorrow." She moved toward the door. "And I'm going with you on *your* rounds. You're not exactly John Wayne, you know."

"What's that supposed to mean?"

"Maggy got the drop on you, cowboy."

"But—"

"And I think Goose can take you two falls out of three." She let the screen door slam behind her.

# Chapter Eighteen

Monday morning brought no relief from the heat. To make matters worse, it brought a renewed attack of the earthmovers. Their seemingly endless grading of the parking lot across the creek raised clouds of yellow dust that drifted north to recoat all the surfaces that Abby had wiped and vacuumed. She gave up in disgust and went looking for Mac.

She found him in his office. The turret at one corner of the house formed a large bay in a second-floor bedroom. Mac had dubbed it the tower room, and claimed it as his own. He sat with his back to the door, feet on the sill of the bay, phone held against his ear by one shoulder. As Abby entered he swung around and placed the phone in its cradle.

"And what has the great detective accomplished while his wife attended to woman's work?"

"Abby, I hate to say it, but you're developing an attitude problem. You know I'd be glad to help with the house cleaning, but I had all this important stuff to do."

"Such as?"

"Write up my notes on the case—"

"You hardly ever take notes."

"Which is why it's so hard to write them up. Then I did my filing."

Abby looked over the cluttered desk and the stack of

191

magazines, newspaper clippings, and folders overflowing the top of the file cabinet.

"And I just got through reporting to Metlaff."

"Which took how long?" she asked. "Never mind. Just tell me—will he be able to get Daugherty out of jail?"

"The bond is pretty steep, but he's working on it."

"Well, then let's get out of here before we're buried by the fallout from across the creek. We have people to see, clues to find. By the way, do you have a clue box?"

"A what?"

"That's what I thought. I'll make you one for Christmas."

"About today—why don't you stay here? Somebody has to answer the phone. And if you want to open for Labor Day there's still lots—"

"Forget it."

Mac sighed and unlocked his gun cabinet. He selected the Smith and Wesson Airweight in a clip-on holster and said, "Okay. But if we run into Ingram you stay clear."

"I'm more worried about Magdalena."


At first it seemed Abby had no need to worry, since Magdelena flatly refused to let them in. Or, more accurately, refused to let Abby in.

When the McKenzie's had arrived at the Kazmierski's apartment building on Winslow, Mac suggested a woman was more likely to gain entrance. So it was Abby who spoke on the lobby intercom and received an obscene response. Thereafter Maggy ignored the buzzer.

Abby raised her eyebrows at this. "Well, sir. Just how does a clever, professional investigator go about interviewing a suspect locked in her apartment? Shall we break down the door?"

"We revert to Plan B."

"Which is?"

"Give me a minute to think of one."

They drove to the nearest pay phone. Mac called Maggy and said he had information about Bennet that she might like to hear. He received an invitation to come right over.

Abby noted a flash of anger as Maggy opened the door and found Mac wasn't alone. Abby also noted that while Maggy was still in robe and nightgown, she had managed to apply lipstick, eye shadow, and mascara.

Maggy recovered quickly. Nodding to Abby she said, "Sorry if I seemed rude before. I slept in this morning and I'm not at my best when that damn buzzer wakes me up." She cinched the belt of her robe more securely and said, "What is this information I'm supposed to be interested in?"

"You remember that I followed Bennet to the motel where he met you. And then I followed you as you followed him."

"No law against curiosity. Yours *or* mine."

"It looks to me as though you were getting ready to hijack him."

Maggy smiled. "You can't prove that."

"And, when you couldn't find the money, you decided he was getting ready to skip without you."

Maggy sat on the couch and crossed her legs. "Assuming, for the sake of argument, that I was going somewhere with him." She leaned back and smiled directly at Mac. "Why would he leave me behind?"

Abby smiled at Maggy and supplied the answer. "It would be cheaper to find a companion where he was going, than to take one along who wanted a share of the money."

Maggy's controlled performance slipped a bit; her jaw tightened and she abruptly turned to Abby.

"Getting back to your movements," Abby said, "you followed him again at the fair. I know, because I watched you the whole time. Then you disappeared, and a short time later Bennet was dead."

"That has nothing to do with me. Besides, the killer's in jail."

"And the next time I saw you, you were soaked to the skin."

Maggy got up, strode to a small table near the entry, and got a cigarette from a lacquered box. "Of course I was wet, stupid." Her hand shook slightly as she lit the cigarette. "It was raining."

Abby nodded. "Soaked your clothes and ruined your hairdo. Why didn't you take shelter? In the food tent, for instance?"

"I didn't want to stick around."

"If you were anxious to leave, and already as wet as you could possibly get, why stop at my booth?"

"I like pictures. Not that yours are so great."

"You wanted a witness to the fact that you came from the far end of the fair. As far as possible from Madame Gladys's tent."

Maggy, still standing, reached for an ashtray on the end table, dropping a quarter inch of ash on the rug in the process. She rubbed the ash into the nap with her slippered toe. "Okay. So whether I wanted a witness or just like pictures, the fact is, I *have* a witness. You."

"But a witness to what, Magdelena? You coming down the walk after inspecting quilts and handmade candles? Or after leaving the rear of the tent and scur-

194

rying along behind the hedge to make it look as though you were somewhere else?"

"*I* say I was never in the tent. Prove otherwise."

Abby, her abrupt tone matching Maggy's, said, "Your shoes were muddy. They didn't get that way on an asphalt walk."

"Guess work." Maggy stubbed out the half-smoked cigarette. "Doesn't mean a thing."

Mac grinned. "You're right. But that's what detectives do. Only they prefer to call it a theory, not a guess. When they hit on a theory that fits all the facts, they have a case for a jury." He shrugged. "I'd say this theory is pretty close to jury caliber, wouldn't you?"

Maggy walked to the window and stared out silently. Abby feared they had lost their chance at getting anything from her. "If we put this theory to the police, you may find yourself in real trouble."

"Yeah? Then why didn't that cop bring all this up when he questioned me?"

"Which cop was that?" Mac asked.

"Big and ugly. Bad temper."

"Almeir," Abby said. "He doesn't know everything we know. And so far the police have been satisfied with Roy Daugherty." Hoping Maggy wouldn't know the difference, she said, "But as a matter of fact, I expect him to get out today. Then they'll be looking for a new candidate."

Maggy swung around to face them. "They can't pin anything on me."

"But they'll try like hell," Mac said. "Of course, you could tell the truth. Sometimes that works."

Maggy's laugh was bitter. "That'll be a first." She got another cigarette and returned to the couch. "Okay. I'll tell you. You'll see there's nothing illegal about anything I did."

195

Abby sat in the chair opposite Maggy. "If you had nothing to do with Bennet's death, telling us the truth could save you a lot of grief."

"Yeah. Grief. Tell me about it. That's all I had out of that bastard. Not that I should be surprised. That's all you ever get from a man."

Abby nodded sympathetically. Mac eased himself around behind Maggy, out of her sight. Abby took this to mean she had the ball.

"Bennet was full of promises and grand plans," Maggy said. "According to him we were going to Rio in the spring with half a million. It sounded good at first, but the longer I knew him, the less I believed."

"Did he say where all that money was coming from?"

Maggy shook her head. "Nothing specific. Just vague talk about big deals and how everybody but him was a fool. You know the type."

"I sure do," Abby said. "I was married to a con man for years."

Obviously surprised, Maggy said, "I'll be damned. Mrs. Marvelous? Well, then I guess you do know." Maggy laughed. "We fall for the same type every time, don't we? Look at you. First a scam artist and now a gumshoe. When will we learn?"

Abby wasn't sure how Mac would react to being compared to her first husband, and hurried on. "Wasn't Kaz a little out of your line?"

"That was business. He had some bucks he didn't know what to do with and I had some bills to pay."

"I know you said Bennet didn't tell you where the money was coming from, but you must have known what he had your husband doing."

Maggy looked severely self-righteous. "I don't know anything about my husband's business." Then she grinned wryly. "That was penny-ante stuff. I got the

196

idea Bennet had been socking it away for a long time. And I suspect—that's *suspect,* not know—that he was running some insurance scam too." Maggy paused, her brow wrinkling. "And he said something about making a big score out of Daugherty. Something to do with real estate."

"What did he say, exactly?"

Maggy shrugged. "I was beginning to get the feeling that I was going to be left behind, so I was busy with my own plans."

"What were those?"

"I asked him once if his wife wouldn't clean him out in the divorce. He just laughed and said 'she can't get what she can't find.' So he must have had it stashed somewhere in cash. And I was going to get my cut."

"That's why you followed him?"

"Right. He waved this cash around when he came to the motel, bragging how he'd found another sucker. He dropped two hundred on me and said to get a new dress. So I figured when he left me he'd be heading for his private cookie jar. Thought I had it made when I saw his light go into that shack down in the pit."

"But next morning the money was gone."

"Yeah. First I thought he might have spotted me and moved it. It wasn't till later that I decided somebody else got it. Although I still don't see how anybody could have known where it was."

Abby sighed. "Lawrence Bennet was a fool. The money could have been found at any time. Children go down there to play, there's an occasional fisherman, and if someone suspected what he was up to, all they had to do is follow him."

"I guess." Maggy took a deep drag on the cigarette. "It just seemed such an isolated place to me."

"What happened after you met Mac at the shack?"

197

"I went to Larry's house to see what he'd do next. I figured if he'd taken the money he might be ready to make his move. If he headed for the airport I was going to be at the ticket counter right behind him. He could hand over half, or talk to the cops."

"But instead he went to the fair," Abby said.

"Yeah. That confused me until I saw him go into the tent."

Now Abby was confused.

"Well, it was obvious," Maggy said. "He was taking that phony fortune-teller to Rio." She gave an unladylike snort. "Thought he had better taste."

Abby noticed Mac about to comment and silenced him with a frown. "I saw you watching the tent from the leather goods booth. Then you disappeared. Where did you go?"

"I could see a little of the back of the tent from there. After a while Gladys came out and went through the bushes. A minute later Larry stuck his head out and I slipped around back and cut him off."

"You went into the tent?"

"No. I told you. I was never in the tent. We talked outside."

Abby raised an eyebrow. "In the rain?"

"It hadn't started yet. Or maybe just a fine drizzle. I don't remember. Anyway, I lit into him. Wanted to know what the hell he was pulling with this broad. At first he seemed confused about why I was there and everything. Then when it got through to him that I'd followed him to the pit he got mad. I thought he'd kill me."

"What did he say exactly?" Abby asked.

"He grabbed my arm." She raised the left sleeve of her robe. "I've still got a bruise. He stuck his face right up to mine and said, 'What did you do with it?'"

198

"Did you take that to mean the money?"

"Right then I was too scared to think. That man had murder in his eyes. I said, 'Somebody's coming,' and he let go. Then he said 'I'll take care of you later.' I beat it."

Abby frowned. *"Was* someone coming?"

"I just said that." Now Maggy frowned. "But maybe someone was. Because before he turned me loose he cocked his head, like he was listening. So maybe he heard something I didn't."

"You left—through the hedge?" Abby prompted.

"Yeah. I followed it round and came out between a couple of booths. By then it was raining pretty good. Like a dummy I stood there trying to figure what was going on. Then I ducked into the beer tent to wait for the storm to let up."

"But you didn't wait. It was still raining when I saw you. What changed your mind?"

"Gladys. I saw her, but I don't think she saw me. She had a shiner you wouldn't believe."

"What did she do? Stay there? Leave in the rain?"

Maggy shook her head. "I don't know. This was a new development and I had the idea I'd better get back to watching Larry. So that's why I stopped off at your booth."

"Not for an alibi?"

"I didn't know one was required. No, I was just hoping to catch sight of Larry by heading up the path towards the entrance. When I got to you I stopped, hoping you might mention seeing him. I couldn't come out and ask, of course."

Abby thought back over their conversation that rainy morning. Maggy had asked if she had seen "him" around. Had that been a reference to Kaz, or the mayor?

199

"I finally decided he'd left, maybe to go to his office in the village hall since that was close. While I was up there all the commotion started and I heard he was dead."

Abby fell silent as she tried to decide if she believed Maggy's story. Everything she had said fit into what they knew. It all sounded plausible. She noticed Mac move back to where he could confront Maggy.

"Did you see anyone else on the path when you came back from the beer tent?" Mac asked.

"Yeah. Nobody I know."

"See a tall, white-haired man in a black suit?"

"Oh, sure. Can hardly miss that guy, can you? He was standing on the path talking to some woman."

"What did the woman look like?"

"Shorter than me. Nice figure for her age. And intelligent."

"Intelligent? How do you know?"

"She was the only one I saw with an umbrella."

As they left the apartment Mac said, "You did good, Junior."

"You're just lucky I was along. If you had gone in there alone, that woman would have eaten you alive."

"Listen, you're talking to a professional here."

"At the risk of sounding catty, I'd say Magdalena Kazmierski is the professional."

Abby got into the car and adjusted the vent window to catch the breeze as they began to move. If what they had heard was true, it seemed to put Gladys in the clear. Bennet *had* been alive when she left the tent. And the fact that Maggy and Bennet carried on their conversation outside would corroborate Daugherty's statement that the tent was empty when he looked in.

Mac reached over and patted Abby's leg. "Getting back to your handling of the witness, Junior, you only made one mistake. You forgot to ask her about Bennet's book. The one he threatened Kaz with."

"Damn! So why didn't *you* ask her, Dick Tracy?"

"I forgot."


The office to the right of the Village Hall entrance housed most of the departments that dealt with the public; billing for water and sewage, licenses and permits. A counter faced the door. Behind it village employees were seated at desks crammed together in space they shared with several rows of file cabinets. Douglas Kazmierski occupied a desk at the rear of the room.

Abby followed Mac through a gate in the counter and slalomed between ancient, gray furniture that seemed to be placed with an eye to creating obstacles.

As they approached Kaz he glanced up, then stood quickly and looked around as though for an escape route. Trapped in his corner, he slumped back in his chair and smiled weakly in greeting.

"Hello, Kaz," Mac said. "Things going along okay without the mayor?"

"Yeah. Sure." Kaz drew a handkerchief from his hip pocket and wiped his brow. "Air-conditioning don't work worth a damn. They tell me it's been like this since the place was built."

"Should have had a good, tough inspector like you on the job, right?"

Kaz squirmed in his seat. "What can I do for you folks?"

"Just stopped by to ask a few questions, Kaz. You don't mind do you?"

"Mind? No. What about?"

201

"Bennet's murder. We thought you might be able to help us."

"Murder?" He picked up a pencil and sketched a rectangle on the pad in front of him. "Bennet? What's that got to do with you? I mean, sure, but—"

"But what does it have to do with us? See, we work for Daugherty's defense. And his lawyer wants us to talk to all the witnesses."

Kaz began furiously filling the rectangular box with short strokes of his pencil. "I'm not a witness. I was at work that day. Here in the office."

"It was a Saturday. I don't suppose there were many people here."

"Not *too* many. No."

"Maybe none."

"Well, maybe." The box had been filled several times over and Kaz drew another. "No. Wait. The cleaning crew. They were here."

"What time was that, Kaz?"

He now had four rectangles in a row. "I don't remember. You could ask them." He began filling the first box.

"The thing is, Kaz, you were seen at the fair."

The pencil paused, then began again, more slowly. "I might have gone over. For lunch. Yeah. They had good hot dogs."

Mac sighed loudly. "I was hoping we could keep the police out of this, Kaz. But if you're going to lie—"

Kaz dropped his pencil. "It's the truth. I went over—"

"And followed your wife, ducking into booths, hiding every time she turned around. You knew she was having an affair with Bennet and you thought she went to the fair to meet him."

202

Kaz's eyes darted around the room as though he were looking for help.

"We've been keeping an eye on you, Kaz, ever since you tried your scam on us. Didn't Bennet warn you about that? He knew we were investigating you."

"He didn't say anything. Why me? I just work here." Kaz took out his handkerchief again. "I don't know anything about what Bennet was up to. The police already asked me."

"Just tell us what you did Saturday at the fair. We pretty well know, but we want to be sure you're being straight with us."

Kaz sighed and wiped his brow. "Are you going to tell your buddy, that Pawlowski? I guess I forgot to mention anything about being there."

"Did he ask you?"

"Mainly he wanted to know what kind of deals Bennet was into."

"Well, I'm not interested in that. I want to know everything you did, and everything you saw Saturday."

Kaz returned to filling boxes, slowly, with careful attention to uniform shading and staying inside the lines. "I decided to quit and go home. Maggy went by as I came out, so I followed her. She walked real fast until she saw Bennet, then she slowed up and stayed behind him."

"Go on."

"He went into that fortune-teller's tent. She hung around watching."

"Why do you think she did that?"

"With Maggy you never know." Kaz sighed. "I don't know why I bothered. She'll be leaving me pretty soon anyway." He seemed close to tears. "If it ain't him, it'll be somebody. Or nobody. But she's going."

Abby began to feel sympathy for him for the first

time, but Mac pressed ahead. "Then what did she do?"

"She went around back. You know, the tent. Bennet came out and they talked. I think they were both mad."

"Could you hear what they said?"

Kaz shook his head. "I was too far away. Then she went through the hedge and Bennet stood there."

"What did Bennet do then?"

"I don't know. I couldn't think of any reason to follow Maggy after she'd already seen Bennet. I turned around and started to leave." Kaz stopped doodling and looked up. "For some reason I got worried. Maybe because Bennet seemed so mad. I got as far as the merry-go-round and I thought maybe he went after Maggy. So I went to take a look where Maggy went through the hedge. I heard voices in the tent."

"What did they say?"

"Somebody said, 'This is going to cost you fifty grand.'"

"Recognize the voice?"

"No. It was almost like a whisper. Then the same whisper said, 'Get out of here. I'll take care of this.' That's all I heard, 'cause I didn't want to get caught listening, so I beat it."

"Didn't stick around to see who came out?"

Kaz shook his head and went back to filling his boxes with a pencil.

Abby tried to fit this new information to the list of suspects and came up with Daugherty and Ingram. She refused to believe it was Daugherty. She glanced at Mac. He was gazing at the wall over Kaz's head, lost in thought. "Do you know Charles Ingram?" she asked.

"Ingram? No. I don't think so."

Mac returned his attention to Kaz. "Now tell us about Bennet's book."

The point of Kaz's pencil snapped. "What book?"

"The one he mentioned when you two were arguing down in the gravel pit."

"How did you know about—You been following me that long?"

"The book, Kaz."

"He just mentioned it the once. I don't even know if there *was* a book. Maybe he just made it up."

"But you knew where he kept his money."

"No. Honest. I figured it was down in the pit some-place, but I don't know where."

"You've been looking for it, haven't you?"

"No!"

"Why not? Everybody else has."

Kaz picked up his pencil, looked at the broken point, then shoved his doodle pad away. "Look, I tried follow-ing him the one time. He just fished, is all. And he caught me. That's when we had an argument and he mentioned the book. Later he came around and said if I followed him again he'd get me fired."

"He's dead, Kaz. Nothing to stop you from looking now."

"That pit's a big place. Where would I look?"

"Maybe in Bennet's house? Or Daugherty's?"

"I ain't no burglar!"

"Okay, Kaz. Now tell me why Bennet went to Daugherty's house and tried to frame him for attempted murder."

"I don't know. Honest. He didn't even tell me where we were going. Just said, 'Get in the car. I need a wit-ness.' When that crazy Daugherty came at us with a shotgun I thought it was all over."

"Did he actually point the gun at Bennet?"

"Well, not exactly." Kaz wiped his brow. "But it was lucky that cop came along. No telling what he might have done next."

205

* * *

Abby waited while Mac unlocked the car. "The inside's going to be like a furnace. Did you have to close the windows?"

"The gun is in the glove compartment."

She got in and sat down gingerly. "Who do you think that mysterious voice belonged to? I prefer to think it was Ingram, but the words sounded out of character for him. More like something Daugherty might say."

"An even more interesting question: who was the mysterious voice talking to?"

"Bennet, of course."

Mac touched the steering wheel and swore. "You can raise a blister on this wheel." He started the engine and backed up, steering with his fingertips. "The voice said, 'Get out of here. I'll take care of this.' Take care of what?"

"Doesn't make sense, does it?"

"Kaz took his time deciding to go back to the tent. A lot could have happened. What if Bennet was a silent witness to that conversation? What if the thing to be taken care of was Bennet's body?"

# Chapter Nineteen

After lunch Abby left for the Daugherty place and Mac called Stan's office. He was told Capt. Pawlowski hadn't been feeling well and had left early. He was also told that the crime scene had been released. Unless he wanted to abandon Abby's booth to the local kids to use as a fort, he had better pick it up.

The section of park that had doubled as midway was deserted and littered with styrofoam cups, candy wrappers, and other assorted trash. The craft booths were also gone, except for a cluster of three: Abby's, the leather worker's, and Madame Gladys's tent.

Mac parked next to a blue station wagon with a rusted quarter panel and a bumper sticker that said, THE REST OF YOUR LIFE IS IN THE FUTURE. He marveled at this revelation.

He got out of his own wagon and opened the tailgate as Madame Gladys came out of the tent. She was dressed in a sleeveless blouse and faded jeans and carried an umbrella.

"Can I give you a hand?" Mac asked.

"Thanks. Taking the tent down alone can be tricky." She shoved the umbrella into the wagon. "The first time I did it I wound up trapped under collapsed canvas."

Mac examined her blonde hair, freckled nose, and slim figure. "I can see how, dressed in bangles, beads, and a wig, you can pass as Madame Gladys who tells all. But some of your clients know you in real life. You look like Gidget's mother—"

"Older sister."

"Sorry. Older sister. How can they take you seriously?"

She grinned, and taking a deck of cards from a bag in the wagon, said, "Let's find out." She turned and entered the tent.

Mac retrieved the umbrella and followed her. "I see you were one of the few that came prepared for rain last Saturday." He examined a small rip in the fabric. "Strange how optimistic most people were that day. Considering the overcast, you would have expected more of these."

"Bad forecast." She sat at the card table. "Radio said the squall line would pass to the north."

"The cards any good for weather predictions?"

Gladys laughed. "It's never worked for me." She riffled the cards. "Although, come to think of it, I did predict the blizzard of '67."

"You should have spread the word. Might have saved a political career."

"I did a reading for the wife of a Streets and Sanitation worker. I told her not to expect him home for two days." Gladys passed the deck to Mac. "Shuffle."

Mac sat down and shuffled. "How did she react?"

"She threatened to kill the bitch when she caught her." Gladys chuckled. "Took some doing to convince her I was talking about snow, not romance."

"Must be a serious problem in your business. I mean, people acting on what you tell them."

"Yeah. That's why I don't always tell everything I know."

"Me too." He passed the deck back to her.

208

Gladys took the deck and held it a moment. The air of hard-edged cynicism dropped away, her face smoothed, and a stillness descended on her. She turned the first card. "The Emperor. That's you, the questioner. Interesting. The same card represented you in your wife's reading."

"From a cold deck."

Gladys gazed at him for a moment before returning to the cards. "Yes. But this one isn't." She turned the next card and laid The High Priestess across The Emperor.

Mac grinned. "Is that the female version of the tall, dark stranger?"

His attempt at humor failed to break Gladys's concentration. "It means you are not yet in possession of all the facts. Further study is necessary."

"I'll buy that one without question. For instance, why did you come to Sarahville?"

Madame Gladys looked at him and blinked. After a moment she said, "I ran into Mrs. Bennet at a psychic fair. That's how I became aware Lawrence Bennet was here, and much too successful for my taste. It occurred to me that my presence in his town would complicate his life." She returned her attention to the cards. "You will be influenced by a woman of intuition and clear sight. Trust her."

"You?"

"No." She started to turn the next card. "This reveals your destiny." She placed it at the top of the spread and hesitated, frowning. "Judgement. Perhaps its meaning will become clear as we go along."

"Isn't judgement supposed to be everyone's ultimate destiny?"

"In this case we're not dealing with anything so final."

"That's encouraging. I can stand a lot of improvement before judgement day." He reached over and touched her hand as she was about to turn another card. "Tell me something else. Why did you con the Daughertys into coming here?"

Holding the card facedown, she said, "I'm sorry about that. He had more reason than I to hate Bennet. It seemed like a good idea for both of us to be here. But now he's in very serious trouble and I must help him. And others."

"What others?"

She placed the next card on the table. "This is your past. The Tower indicates there has been conflict and disasters. Death and destruction. You have suffered a great loss and gained new understanding as a result."

"Do you know anyone my age that doesn't fit that description?" Mac tapped the center card. "Let's get back to the Questioner's questions. When you were setting up Bennet with a gathering of his enemies, did you worry at all about the effect on Mrs. Bennet?"

"I did readings for her over a period of time and got to know her well. She is clear-eyed, cold, and self-possessed. Whatever happened to her husband wasn't going to hurt her. And nothing I could tell her would come as news."

"Did she know about you?"

"She knew the story. But I never told her I was the pregnant girl he abandoned." Gladys turned another card. "The World, and your recent past. You ended a phase of your life and started anew. There is great hope for the future." She looked up from the card. "I think the significance is self-evident."

"Did you tell her about Daugherty?"

"She knew. I believe she must have had a detective investigating her husband."

210

"So she'd been planning a divorce for some time. I thought you might have influenced the decision."

"No. That was settled in her mind before we met." Gladys placed a card to the left of the display. "The Hanged Man is your future."

"Terrific."

"It merely means that the future is in suspense. The outcome will depend on your reactions and on the actions of others."

"There's a news bulletin for you! The future depends on what happens in the future."

Gladys ignored him and turned another card. "Death. Can it be—" She shook her head. "No. This means change. Endings and beginnings. Your future will be influenced positively if you accept a change, perhaps a change in thinking or in the way you now see a problem."

"So help me change my thinking. How did you bring Prestwick and Quill into your scheme?"

"I suspected Bennet was using his insurance agency to defraud people. Mrs. Bennet mentioned that Estelle Prestwick recently bought an annuity. She had seen the check. Estelle, it seems, believes in a lot of strange things. It wasn't hard to get her as a client. As for Goose—where one goes, the other goes."

"What about Ingram?"

"Estelle brought him to me. He's a witch, you know."

"And dangerous."

"Perhaps." She turned over The Moon. "You are being strongly influenced by the deception that surrounds you. This will interfere with your ability to accept the change in thinking that is necessary."

Mac nodded. "Hold that thought." He picked up the umbrella. "Clear away some of that deception for me and tell me who this belongs to?"

211

"Somebody left it."

"Who?"

Gladys shrugged. "Can't be important. Otherwise the police would have taken it."

"John Almeir has a one-track mind. But I'm surprised Sergeant Henderson didn't take it when he first searched the place."

"They took my costume, cards, and crystal. As far as I can see, that's all."

"You didn't find the umbrella here. It must have been some distance away, or Henderson would have bagged it as evidence."

"That's right." She drummed her fingers on the card table. "Probably doesn't have anything to do with anything."

Mac leaned back, hands in pockets, ankles crossed, looking as if he were settled in for the rest of the day, if necessary. "So you went looking for it. Why?"

"Why are you so interested? It's not even a very good umbrella. It has a rip in it."

"It belongs to Estelle Prestwick. She came to this tent, entered from the rear, put on your costume, and left the way she came, complete with umbrella. Then, before stepping through the hedge to return by way of the path, she hid the umbrella. She didn't want it associated with the gypsy. Since then she's been afraid to come for it. So you're doing the job for her."

Gladys's eyes narrowed. "Why would she do that?"

Mac straightened up and leaned over the table. "You tell me, Gladys. Or would you rather see Daugherty take the rap?"

"Estelle didn't kill anyone. She has a problem swatting flies."

"I'm sure you're right. Well—pretty sure. But I still need to know why she did it. I'll ask her, of course.

And if she doesn't tell me, she'll have to tell Captain Pawlowski, or sit it out in a cell." He smiled. "Come on, Gladys. Save me and Estelle a lot of trouble."

Gladys got up and stepped behind her chair. She leaned on the back. "I can't do that. But I'll talk to her. Maybe I can convince her to tell you."

Mac leaned back. "Good. Can you finish the reading, or did this whiff of reality break your trance?"

"We'll see." Gladys sat down and picked up the deck. She sat quietly for a moment, then shook her head and turned the next two cards. "Strength and the Wheel of Fortune." She drummed the table impatiently. "I'd say you're about to overcontrol the situation—"

"What situation?"

"How the hell should I know? And the wheel is about to take a turn. When it does it'll dump you on your ass." She gathered up the cards and, grinning, said, "I have no idea whether that's good or bad."

"And you were doing so well, too."

"The cards aren't talking to me any more. Well? Are you going to help me strike this tent, or should I bring it down with you in it?"


Mac returned home with the tailgate open and the folded booth extending over the edge. Seeing the car parked in his drive, it was no surprise to find Elmer Johnson seated on the porch steps smoking a cigar.

"Glad to see you, Elmer," Mac said. "After you move your car you can help me haul this stuff into the garage."

Elmer got up and made a show of straightening a sore back. "Might ruin my image as a politician to be seen actually working at something useful." But he backed his car, and when Mac pulled in, followed along and parked behind him.

Mac raised the garage door. "What brings you here, Elmer?"

"I was in hopes of a cool beer and a little quiet conversation."

"Grab an end of this thing and we'll see what we can do about the beer."

They carried the folded booth inside and leaned it against the wall. Elmer dropped half an inch of ash on his shirtfront in the process. "How's the treasure hunt going?" he asked.

"Not too well. That's not my main problem anyway." They carried the table and chairs in and put them next to the booth. "My immediate goal is to get the police off of Daugherty and on to somebody else." Mac pulled down the overhead door and led the way into the house.

"Well, how's that goin'?"

Mac got an ashtray for Elmer's cigar and began washing his hands at the sink. "I've got lots of people that might have wanted Bennet dead, but nobody that could have planted Daugherty's knife." He dried his hands on a dish towel. "Except—no, better not speculate out loud." He got two cans of Stroh's from the refrigerator and popped the top on one. "You might be able to help me, though."

Elmer took the other can and a seat at the kitchen table. "Shoot."

"You know anything about a real estate deal that involves Daugherty's property?"

"Seems like I heard something." Elmer sipped his beer and gazed at the ceiling. "Sure, I remember. A while back this fella from Florida come up with a scheme to turn that old gravel pit—you know the one?—into a lake. Put up a high priced lakeshore development around it. Take a lot of capital and a lot of red

214

tape with the state, county, village, and the Corps of Engineers, but should turn a nice profit too, if he could get the land cheap."

"So what happened?"

Elmer re-lit the cigar that had gone out in the ashtray. "He had an option on everything but Daugherty's piece. Daugherty wouldn't sell, at least not cheap enough to make the difference in the bottom line. So the fella went back to Florida."

"How does this sound." Mac sat across the table from Elmer. "Bennet offers to get Daugherty to change his mind for a finders fee. Enough money in it to make it worth our deceased mayor's time?"

"Could be. But Daugherty and Bennet weren't on friendly terms. How would he go about it?"

"Frame Daugherty for assault. Because Daugherty is so hotheaded it turned into attempted murder, which is even better. Then he gets Daugherty to sell in return for dropping the charges."

"That'll work. He might even push the price down and up his fee."

Mac relaxed and tended to his beer. "Thanks, Elmer. You just cleared up a point that's been bothering me."

"Getcha closer to the killer?"

"Don't know. Now what's *your* problem?"

"Wanted to talk a little politics." He scratched his head. "The way things turned out, it looks like I'm a shoo-in for mayor. So I've been givin' some thought to a real housecleaning. Wanted your advice."

"Me? Politics ain't my game."

"You know a lot of the people. What do you think?"

"Kaz has to go. But you knew that." Mac thought about Stan. Would he want to be chief? They'd never discussed it. Well, he could always turn it down. "I hear Venlow wants to retire. If he does, do what you

215

can to put Stan in his place. And it wouldn't hurt to see if Almeir can be talked into retiring."

Elmer nodded. "My biggest problem is, some of the trustees been too close to Bennet. I hoped the investigation of Bennet's murder would turn up some dirt that'd get them to drop out. Trouble is, with an open-and-shut case against Daugherty, there ain't much investigating going on."

"And you want me to turn up the dirt."

"Just a pinch."

Mac laughed. "Okay, Elmer. But it'll cost you."

"I figured you could write off part of your fee as community service."

"No way. The Daugherty case will probably wind up on the cuff as it is."

Elmer's customary sly and knowing half-smile slipped a bit. "There's another angle, might make a difference. See, it ain't enough to get the deadwood off the village board. You got to find somebody to replace 'em. That ain't easy in this town."

"So?"

"Maybe a McKenzie on the ballot would—"

"You're crazy!" Mac swallowed the rest of his beer. "I have absolutely *no* interest in politics!"

"Well, I know that, Mac. No. I figure Abby's the vote-getter in the family."

Stan lived just over the western edge of Sarahville in an area that had few houses, each served with its own well and septic system. The drive over gave Mac time to put Elmer's ridiculous suggestion in perspective.

Abby in politics? Between running her business, and trying to run his, when would she find time? And there was the Historical Society; that was a meeting every month not to mention poking around the archives try-

216

ing to add to Sarahville's meager history. And she frequently complained about not having time for her painting.

Of course, she was an excellent cook. And they had been eating out more than was good for them. But he'd never let a little thing like that stand in the way, if she *really* wanted to do it.

But it was just as well that he *knew* she had absolutely no interest in politics.

He paused at Stan's driveway to let a car exit. The driver glanced his way in passing and he saw it was Chief Venlow. Probably come to see if Stan was all right.

Mac parked back near the garage and waved to the tall woman hanging wash on the line. "Hi, Julie. How's Stan doing? Up to visitors?"

Julie Pawlowski removed a clothespin from her mouth and brushed a wisp of black hair from her brow. "Stan? He's fine. Go on in. I'll put the coffee on as soon as I'm done here."

Stan, wearing paint-stained pants and a tee shirt, was sitting in the family room, bare feet on the coffee table, doodling on a yellow note pad. He turned his head as Mac entered. "Just the guy I want to see. Pull up a chair."

"What excuse did you use with the chief? I remember your grandmother died three times in high school, and once you knocked off an uncle."

"Only for really important reasons."

"Yeah. What was her name? Thelma? Erma?"

"Erma Bodine. Thelma was the waitress at Koslowski's Kafe specializing in kielbasa."

"Thelma specialized in—"

"No. Koslowski. Thelma didn't have a specialty. What you might call a generalist."

217

"What really important reason caused today's goof off?"

Stan drummed on his pad with the eraser end of his pencil. "A little meeting with the chief. If we spent two hours in an office with the door closed the rumors would range from Pawlowski's imminent dismissal to cancelling the department bowling league."

"I don't suppose you can tell me about it?"

"As a matter of fact, the chief particularly wanted me to talk to you. He figures you can help. Off the record. No pay. Civic duty."

"Why is everybody after my civic duty? Elmer tried that scam on me just a little while ago."

"Elmer? What did he want?"

Mac chuckled. "He's counting his chickens. And come election day he doesn't want any of Bennet's chums around. I'm supposed to find suspect connections between them and Bennet's graft."

"Did you take him on?"

"Sure. But that's not all. Wait till you hear this. He—"

"That complicates things." Stan tossed his pad on the coffee table. "Maybe I better talk to Venlow before we get too deep here."

"What's the problem?" Mac leaned forward. "You're not after Elmer, are you?"

"Nothing like that. It's just that—oh, hell. I'll tell you." Stan removed his feet from the table. "This business with Bennet, it looks like some other people could be involved. There were rumors before, and what we know so far confirms them."

Stan picked up a full ashtray and an empty cigarette pack. "Just a minute." He left the room and returned quickly with an empty ashtray and a fresh pack.

"The chief wants to clean up the mess before the

218

State's Attorney gets on to it. Especially since it affects the department."

"Almeir?"

"Sure, Almeir. Maybe not enough for a felony beef, but enough to bring charges before the Police Commissioner. Or at least get him to resign."

"So Venlow can retire with a clear conscience."

"Yeah. The Commissioner is a Bennet appointee, but with Bennet gone he may not give us any trouble. But working undercover in your own town with a small department is tough. Everybody knows everybody."

Mac shrugged. "Why not an open investigation?"

"Two reasons. It would bring in the State's Attorney at a run. And with an election next April, Venlow doesn't want the department accused of mixing in politics. That's why you working for Elmer could be a problem."

"I can get around that. But why me?"

"You're working on the Daugherty defense. That gives you a reason to poke your nose in."

Mac leaned back, frowning. "What *about* Daugherty? If the chief figures Almeir for a crooked cop, tied to the victim, why let him handle the case?"

"It's open-and-shut. Not even Almeir can screw it up. And it keeps him busy looking in the other direction."

"It also gives him an excuse to dig into Bennet's business. How do you know he isn't disposing of evidence of graft?"

Stan shook his head. "Bennet wouldn't be fool enough to keep records."

"I heard different. There may be a ledger somewhere. It disappeared with Bennet's money."

"Damn! Why didn't you tell me?"

"That's one reason I came here." Mac outlined what

219

he had learned to date. "Nothing there that helps you, I'm afraid."

"You're convinced Daugherty is innocent?"

"Yes."

Stan shook his head. "If he is, and that's a big if, there's only one way it could have happened."

"I know. Proving it is gonna be a bitch."

# Chapter Twenty

When Abby saw Mrs. Bennet leave the Running Fox Tavern it seemed like an ideal opportunity. She drove into the parking lot as the woman, holding her broad-brimmed hat against a light breeze, got into a car. Before Abby could hail her, the car had left. No doubt Mac would disapprove, but Abby decided to follow along and catch Mrs. B at her next stop.

Next stop turned out to be the Bennet home. Abby parked on the street as her quarry unlocked the front door.

"Mrs. Bennet!" she called, walking up the drive. "Do you have a minute?"

"Why, Mrs. McKenzie! What brings you here? Come in."

Abby smiled. "Sorry to come without calling first. Do you mind?"

Mrs. Bennet ushered Abby into the foyer. "I just had lunch at the Tavern. The idea of sitting here alone, eating cottage cheese—well—I'm glad of the company." She dropped her hat on a hall table and, fluffing her hair, inspected herself in the mirror above it. She straightened her belted, yellow dress, then led the way into the living room.

"Would you like a drink"

"No thanks." Abby chose a straight-backed chair upholstered in green. Mrs. Bennet sat on a matching chair with an end table between them. Not an ideal arrangement from Abby's viewpoint. Both chairs faced the same way, and she had to turn awkwardly to see Mrs. Bennet's face while they talked.

"Have you brought me news?" Mrs. Bennet asked.

"I'm afraid not." Abby looked about. "You have a lovely home. It must have been very upsetting to have someone break in and destroy things."

"It took quite a while to set everything straight. Fortunately, nothing was broken."

"Was anything missing?"

"Nothing. It must be as Mr. McKenzie said. Someone was after Larry's money. It would be a natural assumption that he might have kept it here, but believe me, if it *were* here, I'd have found it long ago."

Abby had no doubt of that. "Did you have any inkling that he had hidden the money down in the gravel pit?"

Mrs. Bennet shook her head slowly. "No. I remember you suggested his interest in fishing was a ruse. That was very clever of you. And, of course, it was a particularly good choice for a hiding place. Larry knew I would never go down there."

"Why not?"

"My dear, have you seen the place? It's an absolute wilderness."

"I wasn't aware that you were familiar with it."

"I've passed it on occasion. And it's been described to me."

"I'm not terribly impressed with Mr. Bennet's hiding place," Abby said. "It seems to me there was always a chance of accidental discovery."

"I wonder about Magdalena and the weasel."

"It's possible, but I'm inclined to think not. Were you

222

aware that Magdalena was having an affair with your husband? And expected to go away with him?"

Mrs. B examined her nails. "No, although it's not surprising. She's the type he preferred. Cheap."

"Did you find it odd that Mr. Bennet's enemies seemed to be attracted to Sarahville?"

"What do you mean?"

"Gladys, for instance."

"Gladys came here because she thought it a business opportunity. I'm sure she didn't like him. Perhaps because of the things I told her. Are you saying she knew Larry, other than from what I had told her?"

"Let's say she had strong negative feelings about him." Abby noted that Mrs. Bennet's face showed only polite interest, but her left hand was unconsciously polishing the arm of the chair. "How did you happen to meet Gladys?"

"I believe it was at one of those psychic fairs. You know the sort of thing? All sorts of strange people promoting astrology, pyramid power, selling books and charms."

"Forgive me, but you don't seem like the sort of person that would take all that seriously."

Mrs. B smiled. "I suppose not. I do think most of them are charlatans. But we all have our idiosyncrasies. My mother was a firm believer in spiritualism and something of that has remained with me. In any case, I found Madame Gladys to be refreshingly honest, and surprisingly accurate."

"What did Mr. Bennet think of all that?"

She laughed, relaxing. "He assumed it was the sort of foolishness one could expect of a woman."

Abby smiled sympathetically. "So he knew about Gladys?"

"In a sense. He knew I was having occasional readings, but by then we weren't communicating. I'm not sure he paid any attention to what I had to say about it." She frowned and half-turned in her seat. "Now that I come to think of it, he *did* press me on the subject once."

"When was that?"

"The day he died. He was particularly agitated that morning. I put it down to lack of sleep. I mentioned going to Founder's Day for the craft exhibits. He asked, 'Don't we have enough junk?' by which he meant my collection of depression glass." Mrs. B waved her hand toward a curio cabinet containing a number of green glass items. "Larry had absolutely no taste."

Abby wondered why the well-off found it fascinating to collect the artifacts of the poor. "They're—interesting. But the subject of Gladys came up?"

"I mentioned Madame Gladys would be there. He asked who Madame Gladys was, and I said Gladys Brett. If he had been a dog, his ears would have pricked up. He questioned me about her, what she looked like, that sort of thing. Then he left abruptly, saying he was on his way to the village hall to check the record."

"What record would that be?"

"I've no idea."

"Village business permits, perhaps? They would show her full name and other identifying information."

"Are you sure you wouldn't like something to drink? I'm going to have a gin and tonic." Mrs. B walked to the small bar at the side of the room.

Abby joined her. "It's a little early for me. Perhaps a glass of water."

Mrs. B poured water from a carafe and added ice from a small refrigerator under the bar. "What do you think of my chances for recovering Larry's money?"

224

"Pretty low, I'm afraid." Watching for some reaction, Abby asked, "And what about Roy Daugherty? Why do you suppose he came here?"

"I don't know why that Daugherty man came here. Although I'm sure he knew Larry from someplace else."

"Why do you think that?"

"You know they once had a fight? Right in the village hall. Something Larry said afterward made me think they were old enemies. He wasn't specific." She mixed a gin and very little tonic. "But it must have been Mr. Daugherty that killed Larry, don't you think?" She looked earnestly at Abby. "I know you work for his defense. But realistically, you must think it hopeless."

"Grim, certainly. But not hopeless."

"Really?" Mrs. B sipped her drink. "Even though the weapon has been identified as his? Even though it was never out of his possession?"

"Despite all that. Or maybe because of all that, if that makes any sense to you." Abby gazed into her glass. "For his daughter's sake, I hope we're right."

Mrs. B added a bit more gin, sipped again, and appeared satisfied with the mixture. "How is the little girl taking it?"

Abby shrugged. "On the surface, pretty well. I'm afraid she's holding too much in. Finding the body was a shock and then to have her father taken away from her." Abby shook herself and drank deeply. "Worrying about it isn't going to help. Let's see, where were we?"

"About the money."

"Oh, yes. Well, if we knew who was breaking into homes, at least we'd know who *didn't* have the money."

"I understand that would clear the Daughertys and Charles Ingram. And me of course. On the other hand, the weasel and his wife haven't been bothered."

"Nor has Gladys. But that doesn't prove anything.

The police have been watching both places, so our treasure hunter hasn't had an opportunity."

"Any other possibilities, do you think?"

"What do you know about Estelle Prestwick and Irene Quill?" Abby asked.

"Nothing, really. We met at Madame Gladys's, and I found they believe Larry defrauded them. I assume that's true?"

"Apparently. What about Charles Ingram?"

"What a strange man! Is he quite sane?"

"He's at least eccentric. You never met him except the one time at Gladys's?"

"That's right." Mrs. B carried her drink to her chair. "The only connection between the four of us is Madame Gladys." She laughed. "You can hardly imagine me associating with someone called 'Goose,' now can you? Or with a professed witch?"

Abby smiled. "It *would* be out of character."

Mrs. B glanced at her watch. "Oh, dear. I hope you won't take it amiss, but I have an appointment with my hairdresser. Are we finished?"

Abby placed her glass on the bar. "I'll walk out with you. There's only one other thing I'd like to ask about."

"What's that?" Mrs. B put on her hat in front of the mirror, carefully adjusting the brim.

"You left my booth when you saw your husband coming. Can you tell me where you went and who you saw? It helps to place people."

She turned from the mirror, frowning. "Let's see, that was—Good Lord—that was just the day before yesterday! It seems so much longer." She tapped her lips with her forefinger. "I continued down the path, looking for the glass vendor, I remember that."

"Did you find him?"

226

"Yes, but I could see at a glance he had mostly hobnail and milk-white glass, so I didn't linger." She turned back to the mirror and applied fresh lipstick. "I believe I continued around the circle, found nothing of interest, and left for home."

"Did you see anyone? Or were you too concerned with getting rain-soaked to notice?"

"Fortunately, I was in my car before the drizzle turned to heavy rain." She held the door for Abby. "By seeing anyone you mean anyone relevant. No, I don't— Yes! I saw Mr. Daugherty. But you already knew he was there."

"Where was he when you saw him?"

"I had completed the oval path and was striking out across the midway when I turned for a moment, looking back toward the fair. He was on the path to Madame Gladys's tent. I wouldn't have known it was he except that he looked over his shoulder at that moment."

"You're well acquainted with him then?"

Mrs. B smiled. "My dear, one doesn't forget the man that pushed one's husband into a punch bowl at a public function!"

Abby smiled in return. "That *would* be memorable." She stepped through the door.

"You *will* let me know at once if there is any news of the money?" Mrs. B asked, closing the door behind them.

Abby nodded. "Did you ever see a ledger or notebook that Mr. Bennet kept? Something apart from his business records?"

"Ledger?" Mrs. B stopped abruptly. "What about a ledger?"

"We believe he kept a private record of his activities. If we can find it, it may implicate others in some of

227

his illegal activities. And it may also be a financial record."

"I see." She stared at Abby for a moment. "How do you know there is such a book?"

"A witness heard him mention it to Kazmierski."

"And this book, it would say where Larry's money came from?"

"We think so."

"I don't know anything about it. Sorry."

Driving away from the Bennet house, Abby realized that if Mrs. Bennet found the ledger, it would quickly disappear. A record of Bennet's illegal income was the last thing she'd let fall into the hands of the IRS.

She wondered how Fran and Kim were getting along, or if there had been any news of Daugherty's release on bail. On impulse she turned into the village hall parking lot. Maybe she could find out, and if the word was encouraging, bring something to Fran that would cheer her up.

Might as well go right to the top. She headed for Chief Venlow's office.

As she entered the building she was delighted to see Metlaff standing in the hall. "Any good news?" she asked.

He stopped in the act of unwrapping a cigar. "Satisfactory news, yes. I've arranged bail. Mr. Daugherty should be out as soon as he's been processed. I was just waiting to drive him home."

"I can do that. I was on my way to see Fran Daugherty anyway."

"Good. Have you met Mr. Daugherty?"

"No, but I've come to know the rest of the family quite well."

228

"I'll introduce you and then be on my way."

"How did Roy Daugherty find the money? I thought his bail would be very high."

"It was. But his property has considerable potential." Metlaff turned at the sound of footsteps. "Here he is now."

Abby recognized him from the craft fair. He was still wearing the Cubs hat, and strode rapidly toward them.

"Let's get out of here before they change their minds," he said.

"Mr. Daugherty, this is Mrs. McKenzie. She has offered to take you home. I have a number of things to do and leave you in her hands." He nodded to Abby and headed for the door without further ceremony.

Daugherty grinned wryly. "He's in a hurry to get the lien registered."

"Lien?"

"Yeah. He put up my bail and took a lien on our property. He already had Fran's signature before he got here." Daugherty shrugged. "Can't complain. It's a fair deal." As they left the building he adjusted his cap to shade his eyes from the sun. "I'm glad to meet you, Mrs. McKenzie. Fran's told me about all you and your husband have done. I don't know when I'll be able to pay your bill, but—"

"Don't worry about it. It won't be as much as you think, and there's no hurry. The important thing is to clear you."

"You sure I didn't do it? Even Metlaff wanted to try a plea-bargain."

"Your wife and daughter are sure. That's good enough for me."

They were silent as Abby waited at the parking lot entrance for a break in traffic. As she completed a left turn he said, "I've been thinking about that knife. And for the life of me, I can't figure how it got into Bennet's back. How about it, Mrs. McKenzie? You got any ideas?"

"Not yet. You know, I've gotten to know your family so well, I think you should call me Abby."

"Okay, Abby. Just don't call me Roy. It's always been just Daugherty. Even Fran calls me that half the time."

"What does she call you the other half?"

Abby was glad to hear he could still laugh. "A thickheaded Mick."

"Tell me something, Daugherty. Why did you go straight from jail to Gladys's tent?"

"Getting turned loose was a surprise. That over-size cop opens the cell door, takes me down the hall to get my stuff, and says the charge's been dropped. I guess that was Mac's doing. So I turns to him and I says, 'Wait a minute. How do I get home?' So he turns to me an says, 'Call your old lady.' I asks him where's the phone, and he points to the pay phone in the hall."

"He's a charmer, all right."

"Well, all I've got is a twenty, and I asks him for change. 'What do I look like?' he says. 'A goddamn bank? Go get it at the fair, or walk.' And he turns around and leaves me standing."

"So you went to Gladys for change?"

"I tried the carnival rides first, but they need the change for when they opened. So I figured maybe the food vendors further back could sell me a coffee and I'd get change that way. Then I saw the tent and decided to try Gladys."

"And what did you see in the tent?"

Daugherty was silent for a time. "I guess I better level with you. Bennet was dead. Considering I just got out of a charge of attempted murder, that was the last

230

place I wanted to be found. I took off like a scalded cat."

"Did you tell this to Metlaff?"

"No. Yeah, I know I should have, but it just gets me in deeper, you know? And he thinks I'm guilty anyway. So I said the tent was empty."

"What was the point of leaving? Weren't you afraid you'd be identified coming out of the tent?"

"Sure, when I slowed down long enough to think about it."

"Did you recognize your knife?"

"I didn't see it."

Abby frowned. "It was pretty noticeable."

"I hear it was in his back. The way he was sitting, leaning back in the chair, his arms dangling, I don't think I'd have seen it."

Abby suddenly pulled off on the shoulder and stopped. She half-turned to face him. "He was leaning back? You're sure?"

"You don't forget something like that. Yeah. I'm sure. What's the big deal?"

Abby drove slowly off the shoulder. "When I saw him he was slumped across the table. Are you sure he was dead?"

"Oh, yeah. He was dead enough. His eyes were open and dead-looking, you know what I mean? And I checked for a pulse at his throat."

"I see." She stopped on the shoulder again.

"We ain't making much progress this way," he said.

"Once I get you home you're going to want to be with Fran and Kim. I need these questions answered right now. Because if you saw Bennet leaning back, and he was truly dead, then someone moved him after you left."

"Maybe he fell forward later."

231

She shook her head. "Think about it. It couldn't happen that way. Did you see the cards?"

"Cards? I don't — wait — yeah. Those fortune-telling cards. There was some on the table."

"The whole pack?"

"I don't know. A lot of 'em anyway."

"None on the floor?"

He shrugged. "I don't think so."

Abby bit her lip and visualized the scene in the tent as she had seen it. Bennet lying forward over the table. One arm outstretched, the other dangling toward the floor, pointing to the spilled Tarot deck. And just two cards on the table.

"Did you see the gypsy costume Gladys wears?"

"I didn't really take a good look around. I just wanted to get out of there before somebody came along and found me."

"Did you think of going out the back way?"

"Didn't know there was one."

"It's pretty obvious."

"Like I say, I wasn't really checking everything out, you know?"

Once again, Abby drove slowly onto the road. "So Bennet was killed before you got there. Then after you left, someone else moved the body, and the cards. Of course, moving the body might have knocked the cards to the ground. No, that wouldn't account for the two that had been dealt. Or could they have wound up in that position by accident, when the rest of the deck fell? Not likely, but I suppose —"

"I don't understand any of that."

"Oh, sorry. I'm talking to myself." Still driving slowly, she turned into the Daugherty driveway. "I wonder — You know it wasn't the knife that killed Bennet. Do you suppose the body was moved in order to

232

shove—" She shuddered. "In order to place the knife where it was found?"

As they came to a halt Daugherty opened the car door. Abby grasped his arm. "Wait. Did you see anyone around the tent? Or on the way? When you were leaving?"

"Sure, there were people around. I didn't pay much attention."

"Did you see me? I was right across the path from you as you came out."

"I saw people. I don't know who."

"I suppose you had other things on your mind."

Daugherty got out of the car and closed the door. Leaning in at the window he asked, "You're coming in, aren't you?"

She checked her watch. "I'll be back later. After you've had a chance to surprise your family. There are still some things I want to ask you."

"Like what?"

"Later. I'm supposed to meet Mac about now."


Mac was sitting at a rear booth when Abby arrived at Sarah's Kitchen.

"I'll just have a small salad and iced tea," she said. "It's too hot for a heavy meal."

"You're right." Turning to the waitress, he said, "Just a cheeseburger for me, fries, and a chocolate shake."

Abby shook her head. "That's your idea of light?"

"I guess you're right. Hold the fries, and make that a double cheeseburger."

"Okay, Nero Wolfe. Ready for some good news? Roy Daugherty is out on bail and reunited with his family."

"That's great. Now let's hope we can keep him out."

"And what great discoveries have you made today?"

233

Mac told Abby how he had come to have his fortune told. "You know, I can see how she hooks her marks. When she goes into her act, the Chicago kid disappears and she's totally concentrated. She almost had me believing it."

"It's not entirely an act, you know."

"Don't tell me you're starting to swallow this stuff? Maybe I should get you a bunch of garlic to ward off Ingram."

"Garlic is for vampires. No, I mean Gladys believes she has psychic abilities. Her premonitions come out when she's reading the cards."

"Yeah? If she can get the cards to match her premonitions, she should be dealing in Vegas."

"That's the beauty of the Tarot. The meaning is always a matter of interpretation. So no matter what cards come up she can usually get a reasonable reading that agrees with her psychic vision, or whatever you call it."

The waitress brought their order and Abby added sugar to her iced tea. "Of course, if she doesn't happen to get one, she gives you the usual bit about coming into money and taking a trip."

"They say the best con artists believe what they're saying at the time." He added ketchup to his burger. "But aside from the cards, I think most of what she told me was true."

"The interesting thing is the discrepancy between her story and Mrs. Bennet's."

"What do you mean? I haven't talked to Mrs. Bennet yet."

"No, but I did. She was coming from—"

"I thought we agreed you wouldn't talk to these people alone?"

"I know, but she was coming out of—"

234

"I don't care if she was coming out of church on the arm of a priest. Stay away."

"Are you going to listen, or would you rather play John Wayne?"

Mac laughed. "You wouldn't catch Duke sipping a milk shake through a straw." He removed the straw and drank from the glass. "He'd take his milk shake straight."

She smiled. "Okay. I can't see that talking to Mrs. Bennet was such a big deal, but I suppose you're right to be careful."

"What did she tell you?"

Abby gave him an abbreviated account. "Now why," she asked, "would Mrs. Bennet say she doesn't know anything about Daugherty, and Gladys say it was Mrs. Bennet that found out where he was living? And Mrs. B said she didn't know anything about Estelle Prestwick, but Gladys said she first heard of Goose and Estelle when Mrs. B mentioned seeing Estelle's check in Bennet's possession."

"Maybe we've been looking at it backwards," Mac said. "We've been thinking Gladys stage-managed everything. Getting Daugherty here, drawing in Prestwick and Quill. But maybe it's Gladys that's been manipulated. Her meeting Mrs. B at the psychic fiesta—"

"Fair."

"Yeah. Suppose it wasn't chance. Suppose Mrs. B knew exactly who Gladys was and went looking for her."

"I'd believe that sooner than believe Mrs. Bennet really puts stock in fortune-telling." Abby frowned. "But why? What's the point?"

"Make trouble for her husband. Push him into a generous divorce settlement."

235

"Or have a lot of ready-made murder suspects on hand."

"That too."

They ate in silence until Mac had finished his cheeseburger. Then he said, "I talked to Elmer. He tells me Bennet was trying to push Daugherty into selling his land. That must be why he provoked the attempted murder charge. It would give him leverage to force the sale in return for dropping the charge."

"But he was foiled by my hero."

"But that's not the good part." Mac grinned. "You'll never believe why Elmer came by." He laughed. "He wanted you to run for village trustee. Where do you suppose he got an idea like that?"

Abby pushed her salad plate aside. "Trustee?"

"That's right. But don't worry. I told him the idea was ridiculous."

Abby stared blankly. "You did what?"

Mac smiled, a bit weakly. "You wouldn't really—I mean, where would you find the time?"

"Did it ever occur to you to ask me?"

"It seemed obvious to me you—"

Abby got up. "I'm going out to the Daugherty's." She gathered up her purse. "And you can go to—"

"I know." He sighed. "No doubt I'm well on my way."

# Chapter Twenty-one

Mac took the Smith and Wesson Airweight from the glove compartment and clipped it on under his loose sport shirt. He bypassed the house and headed for the garage. About to climb the stairs to Ingram's apartment, he paused as a slight sound caught his ear. As if something was passing through the underbrush. On the chance that it might be Ingram on his way to the ladder, Mac took to the path.

A black-clad figure stood at the edge of the pit, looking down. As Mac approached, Ingram whirled to face him.

Mac came to an abrupt halt and took a deep breath. Ingram held a doubled-edged two-handed sword of impressive proportions. The weapon was pointed in Mac's direction, held in Ingram's right hand as easily as though it were a straw.

Ingram said nothing, but after a moment he lowered the sword point and rested both hands on the hilt.

Moving carefully Mac held out the leather-bound book he had found in the pit. "I've come to return your book, Mr. Ingram."

Ingram extended his hand and accepted the book. "Thank you."

"May I ask why you didn't claim it when we met at Farrel's?"

"I did not know then that you could be trusted."

"Can you trust me now?"

"I have been told so."

Mac relaxed a bit. Apparently he was not destined for the chopping block. At least, not yet. "I looked through the book. I hope you don't mind. It's fascinating."

"The lore of Wican is available to all who seek honestly."

"That's a beautiful sword you have. Ceremonial?" Mac hoped.

Ingram nodded. "I must call the Guardians."

"So it doesn't have a real cutting edge, right?"

Ingram lifted the sword in one hand, and with an effortless flick of the wrist sliced cleanly through a one inch sapling.

Mac realized the man's upper body strength must be enormous. The sword was designed for two hands and a full swing from the shoulders. It was definitely not a toy, and might well be a museum piece. "Do you mind," he asked politely, "if I ask a few questions about the death of Mayor Bennet?"

"He was evil and carried the seeds of his own destruction."

"I'm sure that's true, but right now an innocent man is blamed for his murder."

"The instrument is sometimes chosen at random. Had I known, I might have interceded on his behalf, and some other would have been chosen."

"Are you saying Roy Daugherty is guilty?"

Ingram shrugged. "It is what others say. Madame Gladys can tell you if it is true."

"How would she know?"

"She has the gift."

Mac nodded. "I have heard of her gift, but I'm afraid that won't help with the police. Do you know why your place was searched?"

"Yes."

"Why?"

"The time has not yet come."

"Do you know *who* broke in?"

"No. But he cannot escape. It is not necessary for me to know in order to set the elements against him."

"It would be helpful if we could set the police against him." Mac was beginning to understand why the police had left Ingram's apartment muttering. "Maybe you can help in another way. Can you tell me what you did and what you saw last Saturday at the fair?"

Ingram glanced at the sky. "There is little time." He drew a loop of rope from his pocket and fastened it to the hilt of the sword, then slung it about his neck so that the sword hung down his back "I intended to consult Madame Gladys and proceeded to her tent. Lawrence Bennet sat within and after a moment I saw that he was dead."

Mac had a sudden hollow feeling in the pit of his stomach. Daugherty had lied; the tent had not been empty. Or was Ingram lying now? Or did he know the difference? "If you remember, when I asked you about your movements before, you said Bennet was not in the tent when you arrived. Which story is the true one?"

"Bennet was dead."

"Why didn't you say so before?"

"It was not time."

"Okay. It wasn't time, and now it is. What did you see when you went into the tent?"

239

"Lawrence Bennet was sitting in the chair. The crystal ball of Madame Gladys lay on the ground. The Tarot lay scattered about the table and the tablecloth had been disturbed. Madame Gladys's costume hung from a coat rack in one corner. I went to the rear entrance to the tent and looked about. I saw no one."

If Ingram could be believed, someone had altered the crime scene between the time Ingram left the tent and Abby entered. There didn't seem to be any reason for Ingram to lie, but then there didn't seem to be any reason for him to lie when he told his story the first time.

"Mr. Ingram, did you touch anything? Move anything?"

Ingram glanced at the sky again and moved toward the ladder. "Yes. The Tarot beckoned me. I selected two cards. The meaning was clear. The Fool had been destroyed by his own folly. I gathered the other cards, intending to complete the sequence, but a sound from outside interrupted me and I placed the deck on the table and left."

"Mr. Ingram, did—"

"I must go. It is time." Charles Ingram, sword hanging down his back, stepped over the edge and disappeared into the pit.

Mac walked slowly toward the house, trying to make sense of what Ingram had told him. The corpse had been sitting up, not slumped forward. The Tarot had been on the table, not on the ground. At least now he knew why two cards had been dealt. And the crystal had been on the ground, not on its stand. What did it all mean? Or was it all the imagining of a man who carried a sword and had gone to call the Guardians? Guardians of what?

He wondered if Henderson had checked the crystal as a possible murder weapon. The autopsy said "blunt trauma" without speculating on the specific shape of the instrument. The autopsy also said the blow struck Bennet at the back of the skull, fracturing the bone and driving a fragment into the brain. Bennet should have fallen forward across the table. Ingram must be lying.

A crystal ball is a clumsy weapon requiring two hands to swing. It can easily slip, turning murder into farce. It could only be a weapon of opportunity, grasped in a sudden rage.

But if the crime was unpremeditated, how to account for the well-planned framing of Daugherty?

As he reached the house the back door opened and Goose Quill hailed him.

"McKenzie! If you wouldn't mind?"

Mac altered his course. "Is Miss Prestwick in? We hadn't finished our talk."

"Sorry about that." Goose held the door wide. "Afraid we weren't entirely honest with you."

The kitchen table was placed before a double window giving a good view of the backyard. The counters, cabinets, stainless steel sink, and appliances were modern additions to an old house. The tile floor reflected light from the window.

Estelle Prestwick sat at the table with three cups and a teapot. "We were about to have tea. Will you join us?"

"Expect McKenzie would like something a bit stronger," Goose said. "Whiskey?"

"No thanks."

"Beer, then. Just the thing in this heat." Goose took a Pilsner glass from a cupboard and a bottle of Heineken from the refrigerator. She carefully tilted the

241

glass to control the foaming head as she poured. Handing the glass to Mac, she said, "Believe I'll join you."

While Goose poured a second glass Mac studied Estelle. She was pale and her hand, as she held her cup, trembled slightly.

"Miss Prestwick, I'd like to go over your movements at the fair again," Mac said.

"That's just what we wanted to discuss," Goose said. "I'm afraid we haven't been entirely candid, you see. But, I'm sure you know that." Goose drank deeply, resulting in a foam mustache. She dabbed her lips with a napkin. "No doubt Charles has enlightened you, as we advised him to do. Now it's our turn."

"Then why don't you begin, Miss Prestwick? Just start anywhere."

Estelle nodded. "I'll begin where I met Charles on the path. He stopped to greet me and he seemed—elated, I think is the best way to describe it. He said, 'Lawrence Bennet has been dealt with.' At first I thought he meant the police had arrested Bennet. But then he said, 'He is dead.' It was quite a shock."

Mac nodded encouragingly.

"I'm afraid I behaved foolishly. You see, I thought that Charles meant he had killed Bennet."

"A reasonable conclusion," Mac said. "He had threatened to take care of Bennet in his own way. And then he told you he had."

"Yes, but I should have realized Charles's own way is witchcraft, not direct action."

"I understand at one time his actions were very direct."

"You know about—all that?"

Mac nodded.

"He was so different when he was young. So cheerful and self-confident. A fine athlete and really brilliant. I'm sure, if it hadn't been for the war, he would have had a fine career. He had a talent for languages. He spent two years in Paris and spoke French like a Parisian. So naturally—" Estelle's voice faded.

"He was recruited into the OSS?"

Estelle nodded.

"Get a grip on yourself, old girl." Goose leaned forward. "I'll carry on for a bit. You see, McKenzie, Charles was a very successful agent and made several forays into occupied France. His last mission—you understand we don't know precisely what it was about—ended in disaster for Charles. He was captured by the Gestapo. He was in their hands for a long time before the invading force liberated him."

"It must have been a rough time for him."

"I don't suppose you or I can imagine what he went through. He was in hospital for over a year, and he's never been the same since."

Estelle sighed. "He was very withdrawn. There were dreams. Sometimes he was afraid to leave the house."

"He seems very self-confident now," Mac said.

"It's this witchcraft nonsense," Goose said. "He has a source of power outside himself to rely on. He's invincible. At least in his own mind."

"Sometimes it can be frightening," Estelle said. "We really don't know how to deal with him. In a sense it's done him good. And yet, he's deluding himself, isn't he?"

"That picture in his apartment. Charles and a young girl. That's you?"

Estelle nodded. "Charles is my uncle. He was a hero to me as a child. He took me on all sorts of adventures. To the zoo in Chicago. Baseball games." She smiled. "He once took me to the circus where he knew

243

one of the clowns, and we were able to visit clown alley."

"You see how it is, McKenzie. Estelle feels an obligation to protect Charles now that he's fallen on bad times."

"Yes, I can see that. But you went a bit far this time, Miss Prestwick. Tell me about it."

Estelle drew a deep breath. "I told Charles to go home immediately. I'd see him there and we'd discuss it. Then, when he had left me, and I had calmed down a bit, I had second thoughts. Was the mayor *really* dead? I had to know."

She folded her hands, fingers interlocked, knuckles white. "I went to the tent, the back way, and looked inside. It was awful."

"This is important, Miss Prestwick. Exactly what did you see?"

"I saw Mr. Bennet. He was sitting in a chair, and at first I was relieved, thinking he was alive. Then I saw his eyes, and I knew he wasn't."

"What else did you see?"

"Nothing. All I could see was him sitting there, his head tilted back, his eyes wide open and staring upward."

"Where was the crystal ball?"

"I didn't notice."

"The cards?"

Estelle shook her head. "I turned to go, and then I realized that Charles would have come in from the front and had surely been noticed."

"He stands out in a crowd, wouldn't you say, McKenzie?"

"The police would find out Charles was the last person to enter the tent." Estelle said. "They'd question him. He'd—who knows what he'd say?"

244

"And that's when you decided on your masquerade?"

"Yes. I put on Madame Gladys's costume and went out the back way."

"With your umbrella."

"It was raining. But then I had to hide the umbrella. Madame Gladys didn't have one, you see."

"Did it occur to you that your scheme to get Charles off the hook would get Gladys into trouble?"

"At first, all I could think of was getting Charles *out* of trouble. He can't be locked up, Mr. McKenzie." She leaned forward. "Not ever again. I don't know what it would do to him. His mind—it's so fragile. You understand?"

Mac nodded. "I understand about Charles. But Gladys—"

"As I walked toward the tent, I began to think about that. And then it came to me. If I said I saw Madame Gladys somewhere else, it would give her, and me, an alibi."

"What if someone saw her at a different place?"

"That's why I didn't say anything right away. I waited until we all went to her place and I asked her where she had been. She told me—and she also mentioned the police hadn't questioned her yet."

Goose smiled admiringly at Estelle. "Clever girl."

Mac smothered his own opinion of Estelle's cleverness. "Why did you decide to tell the truth now?"

"Well, old boy, I've had the opportunity to watch you in action," Goose said. "Told Estelle it was no good. You'd soon get to the bottom of the matter. Better all round to make a clean breast of it."

"Nice to know I'm appreciated. Any other reason?"

"Madame Gladys has been on the horn. Dispensing advice. She made sense."

245

"And meanwhile Charles told us what happened," Estelle said. "He didn't *actually* kill Mayor Bennet. He just thinks that one of his spells—well, you know."

"Does he actually know anything about witchcraft?"

"Shouldn't think so. I mean, don't they fly about in covens? That sort of thing?"

"So I've heard."

"But he does read a great deal," Estelle said. "And he has all those strange herbs and things."

"Not to mention," Mac added, "a damn big sword. Goose, why didn't we see that in his apartment?"

"He has a place to keep his paraphernalia. No idea where," Goose said. "Wouldn't think of prying."

"Up here, or down there?"

"Shouldn't think it was up here. His apartment and the garage have been searched by the burglar, by us, and by the police. Can't think of anywhere else on the grounds it might be."

Mac, thinking over what he had heard so far, drank his beer. It was by now a bit warmer than he liked, but satisfied his thirst. Could Estelle's story be believed? The fact that it matched Ingram's account was meaningless; they had plenty of time to coordinate their stories. On the other hand, what purpose would a lie serve? Nothing Estelle said removed suspicion from Ingram, or from Estelle herself.

"Okay, Miss Prestwick. So you went into the tent dressed as Gladys. Then what?"

"It was quite frightening. I saw Abby—Mrs. McKenzie—talking to someone. I expected that any minute she'd call me by name. And I really had to steel myself to pass the body."

"Had anything changed since your first visit?"

Estelle paused, brow wrinkled. "Changed? No, I don't think so. I didn't look closely. I was anxious to

246

be done and out of there before someone came."

"Did you hear anything that would suggest anyone *might* come?"

"No, I don't think so."

"See anyone when you left by the back way?"

"No. No, but it's quite overgrown back there, except for the strip that's been mowed. I suppose all sorts of people could lurk about. Don't you?"

"Where did you go when you left the tent?"

"I didn't want to be seen behind the hedge, so I got back on the path as soon as possible and then crossed straight over to the food tent."

"Forgetting about your umbrella."

"Yes."

Goose nodded. "First thing I noticed. I had expected to find Estelle in the food tent where we'd agreed to meet. She wasn't there, of course, so I waited. Then there she came, looking like a drowned rat. Saw at once something was wrong but she wouldn't say a word until we were in the car and on our way."

"And you went along with all this?"

"Well, after all, the fat was in the fire. Nothing to be done but rally round." Goose cleared her throat. "What do you think, McKenzie? Will this foolish little episode have to come to the attention of the police?"

Mac shrugged. "I don't know. As things stand, the police have a solid case against Daugherty so they aren't much interested in these loose ends. And your story certainly doesn't help the defense. But if it becomes important you'll have to give them an amended statement."

"We haven't given a statement yet."

"You mean Almeir hasn't even bothered to question you?"

247

Estelle shook her head. "Just Charles."

"I remember you mentioning that, Goose. So Almeir ignored Ingram's statement that the tent was empty. A false statement, but Almeir wouldn't know that."

"Not quite," Goose said. "It seems Charles had a mental lapse and told Almeir the Elementals had rained down death upon the evil Bennet, or some such slush. Almeir—is that his name?—snorted and stomped off."

"Then no one has given false information to the police, so you're in the clear. And of course there's no law against lying to me. There's also no law against playing dress up." Mac finished his beer and rose. "But I almost forgot. There's the matter of failing to report a homicide. Thank you ladies, for your cooperation."

As Mac reached the door Goose asked, "About the money, McKenzie? Any chance of recovering our investment?"

"Not much. I'd advise you to see a lawyer. Maybe you can get it out of the insurance company."


Abby's anger cooled slowly as she drove away from Sarah's Kitchen. Mac should know better! Did she make decisions for him?

Well, little ones. Like picking out the suit he bought for their wedding. But that was different; the man had no taste. Everything he owned blended into the background. No wonder he spent so many years in the military; all the clothes looked alike and he never had to decide what to wear.

She should tell Elmer she'd run for trustee. That would show him! And why not? She'd certainly do a better job than the current bunch!

What was she thinking of? She had no time for small town politics.

But that was no reason for Mac to assume—assume what? That she had no time for small town politics? Why should she resent it because her husband knew her well enough to anticipate her answer? But maybe that wasn't the point. If he got away with this one, who knows what decision he might make for her next time?

She turned onto Leichtdorf Road and sighed. Because of the argument she had forgotten to tell him about Daugherty's story. Bennet was dead when Daugherty found him, which meant Ingram had lied.

They really must take the time to go over the evidence together. She was beginning to feel that between them, they might have the answer. She turned into the Daugherty drive.

Fran Daugherty stood on the screened porch looking out across the fields. The sun had set and summer's long twilight had begun. She turned as Abby entered. "He's home!" She hurried over to grasp Abby's hand. "I know it's just on bail, but for the first time I feel sure it'll all work out."

"I'm sure it will." Abby patted Fran's hand. "Where is he? There are a couple of questions I need to ask."

"He's out looking for Kim. She doesn't know he's home, and she's still searching for Fidget."

"Kim wouldn't stay out after dark, would she?"

Fran sighed. "Not usually, but she hasn't been her self lately. Poor kid. I wish I knew what to do for her." Then she brightened. "But it'll be all right now that her father's home."

Abby hesitated before saying what she had in mind. "Fran, I know what a shock it was for Kim to find

Bennet like that. And I haven't asked her any questions about it."

"Me too. Better she should forget it."

"I don't think she can, do you?"

Frowning, Fran said, "Maybe not. You think I should talk to her? Kind of clear the air?"

Abby nodded. "Would you mind if I talked to her? You see, your husband told me that Bennet was dead when he went into the tent."

"I know. He said."

"And the way he described the body. That's not the way it was when I went in later."

"It moved?!"

"Somebody moved it. So I need to know what Kim saw."

"Maybe we should both talk to her." Fran's eyes widened. "But Kim must have seen the same thing you did. Otherwise—" She clasped her hands. "You don't think the murderer was there when Kim went into the tent? Maybe out back watching her?"

"I don't think so. But we better find out, don't you think?"

Fran peered through the screen. "What's keeping them? They should be back by now."

Abby thought about the absent Fidget. Mac felt sure that the first time the dog disappeared it was Charles Ingram who had him. Apparently the dog had been well-treated. Could it be that, frightened by the burglar, Fidget had run off to Ingram's place? The idea of knocking on Ingram's door in the gathering dusk didn't appeal to her, but she could ask Goose to go with her. Surely it would be safe with Goose along.

"Fran, I have an idea where I might find Fidget. Why don't I go see? If I'm right we'll have a nice surprise for Kim when her father brings her home."

"Really? Where do you think the dog is?"

Afraid that, should she fail, Daugherty might lose his fabled temper and go storming after Ingram, she decided not to answer. "It's just an idea. I'd rather not say until I'm sure."

# Chapter Twenty-two

Stan and Julie Pawlowski were sitting on the patio at a redwood table covered with soiled paper plates and cola cans. The grill sent up tendrils of smoke to annoy the mosquitos.

"Where are the kids?" Mac asked.

"They went to the mall to read tee shirts," Stan said. "Have a Coke?"

"No thanks. How've you been, Julie?"

"Getting by. And Abby? I guess her art exhibit was a washout, and not just from the rain. Is she worried about opening the store on time? We haven't talked lately, she's been so busy. Why don't you two come over next Sunday? We'll put some ribs on the grill and I'll make potato salad."

Mac sorted out the questions. "Abby's fine. Except she's not speaking to me right now."

"What did you do to deserve it?"

"How do you know he deserves it?" Stan asked.

"Don't be foolish."

"Elmer Johnson wants her to run for the village board. I told him the idea was silly."

"And she wants to run?"

"I don't think so. She's just mad because I didn't ask her before telling Elmer she wasn't interested."

"Well, Stan and I never have that kind of a problem.

We decided long ago that he'd make the big decisions, and I'd make the little ones."

Mac's eyebrows rose. So did Stan's.

Julie nodded vigorously. "Sure. When it comes to foreign policy, who should quarterback the Bears, all the important stuff, that's strictly Stan. I just deal in the piddley little details." Julie ruffled Stan's graying hair. "Ain't that right, honey?"

"Yeah. Where we should live, how much to pay for the house, when to buy a new car. But she lets me pick my own socks every day," Stan said.

"As long as they match, and go with your suit." Julie got up and began gathering the soiled silverware. "I'll put some coffee on."

Stan carried the paper plates to the trash can. "So what brings you here for the second time in one day?"

"Unlike you civil servants, us private businessmen have to work long and exhausting hours. I've been busy." Mac brought Stan up-to-date, including, after some soul-searching about duty to clients, the discrepancy between Daugherty's and Ingram's stories. "Of course, Ingram isn't a grade A witness. Unless you believe in broomsticks and black cats."

"Still, it doesn't do your client much good. Maybe he'd be better off if you quit trying to help."

"You going to pass this on to Almeir?"

"Not yet. As a matter of fact, you should report it yourself."

"That's up to Metlaff. But let's suppose Ingram's story is correct, and Daugherty just lied to protect himself from a bum rap. Where does that leave us?"

"It sounds like maybe the murder wasn't planned. Otherwise it wouldn't be necessary to take the risk of going back later and rearranging things. But why monkey around? What's gained by moving the body?"

"Was the crystal ball checked?"

Stan stood up and stretched. "Sure. And you're right. It was the murder weapon."

"So the killer comes back, wipes the ball, and puts it on the stand. And now it's hiding in plain sight. I'm surprised Almeir had it checked."

"Bob Henderson did that on his own. He found a trace of blood on the tablecloth. The pattern suggested the cloth had been used to wipe the weapon. The only thing in the tent heavy enough was the crystal, and fortunately it had several surface scratches. One of them had collected blood."

"I don't remember any blood on his head."

"Just a little. Broken capillary."

Mac got up from the redwood bench and swatted a mosquito. "Why the body was moved is more of a problem. I can see why it was moved from upright to slumped over. That's so the knife could be put in Bennet's back. But why was he upright? He was hit on the back of the head. He'd naturally fall forward."

"To search his clothes?"

Mac nodded. "Could be. We know there's a ledger and a pot of money somewhere. The killer was looking for a clue. Maybe a key. To a deposit box. Or a locker." He swatted another mosquito. "Don't you ever feed your pets?"

"Every evening about this time. Let's go in."

The kitchen was large enough to accommodate the four Pawlowski's at dinner, provided one of them was willing to move every time the refrigerator door was opened. Three walls were painted yellow and the fourth was covered in wallpaper with a climbing-rose motif. The wallpaper nearest the range had absorbed several years worth of grease spatters.

Coffee was ready, so they settled at the table

254

and Julie poured. "You two solve the case yet?"

"Getting close," Mac said.

"Providing," Stan said, "you start with the assumption that Daugherty is innocent."

"Of course he's innocent," Julie said. "He's got a wife and a darling child. Abby told me all about them."

Stan laughed. "Atilla the Hun had lots of wives and children. What does that prove?"

"That's different. The man was a bigamist."

"Your husband is a hard sell, Julie. Okay, leaving aside ownership of the knife, try to get the facts to fit Daugherty. He comes into the tent expecting to find Gladys. Instead he finds Bennet sitting at the table. They exchange words. He gets mad, picks up the crystal, and brains Bennet. He moves the body, maybe to search for something. Then he leaves."

"I see your point," Stan said. "If he had struck the blow and then stabbed Bennet, to make sure he's dead, that just barely works. But if he goes away, and after a period of time comes back and stabs him, that doesn't make any sense at all."

"Right. Bennet was stabbed to frame Daugherty. That makes sense. Daugherty was the perfect patsy. He had public brawls with the victim. He was known for a hot temper. Who could ask for more?"

Stan added sugar to his coffee and lit a cigarette. "And he'd already been arrested for an attempt to murder Bennet."

"Alleged attempt."

"Whatever. I'm sold, but what do we do about it? Only one person other than Daugherty *could* have done it, and I don't see any chance of proving it."

"Well for heaven's sake," Julie said, "don't keep me in suspense. Who?"

Stan grinned. "You haven't figured it out? After all I told you?"

"Stanley Wojtek Pawlowski! Who?"

"John Almeir, of course."

"Almeir? I never liked the man, but—are you sure?"

"He's the only one that could have framed Daugherty," Mac said. "He had custody of the knife—"

"But he gave it back when he let Daugherty go," Julie argued. "Didn't he?"

"He gave him back a sheath, buttoned down, with a knife in it. Daugherty had no reason to suppose it wasn't his knife," Mac said. "And Almeir rushed him through the release procedure so Daugherty wouldn't be tempted to check things too closely."

"He had to rush things anyway," Stan said. "Almeir was in a sweat to get back to the tent before someone found the body."

"What if he'd been too late?" Julie asked.

"Then the frame was off, that's all. There still wasn't anything to connect Almeir to the murder."

Mac said, "If he had left well enough alone, chances are he'd have gotten away with it. By trying to gild the lily he made himself the only suspect other than Daugherty."

Julie shook her head. "The man must be a fool. Suppose Roy Daugherty hadn't gone to the fair? Suppose he could prove he'd never been there? What would Almeir do then?"

"Almeir knew Daugherty had no change for a phone call. By refusing to let him use a phone he forced him to go to the fair to break a twenty. That put him on the scene."

"What if nobody saw him there?"

"I suppose Almeir would have claimed to see him. The fact that Daugherty actually went into the tent,

256

and was seen by Abby, was just a lucky break for Almeir."

"Not so lucky," Stan said. "Daugherty must have seen Bennet before Almeir had a chance to set the stage. That must have worried him."

"Sure it did. But Daugherty decided to lie and say the tent was empty. Another break for Almeir."

"I wonder why he didn't drop the plan when he saw the way Ingram had rearranged the cards?" Stan asked. "That was a sure tip-off that somebody had been there."

Mac nodded. "The way I figure it, if he didn't notice them until he had planted the knife, it was too late to change plans. Or he figured that since no one had come out of the tent screaming 'Murder,' whoever did it wasn't about to come forward."

"And when he realized Daugherty had been in the tent he'd blame it on him," Stan said.

Julie topped up the coffee cups. She sat down and stared into hers. "Why? What reason would Almeir have to kill Bennet?"

Stan shrugged. "Lots of cases are solved without a motive ever being discovered. In this case, a small fortune in cash could have been the motive."

"Not very satisfying," Mac said. "If Bennet had the money and Almeir hijacked it, Bennet could hardly report the theft. And if the money had already been stolen, as I think it had, Bennet was out of the game."

"That ledger makes a better motive," Stan said. "Suppose it incriminates Almeir and Bennet threatened him with it? Almeir's a hothead. He might have lost his temper. Then afterward realizes he has to get the ledger and starts breaking in wherever he thinks it might be." Stan finished his coffee and pushed the cup aside. "Anyway, we don't have to know the motive. What we

257

need is some way to put Almeir at the scene. Or to prove that Bennet was dead before Daugherty was released."

"That's our best bet," Mac said. "Run down everyone that was at the fair and do the interviews over again."

"Most of them for the first time," Stan said. "Almeir didn't do any checking."

"Venlow has to take him off the case."

"No problem. I'll talk to the chief tonight."

"In the meantime we need a break," Mac said.

The phone rang and Stan took the call at the kitchen counter. He listened intently, hung up and said, "Let's go, Mac."

"What's up?"

"Your wife just found another damn body."

# Chapter Twenty-three

Abby hesitated before leaving her car, wondering if Charles Ingram might be lurking about the grounds. Her fears were put at ease as Goose Quill stepped out onto the stoop to greet her.

"Abby! There you are. Sorry. You just missed him."

"Missed him? Who?"

"McKenzie. Your husband. Seems to be hot on the trail."

"What did he want?"

"Grilled the lot of us. No secrets remaining. Much better that way."

"Did he find out that Mr. Ingram lied?"

"You know about that? Can't put anything over on the McKenzies. Should have known better than to try. Yes, that's all cleared up now. We can go over it all again for you, though I expect you'll receive a full report when you get home."

"Actually, that's not why I'm here. Kim's dog is missing again, and she's off searching for it, and her father's off searching for her, so I thought—"

"Kim Daugherty? Saw her just a bit earlier."

Abby smiled. "Oh, good! Her parents must be getting worried by now. Where did you see her?"

"Crossing the backyard. Children sometimes do. I generally give chase—not that I mind the trespass, but the edge of the gravel pit is just back there. I'm

259

afraid they'll fall in. In this case she eluded me."

"Oh, Lord, she's gone down there!" Abby started for the backyard. "Mac said there's a ladder?"

"At the end of the path behind the garage. But you can't go down! It's twilight and I assure you it will be quite dark down in the pit." Since Abby took no notice and continued across the backyard, she added, "At least wait until I get a flashlight."

Abby paused behind the garage. The light was fading fast, and she didn't know where the path began. She rummaged in her purse for a penlight. As soon as she clicked it on the tree stumps that flanked the path like gate posts sprang into view.

She walked rapidly, eyes on the circle of light that moved along four feet ahead of her. In a minute she had located the ladder. Looking over the edge was not encouraging. The beam of the penlight illuminated the first six rungs and then faded into darkness.

What was at the bottom? She backed away from the edge, her breath quickening. Had Kim really climbed down here? Of course there had been more light then. And no doubt she had come this way before. She knew what to expect. Was she still down there? Lost in the dark?

Abby leaned over the edge and shouted, "Kim! Are you there?"

She heard only the harsh cry of a nighthawk pursuing its prey high overhead.

She tucked the flashlight into her purse and slung the purse over her shoulder. A sense of urgency drove her onto the ladder. She felt for each rung with her foot and tested it carefully before committing her hundred and twenty pounds to Ingram's construction skills.

She knew her caution was foolish. Ingram used the ladder constantly, and he was surely twice her weight.

But climbing into darkness, coupled with anxiety about Kim, was taking its toll on her nerves.

She sighed with relief when her left foot touched rock. She quickly stepped off the last rung onto a steep slope, missed her footing, and slid the rest of the way. By the time she reached bottom her left elbow burned like fire from being dragged through gravel. She felt a sharp pain in her back as she scrambled to her feet.

Her exertions had left her hot and breathless, and she felt a cool, slightly damp breeze against her face. She took out her flashlight. The feeble beam, adequate to light a keyhole when returning home after dark, was swallowed up in this wilderness. She shouted, "Kim! Where are you?"

The air stirred with serenading crickets, croaking frogs, and humming mosquitos.

But no Kim.

Moving cautiously, she approached the saplings and undergrowth that began a few feet from the pit wall. There was a path entrance just to her left, and without further thought she entered, calling out again.

The path into darkness seemed endless. She paused twice more to call, without result, and was about to do so again when she noticed a faint glow ahead. Did Kim have a light? Why hadn't she answered Abby's call?

Or was it Ingram? The thought made her shudder and she turned off her flashlight.

Moving slowly in the dark, she felt her way, and with arms outstretched tried to remain centered between the flanking undergrowth. Each step brought her closer to the glow until she could recognize it as a candle elevated above the ground. She thought immediately of the flat, altar-like rock and black candlestick holder Mac had described to her.

Ingram must be there. And Kim? She moved closer.

A slight rustling behind her brought her heart into her throat and she whirled about snapping on her flashlight. The black-clad figure of Charles Ingram stood before her. He carried a huge sword in his right hand and a wooden box in his left.

He raised the box, upside down, its lid dangling open. His voice boomed in the night. "Have you defiled the sanctuary?"

"No! I just got here. I haven't had time to defile—I mean I wouldn't defile anything!"

He lowered the box and pointed at Abby with the sword. "Why have you come?"

Abby took a deep breath and tightened her grip on the tiny penlight. "I'm looking for a child. She may be lost—or hurt, or—Have you seen her?"

"Child? There are no children here." His voice dropped. "There was a time when they came by day, sometimes by night. But no longer."

A sudden flare of light threw Ingram into sharp silhouette. "I can well believe it old boy," Goose said, "with you patrolling the pit. Do put down the pig sticker. Mrs. McKenzie isn't here to steal your arcane secrets."

Ingram lowered the sword, resting its point on the ground. "Mrs. McKenzie?"

Abby, trembling slightly, raised her light to illuminate her own face. "Yes. It's me. Really."

"And you seek a child?"

Goose stepped around Ingram and lit the scene with a six-volt lantern.

Abby turned her penlight off to conserve the batteries. "Kim Daugherty. She's looking for her lost dog. A white miniature poodle." She hesitated. How would he react? "You know of the dog, don't you? The one that has been in your apartment."

262

Ingram frowned, for the first time showing signs of uncertainty. "You speak of my Familiar. She was given to me as a sign to proceed against the devious Bennet. When the spell was cast, she departed, only returning when its work was done."

How to respond? Challenge his belief? Not a good idea. "Your Familiar came from Kimberley Royal Daugherty. Now that the spell has been completed, it's time for her to go back home."

Ingram seemed to be thinking it over. "She seldom sits still." He nodded as if agreeing with some point he had made in discussion with himself. "And it is unusual for a Familiar to be so—so—"

"Fidgety?" Did he smile briefly? Abby couldn't be sure.

"However, there is still the defiler to be dealt with. He is doomed by his actions."

"What *is* all that defiling business, Charles?" Goose asked.

He held out the box. "It is gone."

"What was in it, Charles? Bat wings? Wolfbane? That sort of thing?"

"The book, and—"

"The book. Yes, well I expect we'll get it back in due course." Turning to Abby, Goose said, "He has this book of spells, quite old. Sets great store by it."

"But—"

"Right now we have the child to think of."

"Oh, Lord." Abby felt a pang of guilt at momentarily forgetting why she had come. "Mr. Ingram, do you have any idea where she might be? Perhaps you heard her call. Did you hear me? I shouted several times."

"There were voices on the wind."

"I think this is hopeless, Abby." Goose swung the flashlight about in an arc, causing the shadows to

263

dance. "The place is too damn big. I suggest we go topside and call the Daughertys. She may be home by now. If not, we can alert the authorities and mount a proper search."

Abby fought the instinct to keep searching. Goose was right. It would take a team with lights to cover the area properly, and by lingering here they were just delaying things. "Let's go," she said, and added a silent prayer that Kim would be found safe at home.

Without a word, Ingram set off into the darkness, Goose at his heels and Abby following the light.

A few yards down the path Ingram turned right into a narrower track where undergrowth snatched at Abby's clothing. "Where are we going? This isn't the way I came."

"Leave it to Charles," Goose said, dropping back to avoid whipping branches. "Knows the terrain like the back of his hand."

Ingram stopped suddenly and whirled to his left, sword raised and pointing.

Oh, Lord. Not Kim! Was she hurt? Abby brushed past Goose and ran to Ingram, flicking on her light. She directed the beam in the direction the sword pointed.

Her knees suddenly felt weak with relief. Roy Daugherty stood there, an expression of shock on his face.

"Jesus, man! You whittle fence posts with that knife?"

At that moment Goose arrived and threw her bright beam onto the scene. And now Abby saw the body at Daugherty's feet. Although he lay face down, and was dressed in slacks and sport shirt instead of his uniform, Abby knew in an instant who it was.

John Almeir.

Goose, her voice showing no sign of emotion in the presence of death, said, "You have a knack for being in the wrong place, Mr. Daugherty."

"I just stumbled over him."

Abby felt a chill pass over her. Questions filled her mind, but one crowded out all the rest. "Where's Kim?"

Daugherty's face looked stricken with fear. "I don't know. I came down here because it was the last place to look. Then it got dark and I got lost. Maybe she's at home by now." He looked around at the encircling darkness. "But if she was here when—Look, we have to get the police down here. They can search with lights and—"

"Wait." Abby pressed her hands to her temples. "Let me think." She turned to Goose. "Put your light on— on the body."

Abby noted that the sparse hair at the back of Almeir's head was matted with blood. She had no idea how long it took for blood to dry, but it still reflected the light. She supposed it could not have been too long since it was shed. Although laying face down, the body was not stretched full length. The arms were bent under the trunk. It looked as though Almeir might have been kneeling when struck from behind.

As tall as he was, he would almost have to be kneeling for someone to strike his head with enough force— unless the murderer was just as tall. She glanced at Ingram.

A leather holster was strapped to Almeir's waist. It was empty. "His gun is missing," Abby said.

The circle of light jerked upward and centered on Daugherty. "Would you mind raising your arms and turning around?" Goose asked.

"I haven't got it." Daugherty impatiently did as he was asked. "We're wasting time."

It was obvious that his jeans and tee shirt offered no

265

place to conceal the heavy revolver Almeir carried, and Goose dropped the light from his face without apology.

"Daugherty can't be found here," Abby said. "Are we agreed?"

"*Would* be a bit difficult to explain," Goose said. "Mum's the word?"

"Mr. Ingram?"

"I am responsible for Mr. Daugherty's difficulty. I will do what is necessary."

"What does he mean?" Daugherty asked. "Responsible how?"

"Don't pursue it," Goose advised. "It will only confuse you."

"All right," Abby said. "Here's what we'll do. If Estelle will help—"

"I'm sure she will," Goose said.

"—she can drive Daugherty home."

"Like hell! We've got to find Kim."

Abby nodded quickly. "Of course. But you said yourself she may be at home. While you're on your way I'll call the police. When they get here Goose will guide them to this spot. I'll wait for your call. If she's not home, I'll get a search organized. Then you can come back, but say nothing about finding the body. Understood?"

"Why can't we just call my place and find out?"

"For God's sake, Daugherty! If you're here, at the scene of the crime, they'll have you back in jail in five minutes. Now, don't worry. We won't waste any time. The police will come directly here, which is where the search has to begin anyway. And if you call, and the news is bad, I'll get down to them immediately. So let's not waste any more time. Lead us out of here, Mr. Ingram."

There was no further discussion until they reached

the ladder. Then Goose said, "I wonder, shouldn't someone stand guard? I don't suppose the killer is still down here, but—"

Ingram, his back to the sheer wall of the pit, rested his hands on the hilt of the sword. "I will stay. None shall pass."

"I believe that," Daugherty muttered.

"No, Mr. Ingram, that's not a good idea," Abby said. "No one is going to come this way. And besides, whoever killed Almeir has his gun. You can't stop a bullet with a sword."

"I will stay."

Knowing argument was useless and time was passing, Abby grasped the ladder and began to climb.

# Chapter Twenty-four

Abby waited on the stoop with Goose, anxiously watching for the flashing lights of the help she had summoned. The first to arrive was Officer Elizabeth Anders. She sprayed gravel onto the flower bed bordering the drive as she slid to a stop.

"Where is he, Abby?"

"Down in the pit, Liz. You'll need a guide."

Officer Anders hesitated. "I should protect the crime scene but—in this case, maybe it's best to get everybody down at once. Not much chance of anyone messing things up anyway."

No sooner had she reached her decision than a van followed by a car arrived. Bob Henderson got out of the van, nodded to the group, and started unloading his equipment. Stan and Mac got out of the car and hurried over.

Mac put his arms around Abby. "You okay?"

Abby nodded, but clutched his shirt.

"What's happening, Anders?" Stan asked.

"I just got here a few minutes ago, Captain. The body is in the pit and I understand we'll need a guide. I know I should—"

"You did right to wait." Stan turned to Abby. "Who's the guide? You?"

"I'll take you there," Goose said. "Familiar with the

terrain. And as it happens, we left someone on guard. Wouldn't want a misunderstanding when you appear out of the darkness."

"Oh? He's armed?"

"You could say that, yes."

"Let's go."

The party started off single file, Goose leading, arms swinging briskly. Mac was about to follow when Abby took his hand and pulled him back.

He watched the group disappear around the side of the house. "You sure you're okay?"

"Mac, we found Daugherty standing over the body."

"Damn! Where is he?"

"Estelle took him home."

"Why? Stan has to know sometime."

"Yes, but right now I don't want to confuse his thinking."

"And the less he knows the clearer things will be?"

"Mac, you know very well what I mean. If Daugherty is in the neighborhood he'll be hauled away and the case will be closed."

"Stan wouldn't do that."

"You mean he'll believe it was just a coincidence that Daugherty fell over the body in the dark, at the bottom of a gravel pit? When he's out on bail, charged with murder? When Almeir is the man out to convict him?"

"Was."

"When he's known for losing his temper? And nobody else has a motive?"

"Listen," Mac said, "I had Stan convinced Daugherty is innocent." He sighed. "The only trouble is, I convinced him by making a case against Almeir. Who at this moment is inconveniently dead."

"Almeir? Mac, are you sure?"

"If Daugherty was framed, Almeir is the only one

that could have framed him. It's as simple as that. But if Almeir is the killer, who killed Almeir?"

Abby shook her head. "We can't worry about that now. Kim is missing. And she was in the pit today. She might have been there when Almeir was killed."

"Why didn't you tell Stan? We should get a search organized."

"I'm waiting to hear if she's at home. She might have left the pit while it was still daylight. Before we started looking for her."

"We'll call. Her mother must be there."

"That's why I'm waiting. Fran must be worried as it is. I'd rather Daugherty were with her when she finds out what's going on."

"I guess you're right. Were you down there looking for Kim?"

Abby clung to him and nodded.

"She's probably home." He stroked her hair. "Good thing you didn't run into Ingram. He'd scare the life out of you."

"We met." Unwilling to admit to her panic, she added, "We had a nice talk."

"Nice talk? About what?"

"About how his sanctuary was defiled and the book stolen. Mac, he means Bennet's ledger. And I don't know for sure, but I think he had the money too."

Mac groaned. "Of course! Who else would know where Bennet stashed it but the Phantom of the Pit of Hell? He probably kept an eye on everybody that came down here. I should have asked Stan to get a butterfly net and collect him for questioning a long time ago."

"If Ingram doesn't want to talk, he won't. But I'm sure Goose knows he has it. She cut him off when he was telling us what was missing from his sanctuary. She tried to make me think the missing book was the old

270

one on witchcraft—but of course I knew you had that."

"I gave it back to him. She wouldn't know about that. Probably never knew it was lost."

The telephone rang and Abby raced into the house and snatched up the handset. "Yes? He's coming here? Don't worry, Fran. We'll find her. The police are here now. I have to run. Is Estelle staying? Good."

Abby hung up and started through the house to the back door. Mac caught her in the kitchen.

"I'll tell them, Abby. There should be some more manpower on the way and they'll need to be told where we are. Watch for them."

Abby started to pull away, then stopped. "You're right. But once they get here I'm coming down."

Mac met Goose and Ingram on his way to the ladder.

"They've ordered all civilians to clear the area," Goose said. "We're to stand by until they have time to take statements."

Ingram said nothing. He climbed the stairs to his apartment, entered, and closed the door silently.

Mac had no trouble finding the crime scene. The work lights were clearly visible from the top of the ladder, and a bobbing flashlight moving through the undergrowth defined the path for him. He descended quickly, turned on his flashlight, and in five minutes he was looking at the back of Almeir's head.

The body was lit from three sides. There were frequent flashes from Henderson's camera as he moved around, covering the scene from various angles.

Stan stood with his hands in his pockets and muttered about the need for a cigarette. "We're having trouble trying to decide how big an area to barricade. Anders started stretching tape to the left and fell in a

271

hole. A lot of this is going to have to wait for daylight."

"Did you put someone on the two entrances? Two that I know of anyway. I didn't see anybody guarding the ladder."

"Shorthanded."

"We need more manpower, Stan. Kim Daugherty is missing. Last seen coming down here."

Stan cursed. "You mean she might have been a witness?"

"That's what I mean." Now that his apprehension had been put into words, Mac's stomach knotted.

"Hey! What're you standing around for?" Roy Daugherty approached at a run. "Let's get this search moving!"

"We will, Mr. Daugherty. But the question is how best to go about it. We don't have enough manpower, or enough light, for a systematic search. We'll have to—"

"So get some more manpower, for crissakes."

"Where is everybody, Stan?" Mac asked.

"Tompkins is on vacation somewhere on the upper peninsula. One car is at an accident scene with injuries. That one should be here in half an hour. Venlow is trying to raise the off-duty people. He should have some called in soon."

"Almeir let Tompkins go in the middle of a murder investigation? Why?"

"Gave Almeir a free hand, didn't it?"

"You going to yak all night?" Daugherty demanded.

"Okay. One of us will follow the tracks back through the tunnel. If she's over there, she might not hear anyone calling from this side of the road. Mr. Daugherty, you try that. And try the shack over there."

Daugherty grunted a reply and started off at a trot.

Mac caught up with him just out of earshot of Stan and ran along with him. "Where did you check before it got dark?" he asked.

"I came down the slope from the road. I didn't know about the ladder. Followed the path. When I got to the tracks, I followed along the pit edge to the west. Found another path into some pretty thick brush and trees. Then it got dark and I lost the path. Who knows where I went after that."

Mac broke off and trotted back to Stan. Henderson and Anders were gone.

"Henderson's following this path to the—what?—northwest I guess," Stan said. "Anders is following the pit wall west. I'll follow the wall that runs along the road. Any suggestions?"

"There's another path, wider than this one, that goes north. If I can find it in the dark."

"Okay, let's do it."


Abby impatiently paced the driveway. Where were they? Surely Sarahville could raise more than three officers in an emergency? What about the neighboring villages? The sheriff's police?

The phone rang and she ran into the house. A cheerful voice was well into a prepared statement about the virtues of water softeners before she could hang up.

Where was Goose? She had come into the house, and on hearing that Kim had still not come home, said, "Time to muster all the troops," and went off to her bedroom. As if in answer to Abby's unspoken question Goose reappeared carrying her lantern in one hand and a pistol in the other. "No need for both of us to wait. Thought I'd join the search party." She slipped the pis-

273

tol into her pocket where its weight pulled her safari jacket down on one side. "Best to be prepared, with a killer on the loose."

"Aren't you afraid it'll tear through your pocket? What is that anyway?"

"Good old Colt Model 1911A. Former property of the United States Army. A properly placed shot will stop a charging rhino."

"Just be careful you don't shoot yourself going down the ladder."

Goose looked hurt as she turned and left.

The waiting wore on Abby's nerves. She started at every sound, and imagined she saw lights approaching a dozen times. To get her mind off her anxiety, she turned to the problem of Almeir's murder. If Mac was right, and Almeir had framed Daugherty, it was only reasonable to suppose he had killed Bennet. What other reason would he have to cover up?

All right, suppose he hadn't killed Bennet? Suppose he had come on the crime in progress? Could he have offered to let the killer go for a price? Yes, that would work.

Then she remembered that Kaz had overheard a few words from the tent. What did he say? Like a whisper. "Get out of here. I'll take care of this." That could have been addressed to the killer. But why the frame-up? Why not just give the killer time to escape, destroy any clues, and then "discover" the body? Nothing more elaborate was required.

Of course, with Daugherty in jail there would be a thorough investigation led by Stan. Who knows what might be discovered? But if Daugherty was free, and Almeir arrested him at once, then Almeir could control the investigation and make sure he and the killer were safe. But he needed more evidence than just Daugherty's presence at the fair, and that's where the knife came in.

What was Almeir afraid might be discovered by Stan? Who would suspicion fall on? Gladys, of course. It was her tent. Was Almeir protecting Gladys for a price? He'd hardly expect her to be rich enough to make it worth the risk. Unless Gladys had found Bennet's money.

No. Almost certainly Charles Ingram had it, until tonight. And Almeir wouldn't take a risk for someone as unstable as Ingram. Besides, the break-ins must have been an attempt to find the money, and that was probably Almeir's doing. He would have known when Fran and Kim were at the jail and their house was empty. He knew Gladys and the Kazmierski's were being watched, so he'd avoid a break-in there.

And hadn't Mac found him actually coming out of Bennet's house?

The way the houses were trashed was indicative of the man's personality. He operated like a bulldozer. Poor Fran's best china smashed just to look in the box.

The next idea startled Abby, and she dropped into a chair by the front window.

Not *all* the burglary victim's were treated alike! She thought of a collection of depression glass, undisturbed in its cabinet. An expensive vase intact though the table it sat on, according to Mac, had been overturned. All the tables and chairs had been overturned, but nothing of consequence broken.

How could that be, unless the break-in was a blind, to put Mrs. B in the same category as the rest of the victims? And who would normally be the prime suspect? Who was always the first suspect in a murder? The surviving spouse.

Abby jumped up and rummaged through her purse

275

for notepad and pencil. She scrawled a note directing whom it might concern to the pit. She pulled a thumbtack from the kitchen bulletin board, sending a cascade of old phone messages to the floor, and pinned her note to the front door.

Mac and Stan should know who they were dealing with. Mrs. Bennet might still be in the pit. She might have Kim.

# Chapter Twenty-five

Abby's second trip down the ladder was less frightening than the first. She stepped onto the rubble-strewn slope at the bottom, holding fast to the ladder's side rail. Her penlight had faded to a yellow glow. She cast it aside. She shouted for Mac, then for Stan, Henderson, and Liz.

There was no response.

They were searching for Kim, but surely they had left someone on guard? Someone with a light to guide her down the slope and through the intervening darkness? She shouted again. "Anybody?"

Just an echo and the thrumming of crickets.

A half-moon rose above the pit's rim and gave some light. The glare of police work lights, filtered through trees and brush, acted as a beacon. Moving with great care, stumbling occasionally, she made her way down the slope. She crossed the open pit floor, where the narrow gauge tracks lay, and entered the dark, twisting path through heavy growth. Her progress was slow as she dodged twigs and branches she could barely see and felt for rocks and deadwood on the path.

At last she came to the crime scene. It was deserted. So Stan had elected to put everyone into the search. Now what was she to do? If she attracted someone by shouting, it would delay finding Kim. Joining the search would be foolish without a light. She'd get lost and they'd have to come find her.

She glanced at the still form of John Almeir and shuddered. He had been covered by a plastic sheet to protect the evidence, but her mind's eye saw Almeir's grotesque, half-kneeling body and crushed skull all too clearly.

What if she were to run into Mrs. Bennet? With the body count at two, would Mrs. B hesitate to make it three?

Or had Abby jumped to an unwarranted conclusion, just because the Bennet home had escaped costly damage? Mrs. B was an attractive woman, in an icy sort of way. Maybe Almeir had a personal interest in her. Maybe that's why he treated her things gently while searching for the ledger.

She strained to hear any sound from the search party. Shouldn't they be calling Kim's name? Unless they had found her and—

No, she wouldn't allow herself to think about that.

If Almeir and Mrs. B weren't in league, maybe he was watching for her to leave the house. Once she was gone he'd have the house to himself until Mac showed up at six.

No, there was something wrong with that. Mrs. B arrived at Stan's office at a quarter to six. She said she went there directly from home. Allowing for a slow pace and missing all the traffic lights, she couldn't have left home earlier than five-thirty. Surely it took Almeir more than half an hour to search an entire house, attic to basement.

But if Mrs. B had been there, leaving just before Mac arrived—or if there was no search, just a hasty job of stage setting?

Was that someone calling Kim? Difficult to tell in this echoing hole in the ground. There seemed to be constant noise and stealthy movements. Leaves rustled, insects hummed, frogs croaked, and her pulse pounded in her ears.

She moved forward out of the ring of lights and waited for her eyes to adapt to the darkness. There was nothing to be seen but the shadowy presence of sumacs and poplar saplings.

Timing. Something else about timing. Yes, Mrs. B's statement about the fair. She said she left before the drizzle turned to heavy rain. Then later, she claimed to have seen Daugherty. But it was raining when Daugherty arrived. Did she leave later than she claimed? Or did she just want to bolster the case against Daugherty? In either case, she lied.

Abby felt uneasy; exposed by the lights behind her, enclosed by the growth around her. Would it be better to return to the crime scene? But there she would be lighted like an actress on a stage. Perhaps she should move down the path, into the open ground before the pit wall.

If only she had a flashlight.

Henderson's equipment case—did he carry a spare? She moved back into the lighted arena, trying not to look at the shrouded corpse. She unsnapped the top of the large case and found a two-cell flashlight clipped inside the lid. She grabbed it, slammed the lid, and moved rapidly down the path with a definite feeling of relief as the bright beam speared the darkness ahead.

Reaching the slope below the ladder, she scrambled up and placed her back against the comforting rock. Now no one could approach from behind, and coming from the front they would announce their presence climbing over the loose rock and gravel. She relaxed and turned off the light to let her eyes adapt to the faint moon glow.

Bennet's wife. What drove her most strongly? Greed

or hatred? Greed probably took her to the back of the tent, hoping to overhear some clue to where the money was. She overheard his talk with Gladys. His talk with Maggy as well. So she would know Bennet no longer had the money. With no reason to hold back, her rage overflowed. She went into the tent and killed him with the first thing that came to hand.

Her hatred for her husband was no secret, and she would have been the obvious suspect. It was just lucky that Almeir had the means to frame Daugherty.

Or had she always planned murder?

She sought out Gladys and Daugherty and manipulated them into coming to Sarahville. She put Goose and Estelle in touch with Gladys. All of this put pressure on Bennet in hopes he'd make a mistake and reveal where he'd hidden the money. It also surrounded him with enemies. Plenty of motives for murder.

Abby caught a movement in the moonlight and clutched the ladder in a spasm of fear. It was an owl gliding along the track in silent search for prey. She breathed deeply, willed her muscles to relax and deliberately turned back to the case against Bennet's wife.

Was it she that had prompted Gladys to get in touch with the McKenzies? But what did that accomplish? More pressure on Bennet? A chance that they'd turn up the money? And in investigating Bennet they'd be sure to turn up his mistress, another murder suspect.

If all that were true, she had played a very deep game. No doubt she would have prepared an alibi for herself when the time came, but then foolishly let her hatred cause her to act on impulse. Only Almeir's greed had saved her. He wanted a payoff, and if the money was found, a cut of that as well.

Or maybe all of it. Was that why he had to be killed?

Her feeling of security in her new position was beginning to ebb as time dragged on. Mac, Stan, and the rest of them were somewhere in the pit, but as far as her senses were concerned she might be the only one alive within miles.

Then the sound of a rock dislodged and rolling down the slope.

She whirled in the direction of the sound and snapped on her light. Mrs. Bennet stood there, face tense, eyes darting wildly. Abby's breath caught in her throat. The woman had a canvas bag slung over her right shoulder and held a revolver in her right hand.

Her left hand gripped the arm of a terrified Kim Daugherty.

Abby instinctively advanced on the woman, ignoring the gun. "Let her go! Let Kim go!"

The woman waved the gun toward Abby. "Don't be stupid! Get away from that ladder."

Abby hardly recognized this woman as the sleek, cool Mrs. Bennet. Her hair hung in disarray and her face was streaked and scratched. Her slacks were stained and ripped.

Abby backed up and put her hand on the ladder. "You can't get out this way. The police are up there." She forced herself to speak calmly. "Put down the gun and let Kim go."

Mrs. Bennet's voice was the snarl of a cornered animal. "This brat is my ticket out of here. Now turn that light on the ladder and get out of the way!"

Before Abby could react, another beam of light caught Mrs. Bennet.

"She's right, Mrs. Bennet," Stan said. "You can't get away. Might as well give it up."

The woman pressed the muzzle of the gun to Kim's head. "I heard you talking! Everybody's down here. That's all the cops this two-bit town can raise."

Another light flared. "There's no place to run," Mac

said. "Even if you make it up the ladder, the police will be right on your tail." Abby felt his arm encircle her shoulders.

The woman jerked Kim along toward the ladder. "With a little start and half a million in this bag, I can go a long way." She advanced another step toward Abby. "Move or I'll kill her."

Abby was drawn away by Mac. "Do as she says," he whispered. The wild look in Mrs. Bennet's eyes left little doubt she would do as she said.

The woman reached the ladder and pushed Kim against it. "Climb, damn you!"

Kim turned her tear-streaked face to the woman. "I can't. You're hurting my arm!"

Another light flashed on the scene. Liz Anders spoke calmly. "Be reasonable, Mrs. Bennet. You can't hold on to the child and a gun while you climb a straight ladder. It can't be done."

"Just watch me."

The woman released Kim's arm and Abby felt Mac's arm slip from her shoulders and he moved a step forward.

The woman pointed the gun at Kim's head again. "Don't try it!" She fastened her left hand on the waistband of Kim's shorts and urged her up the ladder. Kim climbed three rungs and the woman sprang onto the second rung, her right arm looped around the side rail, gun pointing toward Kim. "Remember," she shouted, "if I fall, she falls. And this gun is cocked!"

The woman must be mad with desperation, Abby thought. She's sure to lose her balance, and Kim—She ran to the foot of the ladder and looked up, wondering if she could catch the child.

She was roughly shoved aside. "Bennet, you bitch! This is Daugherty talking! Anything happens to Kim and you die. I swear it!"

"Daddy!"

"Shut up!" the woman snapped. "Move!"

Kim took a step up. The woman followed. Leaning close to the rungs, she slid her right arm upward, swaying dangerously until she secured a new grip. By now they were halfway up and a fall could easily be fatal. And there was the gun to consider.

What would she do with Kim once her usefulness as a hostage was over? Was there no way to stop her? Abby looked around wildly. Bob Anderson was bent forward, his light following Mrs. Bennet. Stan stood behind him, bracing his arms on Henderson's shoulder, the barrel of his revolver following the woman's slow progress.

Mac put his arms around Abby. "It'll be all right," he said, but his voice carried no conviction.

The climbing pair were near the top now. Kim's head was above the edge of the pit. Suddenly Kim rose into the air, floating free of the ladder, free of Mrs. Bennet's grasp!

Abby gasped in astonishment as Kim levitated slowly clear of the ladder to firm ground.

The woman, her grip on Kim loosened, missed her step and swung from her right arm for a moment, then regained her footing and lunged for the top of the ladder.

A dark shape appeared before her, rising as if from the very earth. Charles Ingram stood erect, a hulking silhouette. Arms upraised, a streak of silver leapt from his hand toward the sky as his sword caught the moonlight.

Mrs. Bennet screamed once—and fell.

# Chapter Twenty-six

Wanting to exert gentle pressure on their clients to honor the pledges they had made to the Daugherty defense fund, the McKenzies invited them all to a backyard barbecue. The weather cooperated by providing a cool front that dropped the temperature into the seventies. The charcoal was less cooperative.

"I told you not to leave it in the garage," Abby said. "It picked up moisture while the humidity was so high."

"And where would you keep it?" Mac asked, fanning two glowing coals with a paper plate. "In the kitchen?"

"Well, do something. Our first guests just arrived."

Goose, wearing plaid slacks, a lime green shirt and a narrow-brimmed hat with two golf tees stuck in the band, waved a greeting as she got out of her car.

Estelle, wearing a yellow cotton dress and sandals, followed. "I hope we're not too early," she said.

"No, but we're running a little late. The boy scout seems to have misplaced his fire-making skills."

"No problem," Goose said. She picked up a can of lighter fluid and poured directly on the only spot of red showing. Flames leaped into the air and Mac jumped back to save his eyebrows.

"I could have done *that*, Goose."

"No use toying with it. Direct actions always best. We'll soon have a fine bed of coals."

Abby, reading Mac's expression, decided a change of

subject was needed. "Have you been able to get back the money you paid for the annuities?"

Estelle chose a lawn chair. "We haven't really looked into it yet."

Goose sat at the picnic table. "Too bad your view is spoiled by that parking lot across the creek. Have you thought of planting a line of pine or cedar to block it out?"

"How is Charles Ingram doing?" Abby asked.

"I'm really hopeful," Estelle said. "Since he saved Kim from that awful woman he seems a bit more in touch, if you know what I mean. He's agreed to see a psychiatrist, at least on a trial basis."

"Gave me quite a start when the child began levitating," Goose said. "Almost had me convinced one of Charles's Elementals was about. Quite an exciting conclusion to the adventure."

"I'm glad I wasn't there to see it," Estelle said. "The poor child must have been frightened out of her wits."

"As it worked out," Goose said, "that damned woman confessed by her actions. A disappointment, really. I'd hoped for a brilliant bit of deduction. Gathering the suspects in the manor hall. That sort of thing."

The flames died down and Mac turned to bartending. Iced tea for Estelle and Abby, beer for himself and Goose. "Actually," he said, "Abby figured it out. Unfortunately, she was alone at the time. No chance to gather the suspects."

"Well, that's more like it," Goose said. "Shows Madame Gladys was right to insist we see Abby, and not McKenzie. No offense, McKenzie."

Abby drew up a lawn chair. "It was quite easy once I remembered—"

"Someone just arrived," Estelle said. "The Daugherty clan, I believe."

A yapping bundle of fur arrived first, leaped to the top of the picnic table, and headed for the hamburger

285

patties Mac had optimistically laid out.

"Fidget! Down!" Daugherty shouted. The dog obeyed and ran about sniffing at everyone's shoes.

Kim, grinning broadly, placed a cardboard box labelled CLUES on the table. "This is for you, Mr. McKenzie. Mrs. McKenzie said you didn't have one."

Mac smiled. "Thank you, Kim. Does this mean you're quitting the business?"

"Uh huh. Daddy says I get in enough trouble just breathing."

"Who else is coming?" Fran asked.

"Elmer and his wife, Mabel, were invited, but I guess they can't make it," Abby said. "But Gladys should be here."

Fidget headed for the creek with Kim in pursuit.

"How is Kim doing, Fran? Any bad effects from her experience?"

"She had bad dreams a couple of nights. She seems to be over it now, but you never know with children."

"The kid's tough," Daugherty said. "She'll do okay. Got a beer, Mac?"

"Abby was about to explain how she cracked the case," Goose said. "Clever detective work, I'm sure."

Abby smiled at Goose. "It really wasn't difficult, once I realized that—"

"Hello, folks," Gladys called. "I brought a couple of pies to top off the feast."

"Kurtz's bakery?" Estelle asked.

"You didn't think *I* baked 'em?"

Mac offered Gladys a beer. "Now that you're here, let's talk about the money."

"Sure. Just give me your bill, and—"

"Not that money. It seems that the cash recovered from Mrs. Bennet doesn't quite add up to the total in Bennet's ledger. Comes up about fifty grand short."

"So he spent it."

"Maybe. Estelle, you said you weren't in any hurry to

file a claim for the money you were swindled out of."

Estelle blushed.

"Great deal of red tape involved," Goose said.

Mac turned to Goose. "Between the three of you, you got taken for thirty thousand." He turned to Gladys. "Thirty from fifty leaves twenty."

"Are you a detective or an accountant?"

"I was talking to Myra," Abby said. "You know, at the Happy Traveller travel agency? She tells me you booked a cruise to the Mediterranean this fall."

"Business has been pretty good, and the cards gave me a couple of horses in the daily double."

"Bon voyage," Mac said. "Have another beer?"

"If she won't, I will," Elmer said, rounding the corner of the house.

"We thought you couldn't make it," Mac said, handing him a can of Stroh's.

Abby smiled. "Where's Mabel?"

"Went to see her sister. I'm just out politickin'."

"Thought you were a shoo-in," Daugherty said. "You got appointed to a vacant seat as trustee, and nobody is running against you for mayor next spring."

"But I have to carry some decent trustees with me. Bennet's ledger cleaned out two of the worst, but there's still a couple of deadheads." He winked at Abby. "And I ain't through tryin' to convince this little lady to run."

"Good choice," Goose said. "She was about to tell us how she solved the mayor's murder case."

"I'd be interested to hear that," Elmer said. "I thought Mrs. Bennet more or less confessed."

Abby looked toward the drive to see if anyone else was likely to interrupt. She looked at the group. They all seemed to be attentive, except for Mac, who was rummaging in Kim's clue box. "Well, it all started when—"

"Hey, look at this," Mac said. "Kim drew a map of

the pit." He held up a sheet of notebook paper. "She's got the ladder marked here. And there's the Temple of Black Magic. I guess that's Ingram's hangout." He laid the map out on the picnic table and weighted it against the breeze with two forks. "And over here, on the side nearest the Daugherty place, is the Magician's Cave. Oh, oh."

"What is it, McKenzie?" Goose asked.

"Next to the cave is a list. An inventory maybe. Sword, book—and treasure."

Startled, Abby said "You mean she found the money and didn't say anything?"

"Oh, dear," Fran said. "She was afraid to, I guess. She isn't supposed to go down there."

Abby got up and started walking toward the creek.

"Where are you going, honey?"

"Fidget wants to hear how I solved the case."